← you're not allowed to smile in your passport photo

Passport
do$h
telefoon
pen
notebook
presents for Willa's relos
　　　　　(bird tea towels)
warm jacket (Maggs)
Anne Frank
Dutch for Beginners
possum socks + others
mossy dress (for wedding)
llama pyjamas.
T-shirts (Greta + striped)
long sleeved T shirt
new toothbrush

THE NETHER LANDS

THE FARAWAY NETHER LANDS
MYSTERIOUS GREY WEATHER LANDS
DID CALL 'MAKE HASTE' TO THE
                  ANCIENT ONE
AND THE ANCIENT ONE DID HEED
                THE CALL.
THE ELDERS MET AND THE TRIBE
                MET ALL
AND ALL FOR ONE THE DEED WAS DONE

THE HARDSHIPS ARE MANY THEY CRY
                TENFOLD

A PERILOUS PILGRIMAGE FORETOLD
BUT KNOCK ME WITH A FEATHERLANDS
WE'RE IN THIS TOGETHERLANDS
ANOINTED SCRIBE AND SERVANT
                GIRL

TO THE ANCIENT ONE,
       I JOURNEY AS WELL.

from Stella Street

to Amsterdam

and everything that
happened

~~ELIZABETH HONEY~~

Henni Octon

ALLEN&UNWIN

SYDNEY · MELBOURNE · AUCKLAND · LONDON

Bye
Sweet

Bye

Bye

Six pieces of luggage
Six!

Have
fun

Ready
I'm ready.
Never been so ready
I'm Briquette bouncing at the gate
The sprinter on the blocks
that's me
Take Willa to the moon?
No worries.
Brimming
There's a convex meniscus curve
of instructions
out my ears
It will be amazing
Lucky duck Lucky pig
that's me
Bring it on

I looked at Willa's passport and her name
wasn't Willa de Haan, it was Wilhelmina Roos
Petronella van Veen! But she is Australian.

We stood on footprints in front of a machine and
the instructions said to stare at this spot to have our
photo taken. 'What's all this about?' said Willa, a bit
alarmed. 'I want to see someone about this machine!'
But there was a long queue behind us and thank the
gods she shut up and obeyed the machine.

HAVE A WONDERFUL TIME

Night. No warning. Oh, a bump or two, a sharp jolt.

Then the plane drops like a stone.

A bolt of terror shoots through me. *BANG!* A kid hits the ceiling. *Ding!* Too late! *Screams!*

Willa grabs me. I cling to the armrests. The seatbelt cuts into me. Can the plane hold together? *Oh lordylordy*, lockers pop, lights flicker, screams, groans, pleading, prayers, sick with fear, oh God. Everything is flung up…

> down…
>> down…

Willa's face a wide-eyed stare, each breath a groan…
>> down…
>>> down…

'Night…' Willa gasps, 'always at night…'

An explosion? Things breaking? Engines scream like a million leaf blowers, kids scream. We cling together, blankets, papers, bags, chips, shoes fly *up*.

Willa lurches sideways, breathing in my ear. Oh
lordylord, she wants to *say* something. *Oww* her
fingers hurt *oww*.

'Listen!' she gasps. 'Are you *listening*?'

'*Yes.*'

'*Look after the dog!*'

What? She doesn't *have* a dog! Is she having a heart
attack?

'*WE'RE STILL FLYING, WILLA!*'

'We'll make it, Henni. We're the right kind. Where's
this one?' She's babbling in a squeak, like a kid.
'Papa said we must go down. Papa's eyes are talking.
Moeder! *Please*, Moeder. *Please*, Moeder…'

She's a little girl. She's in *two* nightmares!

down…down…

Eyes are talking, terrified, brave eyes catch other
eyes, ghost eyes shot with fear, eyes closed, lips
praying, masks,

down…

down… How long?

'My heart can't take it,' she gasps.

Oh God, what to do? Mum? Dad? Donna? NOT lucky
pig NOT lucky duck oh silly Danielle. I chant, *This
plane will not crash, we will not die.* I chant with my
fingers, *this plane will not crash this plane will not crash.*

When Frank panicked, what did Donna do? She made him *breathe*. She *counted*.

'BREATHE WITH ME WILLA!' I scream. 'Come *ON*, Willa! *Breathe with me! IN…two…three…four… OUT…two…three…four…*'

down…

down…How long?

'…ghost drifted down the stairs, she didn't care…'

'Shut *UP*, Willa, *LISTEN to* **me**!' I shriek in her ear. '*Breathe IN…two…three…four…OUT…two… three…four…*Don't talk, breathe!'

Her lip trembles. 'I was going home.'

'You *are* going home…*three…four…*Don't cry, Willa, *breathe IN* with me…*three…four…OUT… two…three…four…*'

'In the freezing dark I let her in…never be afraid again. But I'm *afraid again*…' Willa's face is a mask. Her eyes are closing.

'WILLA!' I shake her, pinch her, screaming, '*IN*…two…three…four…*OUT*…two…three… four…' YES! She hears!

'*Safe*…two…three…four…an' **sound**…two… three …four…' I chant I chant I chant and pray to Mum, Donna, Dad, Danielle the plane, the pilot, the sea, the air…Willa and I are a breathing lump, clinging, breathing, waiting...

BANG!

The plane bounces.

A net!

Caught!

Oh, a mighty jolt. Not falling now, going down but forwards, bucking, swinging from side to side, bouncing, jumping.

'*Breathe*, Willa! Big slow breaths.' The plane tips sideways, like jolting down steps. She's crushing me. 'Two...three...four...*Straight!* Two...three...four...'

Willa gasps. 'I was a kid. What did I know?'

The swinging grows less. Oh *thank you* plane, *thank you*. Fly straight now please fly straight plane-bird.

Willa's face is not so grey now, but I chant on. '**Safe**...*two...three...four*...**sound**...*two... three...four...to that house in* **Am**-ster-dam *Safe... two...three...four*...**sound**...*two...three...four...'*

The fear is easing. The plane is flying straight with only little hops. Bit by bit the jolts grow less. The noise is not so deafening, the tension fades. Finally, there's the sound we long for.

Ding!

The crew springs up. The captain makes an announcement which I can't hear for shouting and kids crying. We keep breathing, but loosen our grip on each other. The cabin crew crowd round the kid who hit the roof. He has a broken arm, and maybe ribs. They stop the blood pouring down the face of the woman who was clobbered by an iPad. Uggh, towels covered in blood. When Zev had his accident they said 'heads bleed'. The plane is a hurricane-mess. Who cares? It's flying. Everyone is helpful, relieved. The engines sound normal. We are alive!

And here's a funny thing.

A toddler called Casey, who *screamed* on take-off (probably had sore ears, mine hurt too), and whose mother yelled '*Stop* it, Casey!' a million times, well, that little clown Casey *slept through the whole thing!* And now he's chirping and giggling! Everyone grins and catches each other's eyes. Oh that Casey!

'We have commenced our descent into Dubai.'

Willa is sitting up straight, eyes closed, breathing quietly, her chin on her chest. I think she's asleep.

The flight attendant leans over and asks me quietly, 'Should we get a wheelchair for your friend?'

Willa jerks her head back like a startled horse, awake. 'No wheelchair, thank you,' she says loudly.

SECOND HOP TO AMSTERDAM

Bump!

Oh *joy*! Sweet Mother Earth.

The engines roared and the plane erupted with cheers for the captain and crew. I cheered for the engines.

The poor kid with the broken arm and the lady with the bandaged head left first from our section. Then a support crew with wheelchairs took old and injured people from the plane, then an army of cleaners in overalls and rubber gloves moved in. Poor them.

But I guess you're wondering who *is* this old person, Willa? And what's going on with us being on a plane to Amsterdam? I'll tell you later.

Dubai.

I *never* wanted to fly in an aeroplane again, *EVER!* And by EVER I mean **EVER!**

And Willa? Well, she wasn't saying anything, as she heaved her big body out of that horrible squashed-up godawful mess into the shuffling queue to get off that plane.

Keep an eye on the luggage. Six pieces, remember, six pieces. Two in the hold. Remember Willa's wedding present parcel.

I checked and triple-checked. Weird to be checking for your luggage when not long ago you were checking for your *life!* Yep, we had everything but... I had a funny feeling I'd forgotten something.

We were shuffling out when I heard voices behind me: 'Excuse me.' 'Pass this on.' 'Excuse me.' 'Pass it to her.' 'That girl.' I felt a tap on my shoulder and the woman behind me handed me my notebook! *Phew!* It had slipped right to the back of the plane. It was a bit wet. Not as wet as it could have been... I patted my pocket for my pen. *Double phew!*

Dubai rhymes with *cry.*

What was I supposed to do now?

A small group of passengers from our flight squawked at the cabin crew: 'What *caused* it? Why *weren't we told? Twenty years off my life! FAULT! BLAME! ET CETERA!'* Why were they angry at the crew who looked after us? I wanted to yell, 'Not fair!'

'I need a toilet!' said Willa, looking desperate.

'Me too!'

CURSES! Everybody on that flight needed a toilet. (You don't read about this in books.) We were facing the Queue from Hell!

'Come on, Willa, we'll find another toilet.' It was excruciating. I shuffled Willa along a marble aisle to another lot of toilets and got her in this still-long-but-shorter queue, up the front because she was old.

I sat with the luggage until she came back, then I parked her with the luggage while I waited and waited in the queue, thinking, *Mum! Help! We're in a white marble airport with hundreds of people who thought they would die, but we're walking around looking normal. Dad, what do I do? I don't want to fly.*

We had three hours before the next flight.

Willa looked at me in a blank way, like she'd handed me her brains, and what did I decide for her? Oh *jeeps!* Her relos were meeting us at the airport in Amsterdam. Everyone at home was waiting to hear that we'd arrived safely. Everyone wanted us to be a success. *I* wanted us to be a success. Could I forget

the turbulence??? Could I ever get back on a plane???
NEVER! Could I get Willa back on a plane? Who
knows! And her babbling like a frightened kid, what
was *that* about?

I felt scared and empty. I wanted to flop down and
cry, 'Poor me, poor me.' I wanted someone to put their
arms around me and give me a hot Milo and make the
problems go away. 'We're only a phone call away,' said
Mum and Dad a zillion times, but my phone was as
useful as a dead fish. No chip. No money for Dubai.
No idea how to get reception.

When my body heard that my brain was thinking
about getting back on a plane, I needed the Dames
again, and the huge stupid waterfall in the airport
didn't help. I left Willa chatting to a cheerful Italian
guy. He didn't look like a robber, but they warned me,
'Robbers don't look like robbers.' Too bad. *I gotta go!*

What could I do? Borrow the Italian guy's phone
and call home? *We're in Dubai. Come and get us.*
We want to come home right now, but NOT ON A
PLANE! Could I do that? Like I was six and got
spooked at a sleepover? And everyone in Stella Street
had been so kind. But I never wanted to fly again.
Holyjeepersmoley, what could I *do*? Faint? Steal
whisky and drink it all? But what about Willa?

I thought of Dad's advice. 'Henni, if you ever have to eat cooked horse's eye, *pretend* you enjoy it. You're good at pretending, Henni. *Fake* it.'

A woman two cubicles up from me was getting hysterical on the phone to some poor relative. '...*we were going to die. It went down and down...oh...*'

I couldn't stand it.

Willa looked at me like a tired old dog waiting for the next command. I took a deep breath.

'Okay Willa, now we find the plane to Amsterdam.'

She didn't freak out.

The Italian man said, 'The flight, she will be good. Pilot is clever. Plane is modern.' What a nice guy.

We gathered everything up, yes, all hand luggage, yes, the wedding present parcel, yes, notebook, liquid gel pen, yes, everything. Ciao sweet Italian man. We set off.

Dubai airport is a real-life horror-maze computer game, where you have to find Gate B5. Willa would have been hopeless on her own. *H o p e l e s s !* She wandered in a befuddled daze into the luxury duty-free shops. Did she want a watch for three thousand dollars? I grabbed her arm and steered her out.

I searched for our flight on the electronic

information boards... *Yes!* Gate B5, but poor old Willa dog kept straying...

'Do you want something, Willa?'

'No...' she said vaguely, wandering towards a shop of exclusive beauty products.

Okay. I steered her to the counter.

'Can I help you, madam?' said the delicate assistant.

'Yes. I would like hand cream with the perfume of roses...'

Huh!

'...and lipstick for a wedding.'

Huh! Then she wanted a particular brand because Donna said it was good. I found her credit card and gave it to the assistant who fussed about wrapping this perfect little parcel, which took ages and probably cost a fortune. Then Willa bought a pair of toenail clippers, which took even longer.

Why couldn't she just *tell* me? Was this the new brain-dead Willa? Anyway, she seemed happy now, but I was *really* worried we'd miss the plane to Amsterdam. Everyone had told us, 'Get to the gate early.' On the next noticeboard I desperately searched for our flight. *Yes!* Oh no! It vanished! There it was. Gone *again!* Another number and destination flashed up. It was so confusing. Where was Gate B5?

'Nearly there,' I said. *Ha ha ha.*

We charged around, well, shuffled through Dubai airport, through crowds of all colours and shapes and sizes and languages and kids and hair and robes and legs – up escalators, stairs and lifts, following the arrows, trying not to get caught in a rip of travellers streaming the wrong way. My stomach chewed me up inside. I was scared of missing the plane, and terrified of catching it.

'Donna said we should stretch our legs in the airport,' I chirped mock-cheerfully. (Dad, you would be proud). Dear old Willa struggled on as we followed the signs into a train, through a dark tunnel, onto a bus, which drove for ages beside a high barbed-wire fence through a hot-looking sandy landscape till we were delivered *straight to the plane*! There was *NO Gate B5!*

We were the first to board. Willa was just glad to sit down. The flight attendant helped me shove our stuff in the overhead lockers. We were <u>back</u> *on a plane!* I jammed that fact into my brain's overhead locker and slammed it shut.

'What alcohol do you have?' Willa asked the attendant.

'Sorry. We can't serve anything till we're in flight.'

'We were on a plane that hit turbulence,' I said.

'Oh, that flight from Australia,' he said. 'I heard about it.'

'We hit an air pocket.'

'Oh, it's actually not a pocket with no air,' he said, 'it's just bad turbulence. Don't worry, planes are safe.'

Oh yeah? Tell that to my bum.

We sat.

And sat.

I kept thinking about Willa's ramblings. Did I hear right? It was important. She *made* me listen. She must have read my thoughts. 'I was younger than you,' she muttered, staring at her old, wrinkly hands. 'I was twelve when it began.'

It's something from when she was a kid. 'What happened?'

I was sure she heard me. I was about to ask again when she gave a snort. 'Okay, okay. I'll tell you some Dutch history, which young people don't find interesting...'

'I'm interested.'

Another long pause.

'In the First World War, Germany, England and France went killing each other, but the Dutch were neutral. We watched. When the war was over Europe was a dreadful mess and Germany wrecked, but that evil little Hitlerman was screaming his promises. He built up his army and people could see another war coming like a dark storm. *Okay*, the Dutch thought, *we stay on the side again. Anyway, we have no military machines, just stuff left over from forty years ago.*' Willa gave another sigh. 'But we were dealing with that evil little Hitlerman.'

She was a kid in the war.

Willa squirmed in her seat.

'The Netherlands was pretty tolerant, so when that evil little Hitlerman starts blaming the Jews for everything wrong, some Jewish families came to the Netherlands hoping it would be safe.'

Willa leaned on the armrests and squirmed again.

'Then the Germans, we called them *moffen*, invaded

the Netherlands. For a while, people thought, *Oh it's okay, the moff doesn't bother us, we don't have to decide anything moral.* Some say, "It's pretty good for business, with the Germans." Then the moff start on our Jews. The same old story. Blame them. Encourage us to hate them. Make them separate so they're obvious. I didn't know who was a Jew until they had to wear those Stars of David, oh then we knew. That's *them*! Us and *them*! Round *them* up. Take *them* away to work in a factory in Germany. *Hoh!* My God, those *factories*.' She was angry now. 'Well, some Jews knew about those *factories*.'

What did she mean, 'those factories'? I wasn't game to ask.

'What would you do, Henni, if you were a Jewish mother or father? Hide the family, or maybe suicide together, thinking this is better than the *factories*? Imagine being so frightened and trapped and hated.'

Her hands were fists now and her anger flowed around and it almost felt like she was angry at *me*.

'People say I'm lucky to have such a good memory, well Henni, I tell you, it's a *curse*.'

Willa shut down. Closed her eyes. No correspondence will be entered into. *Whoa!* Donna and Mr Nic back home were right! Something's burning in there. This is not a jolly holiday. Sure hasn't been so far.

The plane was filling up and noisy. The flight was delayed. The waiting-to-fly torture dragged on. Finally, around midnight, we buckled up for take-off. I was so exhausted I was thinking *I don't care if we crash, at least it would be over*. But you know what? The moment I dreaded, the lift-off, was so smooth you could hardly tell we were flying. The crew tucked us up and settled us down like birds in our nests, and turned out the lights.

I woke up, no idea what time, feeling that if I didn't move I would *explode*. I climbed on the armrests over Willa like Spider-Girl, then stretched divine stretches like a cat. I stilted stiffly down the aisle through the sleeping zombies. At the back I found snack-heaven; Maltesers, mini Mars-bars, chocolates, biscotti, which are biscuits, apples, soy rice crackers, juice and drinks. *Free! Help yourself!* Frank would have made himself sick.

I crept up the front. Behind a curtain I heard a *clink-clink* and smelled fresh coffee. I peeped in. A mysterious flight attendant was arranging a delicate little snack. Then a mysterious bearded man used

mysterious sign language to show me how to get a
drink from the tap in the wall. Out a porthole I saw
tiny mysterious dots of light below, in mysterious
towns, in mysterious countries, where mysterious
people slept. How mysterious it all was. I liked
thinking that, instead of thinking I was in a plane.

I prowled back to Willa, who was snoring quietly,
her mouth open, her head slumped sideways. Her
blow-up neck cushion had slipped around, and in the
dark she looked like one of those old Dutch women
wearing weird doughnut collars in those gloomy
paintings.

Quietly as I could, I Spider-Girled back to my seat,

'*Arrrrrrrgh! Oh Henni!*'

'Sorry, Willa. There's food and drinks down the back. Free. Go for a walk. It's worth it.'

Like an old caterpillar easing out of a clinging cocoon, she extracted herself. She swayed for a moment, surveying the zombies, then shuffled down the aisle, steadying herself on the seat backs. She was away for ages. I was about to go looking for her when she showed up, then sighing and groaning she squeezed back into her seat. Willa and me. Wide awake in the dark sea of zombies.

'Willa, you know in the...when the plane was...when it was rough, what did you mean when you told me to look after the dog?' I asked quietly.

'Did I say *that*?'

'Yes.'

'What else did I say?'

'Your parents were going down somewhere...and a ghost went down the stairs?...and someone pushed in?'

She snorted and waved her hand, dismissing it.

'Willa, you nearly *squashed* me. You *made* me listen. It was *important*.'

'I don't even know what it is.'

1

'What?'

'The damn blue dog.'

The *blue* dog? What a weird conversation.

'I think the blue dog *is* important,' sighed Willa, 'but I don't know what it is. It's not an animal.'

I started guessing. 'Oh, code! Like when Mr Nic says *cabbage*, he means *money*.'

'No.'

'A place! The Blue Dog Cafe? or Blue Dog Hairdressers?'

'It was a *thing*, in our house.'

'Like an ornament? A toy?'

'I don't *know*!' she snapped.

'If it was important, why didn't your parents tell you?'

She glared at me. 'There were so many secrets back then.'

'Maybe your sister Hyacint will know about the blue dog?'

'No. Hyacint is a lot younger than me. She and Jacob were only babies, I was twelve or thirteen. Anyway, Hyacint's memory's going now.' She sniffed, and searched for a tissue. 'Hyacint asks a question, I answer it, and five minutes later she asks it again. Jacob says it got worse a year ago.'

'Would Jacob know about the blue dog?'

'I *told* you. They were *babies*! Maybe something will come back to me in Amsterdam.' She flicked her hand at me. 'You're Miss Curious, you solve it.'

'What about the ghost?'

A determined shake of her head.

'Was that in the war?'

She ignored me.

'Did you *see* the ghost?'

'You wouldn't understand.'

'I could try.'

She groaned. 'For goodness sake, Henni, everything was out of control. Something you have never known. It was a different time.'

'I got caught in a rip once.'

'That's the sea,' she snapped, 'that's understandable.'

'What about the turbulence?'

'Same as the sea.' She softened a bit. 'Henni, I'm talking about a time when the worst side of human nature was in control. You've never had brutes force their way in…*Oh! Dom!*' She was mad at herself. 'All right, I'll tell you. But don't you ever talk about it, not in Amsterdam, not back home, not anywhere. Okay?'

'Sure.' We were conspirators in the dark.

In a sullen voice Willa began.

'Moeder – my mother – was a dressmaker, and once, when she had too much work, she looked for someone to help her, and found Sara who lived down the street. Sara was funny. They loved working together. They were a good team. Moeder had the clients and was clever with the technical stuff. Sara had style. But, and here's the catch, Sara was a Jew. She and her husband Matius had come from Berlin years before, after Matius read a book written by that evil little Hitlerman.'

Willa crossed her arms.

'Well, the laws against the Jews got worse. Moeder was furious about what was happening to Sara and Matius. "*Hypocrites! Christian hypocrites!*" she raged. "Whatever happened to 'Do unto others'?"

'I heard Papa tell Moeder to shut up. He *never* spoke to her like that. Papa was frightened of Moeder's rage. Moeder held her tongue, but she started doing risky things. Once I found her coat behind the door, dripping wet, and when I peeped into the bedroom she was putting ointment on a big purple bruise on her hip. One evening I will never forget, out the bathroom window I saw a man climbing across the roofs in one of Moeder's dresses!

'Oh there were terrible arguments. Moeder didn't

like authority, especially if she thought it was stupid.

'"Now they're saying Jews can't grow vegetables!" she ranted. "Can they behave like that?" Papa, who was tired of all this, snapped, "Of course they can and they *are* behaving like that. What do you propose to do about it? Go out there are get yourself shot?"

'Moeder didn't say anything but her mouth pinched up and her blazing eyes flicked round and down to the skirting board, which I thought was weird, so when no one was home I levered the skirting board out with a screwdriver. I found bundles and bundles of food coupons. I put that board back quick smart.

'The next day my parents had a blazing row. Then two days later Moeder told me, "Sara and Matius are going to live with us in secret." A friend of Moeder's brought them to our place. This guy was like a postman, secretly delivering people to houses all over Amsterdam.'

'How long did they stay with you?'

'A year. I remember the night they came, their whispering woke me up and I pretended to be asleep. Next morning we settled into our lives together. They never went outside, and if someone came to the apartment, they hid. We were especially careful about opening the door.

2

'The rumour that Moeder and others put around was that Matius and Sara had gone north to Sweden. We prayed so hard for the Allies to crush that evil little Hitlerman. My parents had given up on God, but…' She shrugged. 'Sometimes you pray anyway. I didn't know what was going on half the time. I didn't know what people really thought.'

Willa took off her glasses and cleaned them slowly with the corner of the airline blanket. I was afraid she would stop talking.

'What happened, Willa?'

She took ages to put her glasses back on.

'One Saturday evening, it had been a shocking, terrible day – one of the babies was sick – when Cornelia, an older cousin, knocked on the door. Someone had just left the building, and the downstairs door was slightly open, so she came straight up to our apartment.

'"Hello, it's Cornelia," she called in a friendly voice. It was nearly curfew. I knew Cornelia, and without thinking I opened the door. I left no time for Sara to hide. Cornelia saw her at the stove. That night, the Gestapo took them. They took Papa too.'

Willa's bottom lip twisted and a tear slid from wrinkle to wrinkle.

'My cousin Cornelia betrayed them. She told her husband, who was in the NSB. And I opened the door.' Willa dabbed her eyes. 'Sara was Moeder's best friend.'

'Oh Willa...'

'It was my fault.'

What could I say?

'Did your father come back?'

'*Enough!*' She thumped the armrests. '*Dom* turbulence!'

The plane's engines droned on, a steady rumble, like surf in the distance. I felt so sad for Willa.

I thought to myself, *I will find that blue dog.*

Then we were ripped back to reality.

'Get him to the *toilet*! Get him to the *toilet*!'
A chunky dad tried to hustle along a white-faced kid, while the mum fussed with a sick bag. The kid was frozen in those pre-chuck convulsions (probably too many Maltesers from the free snack-bar, I saw him going back there). Then the kid erupted right by Willa. *Urgggh!*

Willa's guts revolted and she got pains in the stomach and farted like a cannon. 'Be quiet, bottom!' she grumbled. Thank God for the noise of the plane, and the darkness.

I wrote and wrote on that long flight, scribbling whatever came into my head, and some ideas became poems. I guessed at Willa's story of the ghost on the stairs and why Willa was going back.

The liquid gel pen drove me on. In the plane's air it was bleeding, and I wrote faster and faster in the dark to beat the pen from making a blob, swimming in a restless limbo of imagination. I noticed I wasn't afraid of flying right then, in that speck in the sky. We weren't anywhere. My pen gave a splutter and did a blob.

The day dawned. Cheerful daylight faded up in the windows and the zombies turned into ordinary people, squeezing politely past each other to the toilet. ''Scuse me. 'Scuse me. Sorry. 'Scuse me.'

We pulled down our tray tables and waited for the manna to fall from the food trolley. The plane was a rat's nest of rubbish.

My liquid gel pen ran out, and that was the end of the pen and the night and pretty soon, the flight.

'Cabin crew, prepare the cabin for landing.'

———

FIRST IMPRESSIONS

Schiphol is Amsterdam's airport, which sounds like *Ship-pol* but has nothing to do with ships. At Schiphol we were met by Willa's relatives.

An old man shorter than Willa flung his arms around her. '*Roos*! Mijn *Roos*!' They hugged in such an emotional hug they swayed from side to side like a slow old-human rocking thing, like that gnome thing that keeps time on Magg's piano. Anyway, it was embarrassing and I thought they might fall over.

'Roos, mijn *Roos!*'

'Jacobje, *mijn lieve Jacobje.*'

Willa swamped him with her coat, and when they finally untangled she was sniffing and dabbing her eyes and shaking her head and smiling so hard I thought her face would crack. She held him away and stood back to look at him.

'Henni, this is my little brother, Jacob,' said Willa.

'Thank you for bringing Roos,' Jacob grinned at me. 'Thank you a million times.'

'Is she Roos?' I asked. 'We call her Willa.'

'Roos, Willa, the same person.' Jacob laughed. He was a little taller than me, a arty-looking with a short beard. He was pink around the eyes too. I liked him.

'Remember me, Henni?' It was smiley Wendelien, who came and stayed with Willa in Stella Street. She flopped her hands in a *can-you-believe-it*? way. 'I'm a *doctor* now, Henni, I'm doing *research*, and I'm getting *married*!' She looked older but I recognised the wide, cheeky mouth and disobedient hair.

And the last new person was a tall, strong, serious bear of a man named Dirk, a bit older than Dad. Wendelien and Dirk were Jacob's grown-up children.

Oh boy, these names! How can I remember them? Jacob? Jacob, ja ja Jacob. Dirk? Dirk the Bear. 'Welcome, ladies,' said Dirk the Bear, grabbing our cases as if they were packets of biscuits. Wendelien took Willa's bag, Jacob and I had a bag, and Willa had nothing.

Six pieces of luggage, Remember, six…OH NO! The wedding present parcel! Ha ha! Wendelien has it! PHEW!

Willa had never met Dirk before. She was like a different person, excited and laughing. Maybe Willa was different now she was Roos.

They yabbered away in Dutch as we piled on a train for the city. I could get some words, because they sounded like English knocked sideways (*dit is mijn vriend* = this is my friend) but here's what's amazing – everyone could speak English!

Amazing Amsterdam
Sight Number 1

I stepped out of Amsterdam's Central Station into another world, my eyes as big as bike wheels! Everywhere you looked there were bikes: office workers, tradies, teenagers, grandmas, hip dudes, *everyone* on bikes and not one helmet! And the station's bike park, WOW! *Thousands* of bikes.

You couldn't see a single bike, they were a *mass*, like coral on the Great Barrier Reef. Every post, fence, corner, pole and rail was crusty with bikes. Sure, there were trams, buses and taxis, but this was bike city.

I couldn't stop laughing. 'Ha ha ha! Will we ride home on bi—'

BRRRRIIIIIING!!!!! 'Let op!'

Wendelien yanked me back.

'Jeetje mina!' yelled the rider.

'STOP!' ordered Dirk the Bear, plonking down the cases. 'Tante Roos, Henni, *listen*! You are in Amsterdam now,' he said in a stern voice, pointing to the strip of the road where we stood. 'Here is for walking. Bikes there. Trams there. Buses and cars there. Okay?'

Whooooosh! Whoosh! Bikes shot past on the bike strip. My head swivelled left, right, left, right. We crossed to the pedestrian strip beside the car strip, and climbed into a taxi. I didn't even think of the luggage.

The narrow houses were like books squashed together on a bookshelf. Picture-book bridges hopped over canals and bikes whizzed along, stopping and going at their own traffic lights. What a toy city.

The taxi turned into a quiet street with trees.

'We're here,' said Jacob. 'Eerste Hugo de Grootstraat.'

No verandah, no garden, no fence, just a little bench chained to a drainpipe beside a black door. Our destination, where we would stay with Willa's sister Hyacint.

Jacob searched through his pockets for keys. Suddenly, like a seagull *plop!,* a baby's sock hit the ground at his feet, with keys inside. Above us, an old woman leaned out of a second-floor window and yelled, *'Roos! AndawholelotofhappyDutchlikemysister you'rebackorsomething.'*

And Willa yelled back, *'Hyacint! It'smeandmore happyDutchlikeyesitsmeIcan'tbelieveit.'*

Amazing Amsterdam
Sight Number 2

The house stopped being a toy house when Jacob opened the door. In front of my nose a narrow staircase rose up into the darkness. The stairs were *incredibly* steep. Not exactly welcoming.

Willa didn't hesitate, she
clambered up those stairs
on all fours like a baby.
A light came on and
at the landing she
grabbed the rail and
stood up, puffed and panted,

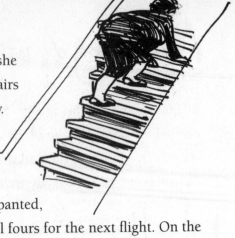

then went down on all fours for the next flight. On the
second-floor landing, her sister stood at her apartment
door with open arms. The old ladies hugged, though it
wasn't like with Jacob.

'Hyacint!' exclaimed Willa. 'You got *old*!'

'You did too, Roos!' There was a lot of laughing.
Hyacint was shorter than Willa, and birdlike thin,
with grey wavy hair. We went inside. It was an old
person's place with big lounge chairs that took up a lot
of space. It looked like nothing much had changed for
a long time.

Willa walked around the apartment sort of smelling
it, and feeling it.

'It's so *small*. Nice colour on the walls…still got
these chairs…there was a dresser here…You got rid
of the table! That was a real nice table. Why did you
get rid of the table?'

'It's *my* place,' said Hyacint.

Willa called from the kitchen. 'Henni, come and look at this.' She pointed to a machine on the wall. 'See this old coffee grinder? I can remember when I wasn't strong enough to wind the handle.' She surveyed it all. 'Hmm, new stove.' The kitchen had blue-and-white tiles like Willa's back in Stella Street and everything was super clean, twenty 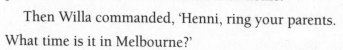 per cent cleaner than our kitchen back home.

Then Willa commanded, 'Henni, ring your parents. What time is it in Melbourne?'

Hallelujah! She has her brain back!

'Mum and Dad said to call no matter what time.'

Dirk the Bear tapped the number into his phone. I heard the spacey doodle-doos, then the lovely sound of our home phone as it rang and rang.

Mum answered, half asleep. 'Henni?'

I was glad she was dopey. Her voice nearly set me off, but I took a deep breath.

'Hello Mum. We're in Amsterdam. We just arrived at Willa's family's place.'

'How was the flight?'

'The first hop was...rough...' I glanced at Willa, who raised an eyebrow, 'but the rest was fine.'

'Glad you made it safe and sound.'

'And the luggage?' I heard Dad ask in the background.

'Yep, all good. Mum, here's the biggest surprise, I'm not tall here. Dutch kids are taller than me!'

They laughed.

'Glad you're normal, sweetheart.'

I couldn't say more with Willa and her family there and it was too hard to keep talking.

'Tell you soon, Mum.'

'Bye sweetheart.'

'Bye Mum.'

Click.

Phew.

Where would I sleep?

In this little apartment with these two old ladies? The living room was crowded. My mind started turning on Willa's story from the plane. We were standing in exactly the space where Willa and her parents and Sara and Matius and the babies had all lived, squashed together for a year. I felt sad and tired.

Willa and Hyacint gabbled away in Dutch, then the tone changed to an argument. You sure could tell they were sisters by the way they spoke to each other. They were talking about me and *Zolder*, whoever *Zolder* was.

'Who is Zolder?' I asked Wendelien.

Wendelien sighed. '*Zolder* means attic. They're arguing about if you should stay in the attic. Willa says: "You can't put her up there. It's freezing. She's not a servant, to live out of sight." Hyacint says: "There is a heater." Willa wants you to stay here, where it's warmer and close to the bathroom, sleeping on the couch and folding it up each morning.'

Jacob leaned towards me. 'They've been together for ten minutes and they're at it already.'

'What do you think, Jacob?' I whispered.

'Personally, I would be far away from these old ducks. They'll drive you nuts. Wendelien made a place for you in the attic.' Jacob interrupted his sisters loudly. 'Please! Can Henni see the attic?'

'Ja!' said Hyacint. 'Take her up, Wendelien.'

'Do you really want to see the attic, Henni?' Willa frowned. 'It's very cold.'

I said my first Dutch word. 'Ja.'

Jacob, Wendelien and I climbed the stairs. After the last landing they were even narrower.

'Everyone lives on top of each other,' said Wendelien.

'...in order of age...' puffed Jacob, '...the old near

the ground...getting closer to the grave...and the young...*Ooff ahh*...up near the stars.'

Wendelien unlocked the little door. We bobbed our heads and went through.

A cloud of doona shimmered like a heavenly vision on the floor. I longed to collapse on it, but Wendelien chattered on. 'Each apartment has an attic for storage. I tossed a lot out, but I kept these Dutch things for you, Henni – this old model ship which Bram dropped, and now it's a shipwreck, and somewhere there's Opa Loobeek's cannonball, and his lanterna magica. Hyacint wants to get rid of everything on King's Day...'

I did listen when she pointed out a grey plastic bucket with a lid, and a roll of toilet paper beside it, tucked under a low table.

'Use the pot,' said Wendelien, 'then bring it downstairs, tip it into the toilet and rinse it out.'

'Oh, I've been camping in the bush,' I said as brightly as I could manage. 'No worries.'

Wendelien rattled on. 'I cleared this little shelf for you. This cupboard was my great grandma's...' Etc etc etc. It was torture. I was so tired I could hardly stand up.

'We should go downstairs,' said Jacob, 'they are waiting.'

'Henni, you're staying in the attic,' said Hyacint.

I looked at Willa. She nodded, but didn't look at me, as if she had betrayed me. Dirk the Bear carried my case up the narrow stairs.

All I will say is that when the attic door closed and I was alone at last, I crashed on the bed and cried huge wrenching sobs. I'd got Willa to Amsterdam, and now I wanted to sleep forever. I dragged the doona round me and fell asleep still crying.

FiRST MORNING

I will tell you everything

but now I say to myself,

to myself I say

How strange to wake up and find me in an attic

And I open my eyes this much = =

And I say to myself

to myself I say

Ja Ja Ja very strange

And close my eyes – –

And I ask myself

To myself I ask

Are you happy? this morning? in Amsterdam? after
everything?

still in last night's clothes? even your shoes? from
Melbourne?

Out of 100?

Be honest

And I say to myself
to myself I say
Ja Ja Ja
which is Dutch for Ja

continents, oceans, hemispheres,
date lines, equator, the planet
we crossed
Willa and I
we fell through a hole in the sky
No not that

We got vomited beside
met with a metrognome
rocked up to a black door
and scaled the stairs
Unknown Events in the City of Bikes
Have Begun

I poke my foot out and quickly pull it back. It's
freezing! Willa was right. I wrangle the divine cloud
around me, with just my eyes and nose in the cold.
Slowly shapes become clearer and I make out this
zolder place. There's just enough light from the
window to see the old wooden beams of the sloping
roof, like two hands, fingers touching lightly above
me. I'm under praying hands.

The light is changing. I hear seagulls and a car. It's
much quieter than home. And a plane, and pigeons.

And church bells! Oh how beautiful. They're
having a musical conversation. The last notes die
away. Will a big bell toll the hours? I'm waiting...

DONG.....

DONG.....

DONG.....

Deep rich notes take their time to drop like heavy
blessings over the sleeping city

DONG

I count on my fingers like all the others lying quietly.

DONG

listening counting wondering...

Five

My mind roams over the city like the Spirit of
Christmas Past, travelling with the last dong to the
furthest places, to the farmers and the sailors and the
lighthouse keepers…

The bells again. Must have slept. How many dongs
now? Seven. The sun is coming up. Through the
window the patch of sky is gold and pink and pale
blue-grey. Wrapped in the doona I'm a big puffy
caterpillar. I shuffle over and open my picture-book
window.

Yesterday was a horror movie. Today is Hans Christian Andersen.

Once upon a time there was a city, where the roofs flowed together like a sea of red tiles that a man could run over. A magnificent spire pointed to heaven, and the trees in the street were bare, for it was winter.

From her window a young girl watched a marmalade cat, who gazed back and flicked his tail. The girl looked down on a crossroads with bike racks on each corner. Hmm…bike racks…in Hans Christian Andersen? Yep, there are now.

Then the girl looked along the tops of the houses, and saw a row of hooks, like Captain Hook's hook, silhouetted against the sunrise. Each hook hung down from a strong beam jutting out from the top of each building. It reminded the girl of playing hangman, and unhappy things. The girl looked at the pattern of windows in the houses opposite. She saw books and plants on windowsills, and then, as the blinds slid up, and the people stirred, she glimpsed their lives.

I am alone, unless someone is determined to climb the stairs. I know why writers write in attics, because they're so far up, and the last stairs are even *narrower*, if you can imagine that.

In Australia there would be a sign saying *Only people weighing less than 50kg may proceed beyond this point.* STEEP STAIRS! SAFETY HAZARD! In fact, there would be a sign at the bottom saying: DANGEROUS. DO NOT PROCEED BEYOND THIS POINT. In fact there'd be a sign outside the door saying DANGER! DO NOT ENTER

'I could survive on carrots in a garret,' said a cheerful poet. 'Who wants to live under the house with the rats? Give me spires to inspire me. No footfall on the stairs except if Wheezing Pockface staggers up to demand the rent, twenty gilders which I cannot pay until my poetry is published, but Pockface has a failing heart and fears the Stairs of Dread…'

hmmmm

so do I

The closest toilet is three floors down the Stairs of
Dread.

I'm busting. Shut up, bladder! *Wait!*

The bells tell me another hour has passed. Now
listen to me, bladder, stay calm – but bladder won't
shut up.

'In days of yore,' said the poet, *'we trotted up and
down stairs with potties all the livelong day.'*

'Well, poet, this is days of now, and back where I
come from some families have a bathroom for *each
person.'*

If someone saw me going downstairs with that
bucket of wee, I would die of embarrassment.

I hurried down one flight, being extra careful with
the bucket, but I heard a door open and shot back
up, my heart racing. I stood inside the zolder door.
Finally I said to myself, *Are you going to stand in this
attic forever, holding a bucket of wee? Nee. Well, go
downstairs, you big baby. You're not risking your life.*

This time on the Stairs of Dread, nobody opened
a door, and nobody saw me. I slipped into Hyacint's
apartment. The twee oude dames were in the kitchen

talking loudly. *Phew*! I did the bucket thing and had a magnificent shower.

When I came down from the zolder, in clean clothes, the twee oude dames in dressing gowns were looking at a *honderd* oude photos. I'm not being rude – *twee oude dames* means 'two old ladies' (*twee* sounds like *tway*). These oude dames are definitely *not* twee!

'Henni,' said Hyacint, cheerfully reaching out an arm, 'look at this!' It was a photo of a teenage girl with two toddlers. 'That's Roos with me and Jacob, aren't we sweet?'

'Did you use the pot?' asked Willa.

'Yes.'

'Was it all right?'

'No worries.'

In the oude family photos Willa was stunning when she was young, and there was the family in this apartment and children playing in the street outside. Hyacint and Jacob have lived in this building all their lives. That's rare in Australia.

My stomach rumbled loudly, then the twee oude dames squabbled about my breakfast. Hyacint wanted to fuss over me, and Willa wanted me to do my own thing. Breakfast was weird, but at least it wasn't boiled horse's eye. There was a sort of breakfast cake, like soft squishy gingerbread, and a drink called *karnemelk,* which I thought was milk but it tasted sour. *Uggh!* And friendly-looking bread.

'Can I toast this?'

'No toaster,' said Willa bluntly, as she ground coffee in the old machine on the wall. Oh well, at least they had butter and slices of cheese, and the kitchen had a lovely coffee smell like back home.

'Henni, phone your parents tonight. They'll be busy now.' Willa sure was self-managing herself. And me!

Hyacint announced, 'Henni, I have asked a nice girl your age who lives nearby to show you around.'

'Who?' said Willa.

Hyacint said a name. Sometimes, when something catches her, Willa has a way of stopping and widening her eyes ever so slightly for a fraction of a moment, like a bird that suddenly realises danger. I didn't notice it much before this trip. I do now. Anyway, she did that.

I know Hyacint is being kind, but I remembered Tara, a girl who came on a holiday with us once. I don't like this being-matchmade-with-a-friend business.

There was a knock on the door. I suddenly thought of Cornelia knocking at that same door. I looked at

Willa but she didn't notice. It was Jacob's wife. It turns
out she and Jacob live in the same building on the
ground floor, with a different door, and everybody in
the building seems to have a key to the downstairs
front door. And Jacob's wife's name is Floor. Yep,
Floor! (Better than Ceiling!) In Dutch *floor* means
flower, but in English it's floor. And Willa is Roos,
which means Rose, but in English it means kangaroos.
Funny huh?

Floor was quiet and stylish, in pale soft colours,
but boy she was organising, in a friendly no-nonsense
way.

'Good flights?' she asked.

'She stressed for me,' said Willa, waving vaguely at
me.

'Henni, on Monday you will go with Jacob to get a
bike,' said Floor, 'then in the afternoon Wendelien will
help you get your phone working. And it would be
interesting for you to spend one day each week going
to work with a member of the family. Sound good?'

'Yes, thank you. Like work experience.'

'Okay. First you go with Wendelien to her clinic.
Also, you are all invited to a family picnic lunch
tomorrow at our garden house with Wendelien and
her fiancé, Eric. (*Eric. Eric? How do I remember Eric?*

Eric Numeric!) We will go on bikes. Roos, can you still ride a bike?'

'Of course.'

Wow! Not only does Willa have her brain back, but she's up for riding a bike!

'Henni, there's a big central library, and Willa, there is all modern Amsterdam for you to see.'

'And a Resistance Museum,' said Hyacint, 'where maybe you will recognise something of Moeder's.'

'What?'

Hyacint smiled. 'I wonder if you can remember anything of that time.'

> *HO!*

Willa gave nothing away, didn't look at me.

I played it cool. 'Do you have wifi?' (Which I had been dying to ask anyway.)

'No, Wendelien will sort that out on Monday.'

Okay (which is *oke* in Dutch, same sound). *Oke*, Wendelien lives somewhere nearby with Eric Numeric. *Oke*, Dirk the Bear lives somewhere else too.

Then Hyacint walked Floor to the door (funny huh?) chatting about the picnic.

Willa grabbed my arm. 'Did you have nightmares?'

'No, did you?'

'No.'

'Should I call you Willa or Roos?'

'Willa. Do you have the Jet Lag?' she asked, like it was the Great Plague.

'Not sure, do you?'

'Just tired. Old.'

'Did you think about the turbulence?'

She looked me straight in the eye. 'I don't like aeroplanes. It's a ridiculous way to travel, and arriving is too sudden.'

'Ja. We have arriving-shock,' I said. 'Can we visit that Resistance Museum?'

She frowned.

'Have you remembered anything about the blue dog, Willa?'

'No.' She lowered her voice. 'But I need to go shopping without a relative.'

'Hey Willa, we made it!'

'Yes, Henni, we're okay.'

Hyacint returned.

Two conspirators in a too-sudden land.

After lunch, which was like breakfast except with thick rye bread, the twee oude dames settled into an argument. '...those tall plants with flowers coming out all up the stem.'

'*Stokrozen*,' said Hyacint. 'Holly*shocks*.'

'Holly*hocks*,' said Willa.

'Holly*shocks*.'

'Hyacint, *pannenkoek*! I speak English all the time. It's holly*hocks*.'

Stuff this. 'I'm going exploring!' I declared, and before they could say a word in any language I shot downstairs.

Stepping outside on my own was exciting. The door shut behind me. I clutched the keys in my hand in my pocket.

Everyone in the street was zooming off to somewhere. They knew what they were doing. Nobody noticed me.

I decided to look for wifi and watch bike riders. I knew the Anne Frank house was only a few blocks away but I couldn't find it, then I got lost, but I found the tram tracks and followed them home. I felt a little jolt of joy when I put the key in the lock and pushed open the black door.

After dinner Jacob came up for a talk. Ja.

Ja
Say 'ya'
Ja
Say ya-cob
Jacob
... a bit yeah
Ja
... a bit nah
Ja
... a bit up-you
Ja
... in y'face
... drop y'jaw
Ja
Ja?
Jaaaaaaaa!

Cold

turning right nonchalant

left a finger

True fact: In the Netherlands, if a bike and a car have a crash, the car's wrong. That's mostly true.

Best: When Willa called Hyacint a *pannenkoek* she called her a pancake!

Worst: No wifi. They couldn't care less.

Lo, it has come to pass and lo, not holes in the sky, nor double-nightmares, nor vomiting, nor plane delays, nor the past, nor the wedding present did stop us. We are under the tiled roof of the van Veens and as my friend Leo in Berlin used to say, 'It's all in dry towels.' Feels like I've been here a *week*!

Where we live

me

?

a guy who travels a lot

Hyacint + Willa

?

Jacob + Floor

bikes

Where's that part in my notebook where it all began?

Ah! Here it is!

I AM CHOSEN

Can't sleep. My brain is buzzing like fifty bees.
Something extraordinary happened tonight.

We were at Zev's place. Friday night is Pizza Night,
best night of the week, and everyone was talking
about Willa who's away for a couple of days. She's
lived in Stella Street forever but not quite as forever as
Mr Nic.

'How old is Willa?' goes Dad.

'Eighty-two.'

'Eighty-eight.'

'Ninety something?'

'Two hundred and she's a murderous old horse.'
(Ignore my sister Danielle when she's hungry.)

'When you think about it,' says Mum, 'Willa's a
mystery. We know nothing about her life growing up
in the Netherlands.'

'She and Henk came to Stella Street in nineteen

fifty-six, the year of the Melbourne Olympics,' says Mr Nic.

'Henk!' goes Maggs. 'I never knew that.'

So the conversation swings along and the pizzas start to come out of the oven.

'Donna, tell us about Willa,' says Donna's husband, Rob. People tell Donna stuff. Willa and Donna talk gardens, although Donna's jungle is the opposite of Willa's neat patch.

'Well,' says Donna 'she must go to Amsterdam. She just *must*.'

'I've heard that fifty times,' says Dad.

'Well, she can't do it by herself and she knows you make things happen,' says Mum.

True. Dad makes things happen.

'Why is it suddenly so important?' says Dad.

'Her sister's been unwell, plus there's a family wedding. Remember her niece Wendelien, who came here and stayed with her? Well, Wendelien's getting married.'

'Henk!' goes Frank. He thinks it's an exclamation.

'Wendelien's great,' chirps Danielle. 'Remember when she flicked the diabolo into Mr Nic's tree and climbed up to get it?'

'Well,' Donna continues, 'somehow Willa's saved

the fare from her pension, but after her purse was pinched at the supermarket she's lost confidence. She's afraid she'll get ripped off and lost, and catch the wrong plane, but she's determined to go.'

'Well, she can't go by herself,' said Dad. 'Wish her son would turn up and be useful.'

'A *son*?' says Maggs.

'Henk!' goes Frank.

'And there's something else...' Mr Nic is serious now.

Donna nods. 'Yes, we think Willa has a bee in her bonnet about something...'

'She's going home to die,' says Danielle, 'like an elephant.' (Cheerful, that's Danielle.)

'She needs help,' says Mum.

'Why should we help this stubborn old lady?' says Dad.

'Because we like her,' says Mum.

We laugh because that's the truth.

'Well, she's straightforward,' said Maggs. 'Remember when she blew her top at me when I couldn't decide between Bali or India?'

'What do you kids think?' Good old Mr Nic always wants our opinion.

'We should help her,' says Zev.

'She has good teeth,' says Danielle.

'She's fine on her pins,' Mr Nic agrees, 'as long as she doesn't have to hurry.'

'She's generous and stops arguments.'

'Well, she can't go by herself,' says Dad firmly. (Hooray for Dad. He's going to make it happen!!!) 'Donna, she wants you to go with her.'

'Oh, I can't go,' says Donna, kissing little Jim. 'Little Snotball here is teething.'

'I can't go,' says Mum. 'I'm working four days a week and I'm saving up my holidays.'

'I can!' (Ignore Danielle. She's so annoying.)

'I don't know the way to Never Lands,' says Frank.

'I'm no good at this flying business,' says Mr Nic.

Etc etc etc. It was like in 'The Little Red Hen' where all the animals in the farmyard make excuses for why they can't help the little red hen plant the corn.

'Not I,' says Rob. 'I've got a beautiful table waiting for me to restore it.'

'Not I,' says Dad. 'We're installing a new computer system at work.'

'Not I,' says Maggs. 'I'm getting the hang of my new kiln.'

Which left

me !

'Then I will do it *myself*,' says the little red hen.
'*I* will go with Willa.'

'Well, that's all very terribly interesting,' says Danielle,
'but will Willa go with *you*?'

I sit there like a twitchy expectant Briquette,
looking from person to person for a snack. They
argue about whether it was too much to put on my
young shoulders (I sit up straight and make my
shoulders look strong and responsible) and whether
missing school would disadvantage me (I look fiercely
intelligent). Danielle says I shouldn't go because I
would use up all the pens in Holland blah blah blah
until Dad tells her to pipe down.

'Willa likes me. She thinks I'm responsible. I *am*
responsible. I'm the oldest of us Stella Street kids, and
having a sister like you, Danielle, well, *someone* has to
be responsible or we'd be going to jail sometimes.'

They all look at me being fiercely responsible with
my sholders so straight they're killing me. What a
weird moment.

Then Dad laughs. 'Very well,' he says, 'it's decided.
Henni's off to Amsterdam.'

Just like that!

Danielle, next to me, starts chanting quietly so only

I can hear. 'Lucky duck, lucky *pig*, lucky duck, lucky *pig*, lucky duck, lucky *pig*…'

Us kids sat on beanbags in the corner eating pizzas, with tea towels down our fronts, stretching the cheese strings as far as we could.

'Remember when Danielle asked Willa, "Are you a giant?" and she said, "Yes."?'

'She *was* a giant,' said Danielle.

'Remember when you were walking with her,' said Zev, 'and you had to trot to keep up, like STEP trot trot trot STEP trot trot trot…and when she picked you up you were up so high?'

'Remember when the Botfids' stupid dog jumped

up on Frank and took his cake? And Frank, you screamed, and Danielle kicked the Botfids' dog, then the stupid dog went for Danielle and the Botfids kicked Briquette, who wasn't doing anything, and Willa came flying in and hit the roof?'

'Well it was the park so she hit the sky.'

'She was so *mad* at them!'

'Yes, but then, remember how mad she got at herself for getting so mad?'

Old Willa. She doesn't walk fast anymore. She's a bit bent now, and like a big old horse, the ones with floppy hair around their hooves. She's sharp though.

Mr Nic says, 'Getting old is better than the alternative.'

'What's the alternative?' says Frank.

'Pushing up daisies.'

'Being dead,' says Danielle.

Mr Nic says, 'You wouldn't be dead for quids.'

'What's quids?' says Frank.

'It's a fish,' says Danielle.

Okay, old Willa, you and I will go to Amsterdam.

I'm extreeeemely happy to miss some school. I don't like my school much. I have a friend, but we're not *best* friends. When I started there Mum and Dad said, 'Stick it out and it will get better,' but it hasn't.

I know a school I'd rather go to. It's further away, and it's not as well organised and equipped, but the kids who go there love it. They say the teachers are great and it has a writing club. I told Mum and Dad, but they think I should stay at this school because it gets better academic results.

I will learn Dutch.

zeker

AND there's something else that is *T O P* secret, which I am not breathing a word about.

Maggs says things come in threes. Fingers crossed.

I *might* be part of Big Bike Expo and they *might* pay me for it. Not confirmed. Two big 'mights'.

And a woman phoned me about exhibiting my 'Things Squashed Flat by Cars'. I'll try to explain.

Well, I don't know what the rude finger means in other languages, but in English it means '*get stuffed!*' You get *given* the rude finger, and it looks like this.

This happened just after Rob taught me how to ride my bike with cadence. Cadence is like a magic skill where you click through the gears and cruise effortlessly up hills.

I was riding to my cousin's place, on a road I didn't know, when I came to a cutting in a long hill. My cadence was cooking along nicely, but the road had no room at the side for bikes. At the bottom of the hill a footpath shot off at right angles, to who knows where.

Would I keep my cadence and stay on the road hoping for no cars, or take the path to mysteryland? No cars coming, so I stayed on the road.

I was climbing smoothly like in the Tour de France in the mountains, when I heard a car coming up behind me. Oh *NO!* There was nowhere to go. I went faster. Then the car came right up close behind me.

BAAAAAAAARP!

I nearly fell off my bike! I was *terrified!* I couldn't stop. I would have been squashed flat. I lost cadence and momentum. I panicked, pedalling as fast as I could with the car right on my tail.

Near the top of the hill the black ute roared past me, and a big hairy hand shoved out the window and gave me the rude finger.

Shaking with fear, I got off and scrambled up the

last of the hill. And what was at the top? The damn footpath!

Gasping, I flopped down on the grass. When I got my breath back I was still terrified but also angry. Why was that barbarian in a tonne of metal better than me on my bike?

Finally I got back on my bike and rode off, on the footpath. Then just around the next corner, I looked across and saw this on the road:

It could have been me!

Since then I've collected things squashed flat by cars.

Well, Maggs knows somebody who's working on the Big Bike Expo. She told them about my collection, and this year they're having art as part of it, and they *might* want my Things Squashed Flat by Cars.

Yes folks, that junk I pick up is *art!* It's called *objet trouvé*. And if it happens I will get $180 to spend on 'mounting my display', of which I will spend (with Magg's help) $30 and the rest is coming with me to Amsterdam thank you very much.

So how about that! *Ka-ching!* (Possibly.)

shopper

New (possibly) Grand Total Spending Money: $379

Plus I'm doing other stuff for handy cash. Everyone in Stella Street is getting their windows cleaned.

Hey, I could be another person in Amsterdam! John Lennon and Yoko stayed in bed for a week in the Amsterdam Hilton, for peace. I won't do that.

Sunday 29 March

IN THE NIGHT

I'm wide awake in the dark again...giddy and light-headed...like a balloon let go on the edge of a canyon. So much to tell, but who can I tell? Only-a-phone-call-away? Nee. Nee. Nee.

No phone yet

Yesterday was weird

What time is it? *Hoe laat is het?* How late is it? The church bells beat you, Mr Phrase-er Book

DONG............

DONG......

DONG.........

Only Three

At home no one has a zolder. Our house is ground level. You walk in the door and that's it. The house is big though. I bet Danielle is practising her tennis backhand against the front door right now. She'll be getting away with murder without me. (Actually, I like that she hits against the door, it makes the house less 'inside'. She's good, she hasn't broken much.)

Mijn zolder. (*Mijn* means mine, sounds like main.) Mijn zolder floor is made of thick uneven planks, and you can't go into the corners because of the steep slope of the roof. Mijn zolder has a Baby Bear's shelf where I've put Willa's ghost, where it will gather dust, which is slow work. Wonder who lives behind the doors on the stairs where the ghost went down? Is the blue dog here in mijn zolder? Actually, I don't care about the blue dog now. Willa can sort out that war stuff with her sister and brother. That's them, back then.

Wonder where the bells are? And there's a cannonball up here. Who would carry a *cannonball* up those stairs? Reminds me of the balls the Phonies put on their fence posts back home.

Last night in Hyacint's lounge the *drie oudes* were arguing. Why are they fighting when they were so happy to see each other again? They switch to English and are perfectly nice when I enter. I pretend I don't notice. Weird.

I'll never get to sleep. Wish the sun's alarm would go off.

When Alice fell in Wonderland
how was the falling for her?
Could she breath?
frozen?
Did she think of the landing?
No
It was probably entertaining,
a my-goodness-me thing
a magic fall in literature.

I know a falling feeling
strapped in
Willa and I
we fell through a hole in the sky
plummeting
plummeting
down
with

out
a

caught
by blessed solid air

and I returned to myself
and I went on living
sort of

Oh
I know a falling feeling

GARDEN CUBBY

Sunday. First sunny day in ages, they said. There we all were, on the street, with bags of picnic stuff. Wendelien's fiancé Numeric Eric rode up. Numeric is funny because he's not mathematical at all. He's a tall sailor with a lopsided grin, which kind of matches Wendelien's hair.

'You come with me,' said Eric.

'How?'

'*Spring achterop!* I'll show you,' said Wendelien. Eric rode past her slowly, and with a neat skip she hopped up, landing sideways on the little cushion on Eric's bike rack.

'Now you try.'

My spring op wasn't very neat. Eric and I wobbled like a jelly before we got steady, and set off laughing down the road after the others. Silly and fun, adults behaving like this.

'Pretty good for first time!' yelled Eric. 'You okay?'

'Ja.'

'No traffic today. It's not far.'

'Ja.'

I love saying ja.

Jacob had borrowed a bike for Willa and she rode like a queen, sitting up tall on her grandma bike. She waved at me, and rang her bell.

You won't *believe* our destination. The garden house was in a…not a suburb, not a village, a little separate… *domain* of garden houses. Volkstuinhuisjes, folks *volks* garden *tuin* houses *huisjes*. No roads, no cars, no electricity, just quiet paths, small canals and friendly little garden cubbyhouses.

Spring was in the air. Families were clipping, mowing, raking and planting. I bet in their dreams their fingers sprouted buds. Donna would love it.

We feasted on spinach and feta pastries. Some spirals, some triangles, some with mincemeat or potatoes, some big flat wrinkly rectangles like elephant-skin. Totally stuffed, we basked like lizards in the sun. The sun-hungry Amsterdammers stripped off jumpers, shirts and skirts, baring arms and legs, then midriffs. I wondered how far they would go. There was rather a lot of old skin.

'Want to come for a walk?' said Wendelien.

Wendelien, Eric and I wandered down the paths. I stopped to look in a little library made from a cupboard. Wendelien said, 'We'll keep walking, Henni, you can find your way back.' They strolled off arm-in-arm. I heard a dog yapping wildly.

Suddenly, *whack!* Something hit my head! *'Owww! Bloody hell!'* A purple plastic boomerang!

A girl burst through a hedge, followed by a terrier. She snatched up the boomerang before the dog could get it.

'That hit me on the *head!*' I yelled at her.

'Sorry!'

'It *hurts!* Lucky the hedge copped it first.'

'Where did it hit you?' she says, concerned, looking near my ear.

'Here, where my finger is. Am I bleeding?'

She examines the spot. 'No blood.' But now she's trying not to laugh.

'That was a *rotten* thing to do.'

Her mouth is twisting round.

'What's so funny?'

'I hit an Australian with a boomerang!'

'Yes, you *did!* It's for hunting kangaroos, not attacking visitors.'

'Do you think I meant to hit an Australian with a boomerang? ...Sorry...no, no, not funny.' Now she's desperately trying not to laugh.

'This is ri*dic*ulous!' I say.

So she's holding the boomerang high in the air, laughing like mad, and I'm rubbing my head and the little dog's jumping like a jumping machine. It is pretty funny, when you think about it. I start laughing too.

When we finally get our breath back, she goes, 'Oh phew! The stupid thing. I can't fly it. In the instructions it says Guaranteed to Return. You are Australian, how does it fly?'

'I know those boomerangs, they're made in California. We had the same problem. You have to flex it. We figured it out at the beach, then my sister threw it over the sea and it didn't come back and it was too cold to try to get it. Anyway, how did you know I was an Aussie?'

'The way you yelled "bloody hell". I'm Carlijn, by the way.' She said Carlijn like caarrr-lane with a nice aarrrr in the carrrr.

'I'm Henni.'

'Are you staying in Amsterdam?'

I told her about coming with Willa. She looked

puzzled. 'You're not with your parents, or a relative? Or staying with relatives?'

'No, I'm the guide person for this old lady.'

'Is that interesting to you?'

I couldn't tell if she thought I was stupid or brave. 'Better than school.'

'Do you go to school?'

'Yes. Not here. When I'm home I do.'

'Is she paying you?'

'No, she's not rich. The people in my street paid for my flight. I earned my spending money.'

'How?'

'I won second prize in a poetry competition, and my art was in an exhibition and I washed windows.'

'What is your art like, that was in the exhibition?'

'Well, it's a bit weird.'

'Weird like how?'

'It was things squashed flat by cars.'

She pulled a face. '*Jeetje*, that's weird.'

We grinned at each other.

'What was that word you just said?'

'Jeetje? Jeetje mina.' She said it *yait-ya mina*.

'Jeetje mina. I like it. What does it mean?'

She shrugs. 'Gosh. Wow. Something like that.'

I could see the roof of a house behind the hedge.

'Can you live here?' I asked.

'No. It's too cold in winter. In summer we stay. We have solar panels and a TV. Want to see?'

'Ja!'

She put her arms up to push through the hedge when a man yelled, 'Car-*lijn*!' in a why-aren't-you-helping? voice.

'That's my dad. Gotta go now. Maybe another time. Bye, Henni. Have fun in Amsterdam with that old lady.' She gave me a curious look, then disappeared through the hedge.

'Bye, Carlijn. Don't throw the boomerang over water,' I yelled.

I wanted to talk more. I wanted to see the house. I wanted to pat the dog and know his name. I listened to them laughing and yelling as they packed up. It was just like us in Stella Street, except in Dutch. To put it plainly, I wanted to be her friend. Oh well, that's what happens when you travel.

When I got back to the picnic, the oude dames and Floor and Dirk were arguing in Dutch about something called bram. I flopped down near Wendelien. Eric was tickling her arm with a blade of grass.

'What's bram?' I whispered.

'Bram is my nephew,' said Wendelien matter-of-factly. 'He left home suddenly two weeks ago.' (Dirk the Bear's *son*, Jacob's *grand*son, Bram. Bram? Bram the clam.)

'What's the boy like?' Willa asked clearly in English, an abrupt change of channels. Everyone switched to English which meant I could understand too, but I wondered if Willa was just being polite, or trying to shut the conversation down, or if she wanted me to know. Ah, the politics of language.

'He's stubborn, self-centred and has no ambition,' said Dirk the Bear, who was steamed up about his son and wasn't going to drop the subject.

'He's testing himself,' said Floor.

'Totally lacking self-control,' said Hyacint.

controlled enough to leave home

'He's seventeen, for God's sake,' said Dirk.

interesting

'You're too hard on him,' said Floor. 'Give him a chance.'

'Chances?' Dirk snorted. 'He doesn't stick to anything.'

Wendelien, Eric and Jacob said nothing.

they disagree

'You don't like him, that's the problem,' said Floor.

'Of *course* I like him,' said Dirk. 'He's my son.'

you definitely don't like him.

not now anyway

'He just wants to go on his new computer.'

'Where did he get the money for a new computer?'

good question, Willa

'Damned if I know.'

money's not from his dad!

'Did Bram take his stuff? Has he *really* gone?' I whispered to Wendelien.

'Yes.'

I moved to the shade of a tree near the edge of the garden and tried to read my book. Jacob also couldn't stand it and went off into the house, and made clattering noises, doing the dishes or something. They switched back to Dutch as soon as I moved away. I wondered how close I had to be for them to switch back to English. It was still Bram this, Bram that.

Jacob plonked himself down next to me. 'And how are you, Miss Henni?'

He asked in such a warm friendly way I let my politeness down.

'Well, no offence but no one's really my age group.'

He gave a lovely laugh, his eyes crinkled at the corners. 'You're very diplomatic. Sorry. We are not a happy family right now. Personally, I'm glad Bram's gone. Dirk wants him to be someone he's not. Dirk wants him to be an engineer, and step into his big shoes in the family business.'

'What do you think?'

'I'm a *zachtgekookt eitje*.'

'What's that?'

'A soft-boiled egg, that's what they call me. They think I'm too kind. The sky won't collapse if Bram doesn't come to Wendelien and Eric's wedding. They know what this family is like.'

oh the wedding

'What about Bram's mum?'

'Dirk and his wife separated when Bram was four. She went to America. Dirk was building up his business, so I looked after Bram a lot.'

'Where do you think Bram got the money?'

Jacob shrugged. 'Everyone thinks drugs.'

'Do you think drugs?'

'No. You can buy weed from the coffee shops, why would you bother? And hard drugs? No, he's not stupid. Bram would be rich now if he lived back in the eighteenth century when a boy of twelve might leave home to find his fortune. He's a very determined young man, but stubborn. He's like his father in that way. It would help if he saw more the lighter side.'

I thought of some surfer guys we met once, who lived on the beach, free as air.

'Maybe Bram's gone to Australia. Lots of people do. They get any kind of job, buy an old bomb and drive round Australia.'

'No, he's still studying, we know that, but an adventure would be good for him.' Jacob grew even more serious. 'Henni, if you hear anything about Bram, will you tell me?'

'Sure.'

'Okay, that's enough of Bram.' Jacob stretched. 'Hyacint has arranged for you to meet a girl from down the street. If you don't get on with her, I know a lucky spot for making friends,' (*what a funny thing to say*) 'and tomorrow we go to the *fietsenwinkel* to get your bike.'

'Fietsenwinkel?'

'Bike shop.'

'Winkel is so twee! Makes me think of a character called Mrs Tiggy Fietsenwinkel.'

'You pedal with your fiets.' Obviously it wasn't twee to him.

'Jacob, if you wanted to hide something in your house, where would you hide it?'

'Ja, Roos told me about the blue dog. I don't think there is anything hidden in our house.'

'But if it's hidden you don't know it's there.'

Jacob laughed. 'Ask Dirk, he's a builder. My father was a builder too, but somehow I became an architect. What do you want to be when you grow up?'

I was so full of myself, I said, 'I want to be what I am now.'

'What are you?'

'A writer.'

'Really?'

'Yes, and I came second in a poetry competition.'

'Congratulations!' said Jacob. 'I want to read that poem. Know what I wanted to be?'

'A farmer?'

'A movie director. I love the movies.'

I put my arms round my knees and posed like a movie star.

'You're making fun of me,' laughed Jacob as we stood up. 'You can write about this holiday.'

~

Oh boy, at dinner the Jet Lag came on. Quietly it washed through me, pulling my eyelids down, pulling my head to the table, pulling my body to the floor.

I *longed* to lie down and sleep. I heard their voices, but the wooze in my head was torture. I forced my eyelids to stay up. Going to the bathroom I had my eyes open, but I swear I was asleep.

I'm wide awake in the dark again. My body clock's gone crazy and my brain is flitting around like a butterfly in a box.

This morning in the kitchen I was searching in the cupboards and Hyacint snapped at me, 'What are you doing?' as if I was spying on her.

'Looking for sugar.'

Then she gave me a black look. I had offended her. Jeetje mina, after all the advice they gave me back home, I've got a black mark. Jeetje mina. Where's my torch? I wrote down all that advice in my notebook... where is it? Ah, here it is.

Briefing in HQ

Name: Bond. Henni Bond

Mission: Deliver Willa

Death-defying gadgets: Codes, passwords, iPhone, map, phrase book, notebook, liquid gel pen

Advice from Dad

Don't go running around Amsterdam by yourself, well, certainly not without telling someone where you're going, and definitely don't go out alone at night. But if you must go out on your own at night, stick to well-lit streets. See and be seen. Know where you're going. Always have a map. Look at the map before you go out. Always keep valuables out of sight, in fact don't take valuables. Stay alert. Stay away from suspicious people bla bla bla don't don't don't

Advice from Mum

Stick to other people. If you don't feel comfortable, tag along with people going in the same direction. Safety in numbers. Remember that film of the wildebeest where the calf wandered off from the herd and the lions got it?'

Am I crossing savannah grasslands?

They're alarming themselves. They're alarming me!

I'm not getting out of bed tomorrow. Mind you, I have experienced *nearly* terrible things.

'What if something bad happens?' I asked.

'Depends on the situation,' said Dad. 'Do what you think is best at the time. Hide. Scream. Run. Get help. You're a writer. Pretend. Fake it. Okay, let's practise.' He stared at the ceiling for a moment. 'Henni, will you have another spicy horse's eye, boiled in pig fat?'

'Thank you, Mr Octon, it was delicious, especially the blazing chilli sauce, but I won't have another, I'm watching my weight.'

Dad laughed. 'You'll be fine.'

Advice on Technology

Tibor, who is Stella Street's techno guru (I wrote my first book on his old computer) said all I needed was a phone. A tablet or laptop was just another thing to look after.

'A tech detox,' said Mum. 'Fill your eyes with real life.'

Tibor was thoughtful. 'Write about it, Henni, and send us what you've written. You'll find a computer somewhere, in a library or at Wendelien's.'

'Nobody has to tell me to write!' I said seriously.

They laughed. They love my stories.

Misc advice

'It will be cold,' said Maggs. She's lived in Botswana,
Sweden and London. She's an artist. She lent me her
light-as-a-feather coat and her trusty uggboots.

'I was a hippie in Amsterdam,' said Maggs, 'but by
the time I got there John and Yoko had gone. I lived
in a squat though, with flowers in my hair. Go to the
Rijksmuseum, Henni, and see the Rembrandts. Willa
looks like a Rembrandt when she opens the door
wiping her hands on her apron.'

Tonight when Mum and I were alone she insisted
on a chat about boys. (Are Dutch boys different from
Australian boys?) Then she gave me this pre-scruffed
notebook. Ten cents from the op shop, and a new
liquid gel pen which she knows I love, because the
pen glides over the paper.

This morning I found Danielle had scribbled this:

*Henni's little sister Danielle is jealous because she
must stay behind in Boring-Boring but she knows one
day she will get her revenge. Secretly everyone knows she
is actually the beautiful noble and clever sister who will
triumf*

Danielle's writing is improving.

My best friend Zev told me about the electrical wiring in the plane we will fly in. He's fascinated by electricity.

Advice for the Flight

We're only a phone call away

On the plane walk around, wave your feet like this.

Look after Willa.

Drink lots

Don't drink alcohol   ha ha ha

Look after Willa

We're only a phone call away

Make sure she drinks WATER

Make sure she doesn't get drunk.

Use the earplugs for crying babies.

Make sure Willa walks around.

Watch out for thieves. They look like ordinary people.

We're only a phone call away

Don't lose stuff

check the luggage, *count the pieces*, six pieces

don't don't don't don't don't don't don't don't

   …and remember,

We're only a phone call away

Have fun!

I've emailed my friend in Berlin, Leo, but he hasn't replied. *What's up, Leo? I really want to see you.* I rang but I got a recorded message in German that I couldn't understand. I even sent him an actual letter. What's happened? Berlin looks close to Amsterdam. Maggs says it's five hours by train. *You okay, Leo?*

I've been given three copies of *The Diary of Anne Frank*, but I don't want to read about miserable historic stuff.

Donna will look after Willa's garden.

Where are you, Leo?

Monday 30 March

BIKE, PHONE
...FRIEND?

Today I buy my own bike with my own money.

First I would like to give a big thankyou to my sponsors, Kathleen Julia Bates and Big Bike Expo.

I remember coming home from school not long after the famous Pizza Night and finding this:

> *Congratulations.*
> *You have won the Kathleen Julia Bates*
> *Memorial Poetry Writing Competition.*

I *never* win competitions. I can't run. I can't swim fast. I can't do pratfalls like Danielle. I'm not a wizard in electricity like Zev, but I can write.

Dear Excellent Judge,

you got my poem, right when I needed the money.

FANTASTISCH!! (That's fantastic in Dutch.)

Yay, do the sums

Prize money: 200 smackers

Lines in poem: 28

Words in poem: 232

Prize per line: $7.14

Prize per word: 34 cents

Width of smile: 8cm (approx)

Peanut butter sandwiches: 4

Tim Tams: 3

Glasses of choc milk: 1.5

The bells say seven o'clock. It will be dark for a while yet, but I can hear bike chains clunking. I'm trying to write by torchlight and not let any cold air under the doona, which is not easy to say the least.

My last bike was a birthday present from Stella Street, made by Rob. He can make anything. He put together a red frame, Sturmey-Archer gears, a wire basket, a pair of antler handlebars for exactly where my hands

were, and a broad comfy seat. Lo, and I loved that
bike, and lo with that bike I did ride and discover
freedom and lo it was good verily lo lo lo and I did
love it verily

Before that bike, I had to catch the bus to high
school. And on that bus sat Madison, who expected
me to sit beside her every day. I didn't want to because
she talks *n o n s t o p n o n s t o p n o n s t o p n o n s t o
p n o n s t o p n o n s t o p.*

Plus when the bus crawled up steep Trimbroad
Hill (I call it Trembling Hill), it stopped at a bus stop
halfway up, opened the door and tipped to the side.
It felt like it was going to fall over. *Arrggg!* Every
morning I hated that. Then the bus groaned in agony
as it crawled up the rest of the hill. I hate it now and I
will always hate it till the day I die.

Have you ever had that empty crinkling feeling, staring at the empty post where your bike used to be?

'Was it that tree over there?' you say, feeling sick and urgent. 'That parking sign? Did I leave it at the shops? At the station? No, it was *here*! There's the squashed can in the gutter. It was *here*.'

You feel sick.

Then comes the tsunami of achey-sadness. Your faithful, trusty, freedom-machine gone.

I walk home, which isn't far on the bike, but carrying a heavy schoolbag, it's a long way, especially when I'm in mourning. Filthy scumbag thief. I could *bite a piece out of that thieving arm*. The bus zooms past. *Arrgggg!* Guess who waves from the bus?

I *hate* the bus!!!

Rob and I went straight to the police station. Fat lot of good that did.

'Happens all the time,' said the cop. 'Sorry. Sounds like a great bike. They probably liked the handlebars.'

I was sad and angry. I had bike habits. I would go out the front door and turn left to get my bike off the verandah, *Ooh!* Then I had to walk down the road to the lurching crawling crowded bus containing Madison.

Grrrrrrrrrrrrrrrrrrrr!

It's coming light. The sun is hitting the top branches of my tree. Today is my Amsterdam bike day.

I watch the bike shop. The Fietsenwinkel family sure ain't fairy folk. There's a strong middle-aged woman, a thick muscly son, and a *grootvader* (grandfather). They roll dozens of bikes out of the fietsenwinkel, and line them up on the footpath, front out. The handlebars are locked like horns, as if they're guarding the fietsenwinkel, then the son and grootvader thread a cable through all the front wheels so no one can pinch them. Then they hang a bike either side of the door, like two bikes rampant, to guard the entrance, and the shop is officially open.

Jacob and Floor live directly beneath us. Their place used to be a dry-cleaners. It has big windows with blinds. I went downstairs, out the black door, turned left, took six steps and knocked on their door.

Knock knock knock

Jacob got straight down to business.

'How much do you want to spend on a bike?'

'A hundred and twenty-three euros.'

'Exactly?'

'My prize money.'

He laughed. 'Well, the good news is the fietsenwinkel will buy your bike back, when you leave, if you haven't wrecked it. The bad news is you will need to spend more than that.'

Down a wooden ramp and into the greasy bike-cave we went. The muscly son was working on a bike on a stand. He straightened up and waved us to his mother, who had exactly the same potato-shaped nose as the grootvader sitting in the corner.

'I want a second-hand Dutch bike, where I can sit up high,' I said.

She pulled out a red one. 'This one has foot brakes and a basket at the back, which is nice, and guards so it will not chew your pants. Try it. Ride to the corner.'

'Test the brakes,' said Jacob as I wheeled it out.

I tried two other bikes, but the red one felt good.

'You need this too.' The woman handed me a lock and a chain. *Whoa!* It was so heavy I nearly dropped it on my foot.

'Do I have to have this?'

Jacob nodded. 'Unless you want your bike stolen.'

'I thought Amsterdam was a good place.'

'Good place for bike thieves.'

Bike	€140
Chain	€ 35
Bell	€4.50

} *a lot of my Amsterdam money*

Jacob made sure the fietsenwinkel woman wrote on the receipt that they'd buy the bike back for seventy euros.

Out on the street Jacob showed me how to chain up. 'Put the chain through the front wheel, the frame and something solid.'

What a hassle! I guess it's better than having it pinched. At home I had a simple cable with a combination lock, which was fine until...oh well, we know about that.

I had a name ready for my bike – Tasman. Abel Tasman was a Dutch explorer, the first European to see *Tasman*ia.

Mijn trusty fiets Tasman. We'll explore Amsterdam.
I'll put flowers on the basket.

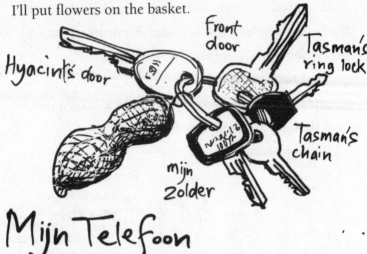

Mijn Telefoon

Wendelien came with me to get my phone working.
She couldn't figure out what was wrong. Dad's old
phone was unlocked. The phone shop was so unlocked
nobody was there. We waited at the counter laughing
about what we'd steal if we were robbers. Above a
glass case of impressive smashed phones there was a
scrawled note saying *Telefoonreparaties* [*I have a nice
phone squashed flat but these were better.]

Finally an old bearded guy in a robe and sandals
shuffled out, straight from the Bible. In the whole deal,
he said three words, maybe four.

'Where?' he growled.

'Australia,' I said.

He took the phone and looked at it doubtfully. 'Old.'

He did something to the phone that I couldn't see because he was behind a poster, then he fished a prepaid pack out of a drawer, ripped it open with his bearded teeth, punched in numbers, listened, more numbers...

'Do I need a password?'

He shook his head and tapped around a bit more.

'Battery.' He gave it the thumbs down. Then he wrote €30 on a scrap of paper and pushed it to me. I paid him, then he shuffled back to the Biblical era. (Three words.)

'I like a man of few words who knows what he's doing,' said Wendelien. 'The battery won't hold much of a charge. We still don't know what was wrong.'

'But it works!'

How long will thirty euros last? Oh well, I'll guess I'll find out. That was expensive. My money's flying faster than crumbs off Hyacint's table. Exciting though. Finally I was back on chat.

Henni

Hello it's me in Amsterdam!
Ja Ja Ja

Suddenly there was *Quack! Quack! Quack! Quack!* as dozens of messages landed. I bet it was Danielle who changed my ringtone.

Quack!   Danielle

> we are not missing you

Quack!   Danielle

> we are not missing you at all

Quack!   Danielle

> still not missing you

Quack!   Danielle

> Saturday still not missing you

Quack!   Danielle

> Saturday arvo still not missing you

Quack!   Zev

> Danielle is not missing you

Quack! Danielle

Sunday still not missing you

Quack! Zev

How was the plane flight?

Quack! Danielle

Reply you lazy pinecone

Quack! Danielle

Reply you lazy tall slug

etc...

I was so happy to be connected again, but I didn't have much time to reply. I had to get home to meet the girl Hyacint had organised.

Right on time there was a buzz on the buzzer. Hyacint leaned out the window and yelled down to a dark-haired girl holding her bike. Down the stairs we went.

'Myrte, this is Henni from Australia,' said Hyacint,

then she said something pathetic like 'I must water my plants,' and shot inside.

Myrte was taller than me, maybe a bit older, with long wavy hair in a ponytail, and eyebrows neat as brushstrokes. We chatted about Australia. She loves koalas. Fine.

I fumbled for ages unlocking my bike. 'Sorry, I'm not used to this yet. I've had two bikes stolen. You never get them back. Your English is good. Have you lived in the States?'

'No, I watch a lot of American stuff on TV,' said Myrte. 'We'll go to a park and meet my friends.'

The park was by a canal and had a long flying fox launched from a small man-made hill. The seat on the flying fox was so high, Myrte's friends had to climb on each other to reach it. They were taking turns, laughing and yelling at each other in Dutch. Myrte introduced me, but I couldn't remember their names.

I stood in the outer suburbs, wearing my easy-going face, grinning at things I didn't understand. One kid was interesting. His dark friendly face was elastic with athletic eyebrows. He would look at me and send his eyebrows right up, which made me laugh. Eyebrow Boy. Yes, I liked him.

There was a weird moment when they were joking

in Dutch and Myrte suddenly asked me in English the meaning of 'loser'. Maybe Tara felt like this when she came to stay with us at Cauldron Bay. No. I think we were nicer to her than these kids were to me.

On the ride back Myrte wanted to know about Willa, which was difficult because we were speeding along and bikes were rocketing towards me. Myrte wasn't interested in me.

'Is your grandmother going to live here?' Maybe I heard it wrong, but I didn't bother to set her straight. I said Willa had a house and friends in Melbourne, and that I didn't know her plans, which was half true because I thought she might stay for a bit longer.

We got home. I said thanks, and went into my clumsy bike chain routine. She didn't say, 'See you on Friday,' or anything, so that might be it. If we don't meet again that's fine by me.

———

'What's she like, the girl from down the street?' asked Willa.

'She's okay. Bit nosy. She wanted to know if you're staying for good, or going back to Australia. And listen to this, Willa, she thinks you're my grandmother!'

'Does she?' Willa snorted loudly. 'Hyacint probably

told her that. Hyacint just says anything.'

'My bike's great. The cobbles are rough though.'

'I learned to ride on cobbles,' said Willa, 'on my father's bike with my leg through the frame, try that for a joke! I was riding my father's bike when we lost it in the war. A German soldier called me over. I thought he wanted directions, but he simply grabbed the bike, swung his leg over and *rode off*! Stole it just like that, leaving me standing there with my mouth open. My father's precious bike! *Jeetje!* Then I had to go home and tell Moeder. This was just when bikes were becoming precious and people were hiding them away.' She gave a heavy sigh. 'Bikes come and go.'

'Is Lodewijk van de Haag still alive?' Willa asked Hyacint at dinner.

'No.' Hyacint replied firmly, 'He died ten years ago.'

Willa went quiet.

'Your good friend?'

'Ja, I wrote to him for a few years but he never wrote back. I thought I might see him again.'

'Happens to all of us,' Hyacint said rather smugly.

In the evening the fietsenwinkel fairy folk took in *all* the bikes.

Funniest: Eyebrow Boy

Worst: Pinching my finger in the chain locking up my bike

Weirdest: Willa being my grandmother

Wish: Myrte was Carlijn.

Jeetje, it was great to be in touch with home at last.

Henni

What's happening?

Danielle

Nothing

Zev

At school we're testing electrical connections to the ground. We're devising experiments on earthing. They're using me.

Henni

Striking you with lightning?

Zev

Gentle lightning

Danielle

Do you know Dutch yet?

Henni

Ja is yes and *Nee* is no. You say them like 'ya' and 'neigh'. My favourite all-purpose expression is *jeetje mina* which means gosh or wow. You say it 'yait-ya mina'. Dutch kids are great at languages, especially English. All the movies and series on TV are in English. Today I met a girl with an American accent, Myrte.

Danielle

Mitre 10

Henni

Willa's sister Hyacint arranged it.

Danielle

arranged friends aren't friends

Henni

I've got a bike it's red. called Tasman

Danielle

I have to go to bed

Henni

Slaap lekker = sleep tight

Danielle

Slap yourself

Henni

Hahaha I'll send a Bulletin about my first bike ride.

Henni

Zev. Earthling. A detective job. Can you research an old friend of Willa's? Lodewijk van de Haag. Dead now. He used to live in Eerste Hugo de Grootstraat. No way am I going to write that all the time. I'll say Hugo. Stay earthed. van = from (Vincent van Gogh – I guess he came from Gogh)
Willa van Veen = from Veen (I just looked it up. There is a place called Veen!)

Henni

Zev, chaining up my bike is a pain. How can I make it easy? Signing off. Henni van Hugo previously Henni van Stella Street

Riding My Bike in Amsterdam
MONDAY 30 MARCH

I stand on the footpath with my foot on the pedal, waiting for a gap in the riders. You must be bold to jump into this fast-flowing river. I slip in. *Phew!* I'm away.

I pass the shop where everyone buys their fruit and vegies, the *Turksewinkel*, even though the guys are from Morocco, not Turkey, then down to the main encircling canal, Singelgracht, the outside onion ring round old Amsterdam. See my map. Then I ride back along a bike lane beside a busier street. I flow along nicely, then I nearly die of fright when a man flies past me so close I can smell his aftershave. Next minute a tourist steps out to take a photo. *BBBBrrrring!!* She jumps away. Ha tourist! *BBBBrrrring!* My turn to ring the bell.

I've had two close shaves. A woman with a big bag on her handlebars lightly brushed my arm, then later I hit the little kerb at the side of the bike lane and wobbled all over the place, but fortunately no one was coming. When I hear someone riding up fast behind me I get right over onto the right-hand side. Flowing along in a stream of bike riders, so close to each other, signalling, talking, carrying stuff, it's scary and exhilarating but you really have to watch out. I love it!

There aren't many things squashed flat by cars here but I find sad, lonely gloves and mittens distressed, missing their twin.

Then suddenly, right above me,

> DONG!...

> > DONG!...

The bells are ringing in the tower of a cathedral. My night-time friend!

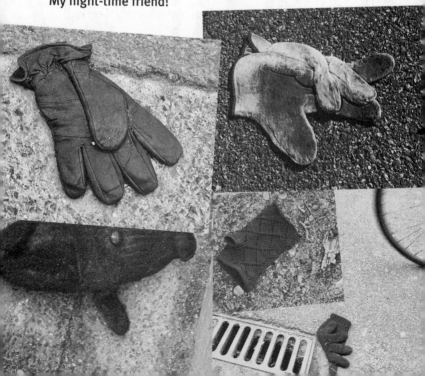

Vesterpark

Schiphol Airport

Central Station

Library round here — ?

Interesting street

the town square

The Dam

Anne Frank House

Westerkerk my night time friend

Prinsengracht
Princes' Canal

Herengracht
Lords'

Keizergracht
Emperors'

Singelgracht — My favourite canal
follow it home

Vondel Park

art galleries

grand palace

Home
X

bike shop

het IJ

NEVER use this map
you'll get lost

Resistance Museum

ZOO

AMSTERDAM

canal + bridge
(gracht + brug)
— street (straat)

Amstel

THINGS ARE NOT GOING ACCORDING TO PLAN

I saved Willa's life this morning. Twice. She had her foot in the air, about to step in front of a car when I yanked her back. She didn't see what a close shave it was. The second time she got angry.

'*Henni*! What are you *doing*!'

Next time I'll let her get squashed.

I thought she'd have long cups of tea with relatives, and I could explore, but nee nee nee, seeing-eye-dog Henni must stay close.

'Tomorrow you go with Wendelien, but this morning I need the chemist,' said Willa.

'Can we go the Resistance Museum this week?'

'Maybe.'

Coats on. Downstairs. Willa double-Dutched at the chemist, who politely asked heaps of questions, but she got loud and grumpy, so he got loud and grumpy. Finally, he went silent and sold her tablets that weren't

the ones she wanted. Then we searched for pills in the
supermarket. We tracked them down to the counter
with the cigarettes, where they're hidden behind a
roller door at night. They didn't have the right pills
either.

'Don't tell the others about this, they'll fuss,' said
Willa.

On the way home, she knew every building. 'That
was a grocer's, that was a tobacconist with a green
door, my best friend Lodewijk lived up there, his
wireless aerial wire dangled down from that window
there, see?' Etc etc etc. Then we came to a square of
tall trees, where she made straight for a bench and
plomped down like a beanbag. She lines up her bum
and lets gravity do the rest. Sometimes I have to pull
her up again.

She leaned back and gazed at the treetops. 'Oh my,
they grew fast! When I left for Australia they were
only as high as my head.'

'They look old.'

'No, they were planted after the war to replace the
trees cut down for firewood.'

'Whoa! People chopped down trees in the street?'

'O mijn God, Henni, the *Hongerwinter* of forty-
four, was a nightmare. The Germans cut off all gas,

electricity and coal. No heat. In the Jewish area, which was deserted because they'd all been rounded up, people raided their empty houses and ripped out anything that would burn, floors, doors, anything wood. O mijn God, we were freezing.

'One day Moeder announced to me, "We have to cut down the tree in front of our house and get the wood before someone else does. We have to do it fast or it will be gone in a flash." This was the tree we played under, where we tied the skipping-rope, like our tree friend. She got a neigbour to do it, and I had to help him. Honestly, it felt like murder. I'll never forget the groan it made as it fell.

Then the neighbour had to duck off urgently and he told me not to let anyone take any wood. First a man came and said, "I'm taking the top." I pleaded with him, but he sawed it off and dragged it away. Like ants, people came and cut off branches and dragged them off. I yelled and pleaded, but what could I do? It was a nightmare. We didn't get any of the wood, and all that was left of our tree was an ugly stump. All the trees were gone.' She sniffed and wiped her eyes. 'Wasn't just trees that were left with ugly stumps.'

Change the subject, fast. I noticed a building with kids' drawings in the windows.

'Look, Willa, is that a school?'

'That was *my* school. O mijn God, Henni, it was cold, and they expected you to sit still and learn! Hyacint and Jacob went there after the war, when I was in high school. That's the high school over there.' She pointed to a solemn building that looked like a bank. A group of grey figures came out of it and stood on the steps smoking. Probably recess.

'Teachers wouldn't smoke like that back home,' said Willa.

'It's not teachers, it's kids,' I said.

'Oh.' She blinked. 'I can't see how old they are. Cigarettes are cheaper here. I'll tell you a story about cigarettes one day.'

'Does Bram go there?'

'No.'

'What do you think about Bram, Willa?'

'Good luck to him.' She shrugged. 'I did stupid things at that age. Bram and Dirk, pig-headed, both of them.'

Later, taking down the rubbish, I was passing the supermarket when who should embarrassingly pop out the door but Myrte! With Eyebrow Boy and a friend. Eyebrow Boy said come with us to the river.

Myrte wasn't pleased but said nothing, so I posted the rubbish and went with them.

They rode fast, Eyebrow Boy in the lead. I'd catch up at the traffic lights, then they'd fly off again. Then the gap between us widened. They turned into streets, left and right, and each time I was mighty relieved when I went round a corner and saw them again. Then they flew over a bridge. I pedalled hard towards it, but just as I reached it, *DING! DING! DING!* The barriers came down. Normally I would have loved this bridge that split and rose up like a road to the sky, but I waited anxiously while two barges of rubbish slid through, till finally, slowly, the bridge came down.

I flew across the bridge, looking everywhere, but they were gone. I stood on the other side waiting, hoping they would show up, Eyebrow Boy at least. No one. What a *mean* thing to do. I *hated* Myrte! I bet she told the others not to wait. I didn't know where they were going. They had really taken me for a ride.

I was lost. I was cold. The long street names were impossible. I was totally miserable. I asked an old man for directions and he sent me off in a way that seemed completely wrong, but I found his road and followed it, and it curved around, and finally I recognised a beer factory. By this time I was late for dinner.

The oude dames sat at the table waiting in silence while I washed my hands.

'I got lost.'

I knew if I tried to explain, it would sound stupid, so I didn't bother. After the dishes, while Hyacint was finding her show on TV, Willa wanted to know what happened. I told how they'd lost me.

'I'm done with Myrte. She's weird.'

'Come into my bedroom,' said Willa. 'I want to show you something.'

She handed me a photo. 'That's me, Henni, two years before the war. I was a good girl. I did what I was told.'

'I have a little story from the war for you, Henni.'
She chuckled at the memory. The teachers wrote on
the blackboards with chalk, we drew in the street with
chalk. Chalk was used everywhere. Well, one night,
on Radio Oranje we heard that Mr Churchill and
all the countries against the moff were using V as a
symbol for Victory, so next morning I put chalk in my
pocket, white chalk it was, and on the way to school,
when I was sure no one was watching me, I wrote
V on a wall, and dashed around the corner. Henni,
without a word of a lie, there on a fence was another
V! In blue chalk. It answered my V! Oh I laughed.
I wrote V on the footpath, on trees, walls, fences. And
I saw the blue V everywhere too. I always wondered
who the blue chalk was. I was careful though. Once
I was beckoned over by a German soldier. I thought
he would see my chalky fingers. I thought the chalk
would burn a hole in my pocket and drop onto the
cobbles at his feet. I was terrified.'

'What happened?'

'He asked where the post office was.' With a cheeky
grin Willa made the V sign. 'Good for moral solidarity.
My friend Lodewijk and I did a few V things.'

Jacob called in and the oude dames fussed over coffee in the kitchen.

'Jacob, tell me about the lucky friend spot.'

He grinned. 'It's in Noord, over het IJ.'

'What's het IJ?'

'Het IJ is not a river exactly, it was a sea inlet, but it was closed off to control the water height so now it's part river, part lake, part body of water, part I don't know what.'

He drew me a little map.

'Here's het IJ. You catch the ferry behind Central Station to Noord. Short trip, free. On the other side, here, there's a little Italian cafe called al Ponte. You'll see the Italian flag. That's the spot. I found two lifelong friends there and that's where I met Floor, waiting for the ferry.' He laughed. 'I bought three cups, no, *six* cups of coffee that afternoon, and we missed about nine ferries.'

'Very lucky spot.'

He smiled. 'My friend Silvia runs al Ponte. Her motto is Make Coffee Not War.' He gave me five euros. 'Have a slice of lemon cake and say Jacob says hi.'

As I cleaned my teeth I heard the three oudes in the lounge. They didn't sound happy, but it's always hard to tell if they're arguing or just speaking Dutch.

I went into the lounge and announced, 'I'm going op mijn zolder, *goedenacht.'*

'Goedenacht,' they said cheerfully enough, but I stood outside the door, and they went straight back to arguing, and if it wasn't arguing it was pretty heavy discussion. It sounded like Willa was under attack, mostly from Jacob.

What a language. Today I saw a shop, Hans Joke. Imagine that for a surname – *Joke*! No one would take you seriously. Sometimes Dutch looks like bad typing. Anyway, whatever's bugging them, I don't care.

I climbed the stairs to mijn zolder. I didn't feel miserable, even after such a lousy day.

Quack!

Zev

Henni, write a bike chaining-up worksong. Get a rhythm to the actions. I'll look for links to heave-ho sailors' songs and prisoners' swinging-sledge-hammer songs.

Henni

Thanks Zev. Anything to make chaining-up easier.

Henni

Today I went for a ride with some kids from round here. I was way behind, they rode over a bridge which went up, but they didn't wait for me. What a low-down dirty trick. In the end I got home okay.

Zev

Forget those creepy kids. Hey Hen, you wrote a letter to that boy in Berlin, Leo. It came back Return to Sender.

Henni

Oh *what?* Bummer!! Wonder what's going on with Leo? That's that then.

Zev

How's Willa?

Henni

Her old self. Some family arguments. Tomorrow I'm hanging out with Wendelien. She's coming at eight-thirty. Doei doei (See ya)

Zev

See ya

Best: V

Worst: Myrte

WORK WITH WENDELIEN

Henni Octon
Re: Happy April Fool's Day, Everybunny!
To: Stella Street

PINCH AND A PUNCH FOR THE FIRST OF THE MONTH and no returns to me! Ha! No way can you get me back!

Today I went to work with Wendelien. You will **never** guess what she's researching. Give up? Kids with constipation! *Ja!* FACT!

On the wall of her office she has a huge print of that mole walking around with a big plop of poo on his head, from that little kids' picture book *The Story of the Little Mole Who Knew It Was None of His Business*. Parents and kids sit in the waiting room, and you feel sorry for them because you know the kid   is   blocked   up.

Mostly the mums bring them in. There was one nanny and a dad. The adults' conversation in the waiting room was pretty blocked up too.

Why are the kids constipated? Not enough exercise, too much screen time, stresssssssss? That's what Wendelien's trying to find out.

Wendelien loves Australia. She says when the weather is cold in Amsterdam she wants to jump on a plane and fly right back. She has a photo on her desk of herself and Eric snorkelling on the Great Barrier Reef.

Here's what I did today: filed files in a filing cabinet. Same alphabet. Then . . . you will never guess!

I made swans.

Wendelien wants the tables at her wedding to look like lakes with white swans, so I folded serviettes into swans. I told her we have black swans in Australia, so she's going to get two black serviettes for Willa and me. The swans took ages, then I sorted medical magazines, which are exceptionally gruesome.

We rode home in the peak-hour flow of bikes. I stuck behind Wendelien.

I can recognise when she's arrived somewhere now. Her bike chain has a particular clinka-clank.

What's going on at home? Zev? Mum? Dad? Danielle?

x H

Swan

I didn't tell them these next things.

Wendelien and I had a picnic lunch in a little park, out of the wind.

'Will you be sad if Bram doesn't come to your wedding?'

'Yes,' said Wendelien simply, 'but I understand. Who wants to be told how to live their life? Sorry you landed in this family mess, Henni – everyone's on edge, and there's unfinished business between the older ones. Jacob chewed my ear last night.'

'What about?'

'Old family stuff. Willa's return isn't all sweetness and light.'

I know that.

'What's Bram like?'

She took a big bite of her sandwich and thought about him while she chewed. 'He's not your ordinary guy. He's serious, intelligent, competitive, super clever on the computer, and sometimes he completely surprises me. He's persuasive, you know. He's social but also a lone wolf.'

We chewed on thoughtfully.

'How was Roos on the flight over?'

I didn't say we were terrified and thought we

might die, or that Willa couldn't breathe, or about the chemist, either. I'm not going to dob Willa in.

'The flights were very very long, but we made it.'

Change the subject.

'Wendelien, did you ever live in Hyacint's place? What do you think the blue dog is?'

'You know, in the Second World War the British prime minister, Churchill, got depressed, and he called it "the black dog". Maybe the blue dog is another form of depression. Otherwise I don't know, Henni, can't help you.'

As I rode towards the house I could see the three oudes on the little bench by the front door, all squashed together like squabbling birds on a branch. God knows why they kept sitting there like that, snapping away in Dutch. Getting fresh air? Maybe they just couldn't end the argument.

'How was it at Wendelien's work?' Willa called out loudly as I chained up my bike.

'Really good.'

She was using me to switch to English and end it, but Hyacint wasn't giving up. '*Roos, I asked* you, what was Moeder like to you before the war?'

I was still struggling with the lock but I was listening hard.

'I *told* you, she was happy,' said Willa. 'You never knew her any different, for you she was the same, but she was good before the war.'

Jacob said, 'She was not the same, Roos. You don't know what she was like after you left.'

'Probably very happy.'

Jacob growled. 'She was *impossible*! There was no pleasing her.'

'What, not even being her favourite?' said Willa.

'Who was her favourite?' said Jacob.

'*You!*' Both sisters pointed at him.

'You got treats,' said Hyacint. 'You slept in later because you were a skinny little stick. You stayed home from school because you were a sick skinny little stick. You got the best piece of meat...'

They're as bad as Danielle and me!

Finally I got the key out of the lock and walked over. The clump of winter clothes stood up and split into three grumpy people, and us dames went in our door, and Jacob went in his.

Hyacint had cooked a warm vegetable stewy thing called *hutspot* with a pork chop, and it was delicious and we felt good after that.

I risked a question. 'What was your father like after the war?'

'Oh, Papa was hopeless,' said Willa. 'Besides, if he protested he'd get his head bitten off. He went fishing.'

'No he didn't,' said Hyacint.

'You *know* what he was like, Hyacint. Don't you remember?'

They watched a show on TV that I couldn't follow so I wrote home.

'Willa, can we go to the Resistance Museum tomorrow? We can catch the tram. It's not far.'

'I'll think about it.'

That's a good sign.

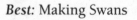

Best: Making Swans

Worst: If there was a Big Bike Expo in Amsterdam it would be ENORMOUS.

Black mark: I left my bag on the landing so I wouldn't forget to take it upstairs. It was in the corner by a pile of stuff that was there already. *Wrong.* Hyacint says I was littering.

The Rolling Parade

They sit up tall
relaxed
enjoying the view
gliding
balancing
a bike
a cake and cello
a dog and toddler
a watermelon
an OAR for goodness sake!
A crate of beer
a friend with sunflowers
two chairs... no, three

A wooden ladder
A carpet
an ironing board
the family
hockey stick and parcel
A stool and a fern
Children singing
Briefcase and shopping
Umbrella
on the phone

Is everybody in Amsterdam
auditioning for the
circus?

Whose fall is it?

I can fall down the stairs
I can fall in the canal
I can fall off my bike
I can fall off the back of your bike
Whose fall is it?
  Mine

THE RESISTANCE MUSEUM

I was jolted awake by a *KNOCK KNOCK KNOCK!* on my door. It was Willa, puffing and gasping. 'Did you leave the heater on all night?'

'Oh *no!*' Desperately I sprang to the knob.

'*Potverdomme,* Henni, when you go to bed *turn it OFF!*'

'I'm sorry, I was tired, I flopped down and...'

'*Another* black mark in the books for you, Henni.' She was furious. 'Hyacint has some sixth sense and she can *hear* if the heater is on, from two floors down. There is some weird connection between this attic and her apartment.'

'I'm really really sorry, Willa, I won't do it again, I promise. And I'm sorry I made you climb the stairs.' I felt like a naughty little girl. I felt like crying.

Willa steadied herself, swept stuff off the chair and with a loud '*Hrummph*' collapsed onto it.

'Oh, it's not just you, they're all cranky.' She waved her hands as if she was shooing away flies. 'And everything worries Hyacint, *everything*! The slightest thing goes wrong, she gets upset. She can't understand why you're in Amsterdam in this precious family time, as if I brought you along as a *guest*. I told her I wouldn't be here without you, but she doesn't understand.' Willa's fury fizzled out. 'I came too late for Hyacint,' she sighed.

She surveyed the zolder, the piles of family junk, with my junk spread on top.

'*Jeetje mina*, all this *stuff*!' She scratched her head. 'I remember those drawers. Moeder kept fabric in them. She'd buy it and keep it for the right time. Henni, pull out that second drawer.'

It was heavy and I could only open it a little. It was jammed with old letters and papers. Willa groaned. 'Close it. Close it.'

'The blue dog could be in there,' I said helpfully. 'A letter? A book?'

'What, search through all that? *Ugh.*' Willa was warming up. 'See that old Jakarta mirror with the pretty pearl inlay? I fancied myself as a film star when I looked in that mirror. This attic is cold as charity, Henni. Turn on the heater, Hyacint be damned.'

We laughed.

'Willa, how could five people live in Hyacint's tiny place?'

'And don't forget the two babies,' said Willa. 'Oh, we got on each other's nerves, especially when a baby cried, but Sara always saw the funny side. It wasn't so bad for us van Veens. We could go about as if things were normal. Read Anne Frank.' She pointed to the book in the mess.

'Sara used to imagine the glorious freedom when the war was over, the picnics in the park, the concerts, the theatre and movies three times a week at *least,* and then she and I were going to be *in* the movies. I was Cinderella and she was the fairy godmother.' Willa made it sound like a sleepover.

'But what about washing, and going to the toilet?'

'You forgot the babies again. O mijn God, they made us work. We had a routine, and a bath once a week. Moeder was very clean.'

'Willa, it was so risky, hiding Sara and Matius. Were many others in the Resistance?'

She drew back and looked at me as if I'd asked the most stupid question in the world. 'Jeetje mina, we weren't the Resistance, we were just saving our friends. Hiding Jews wasn't that rare. Girl, you have no

idea! I told you I was twelve when the war began ...'
she was getting loud, '*that's* the problem. People think
wars begin and end on a certain date. They *don't!*'

'Willa,' I said boldly, 'if we go to the Resistance
Museum I will understand it better.'

'You don't give up, do you?'

'Please?'

'Very well. Today. We go and get it over with.'

We had to catch two trams. I wrangled the map. I'm
not good at navigating in Amsterdam. I said it wasn't
far, but it was far.

'Wonder what I will remember?' Willa was in a
quieter mood.

I was relieved when we climbed off the tram in the
right spot. First thing in the Resistance Museum is a
short film in a theatrette. Thank goodness there were
only half a dozen people sitting in the dark, because
Willa sat bolt upright, exclaiming loudly: 'The radio
was under the stairs, behind the coats. Oh I remember
that! My friend Lodewijk made one like that. Oh, that
despicable man! Oh *yes!*' She got even louder. 'Moeder
was so *angry*. Yes that's how it was.'

Someone shhhhhh-ed us but Willa didn't hear.

When the lights came up everyone turned round and stared at us.

⁓

Willa read every caption for every item, every photo. Before the war the Dutch were in four groups who pretty much did their own thing, and got along okay. The Protestants lived a plain hard-working life, then the Catholics, the socialists who stood up for the workers, and the upper middle class people who just wanted business and life to roll along nicely.

'What was your family, Willa?'

'Well, I didn't go to a religious school. I reckon we were socialists, but not in line with the NSB. Yes. Moeder didn't like the rich getting richer while the poor stayed poor. We were taught to respect our parents, teachers, the Mayor, the Queen. They taught us what was right and wrong, to be fair and tolerant.'

'What happened?'

She huffed at my stupid question. 'How can you be fair and tolerant when that evil little Hitlerman makes it *illegal*?'

'Didn't the Dutch parliament fight against him?'

'*Pfff!* They were naïve! They thought they were negotiating, but after a couple of days he ran out of patience and bombed Rotterdam to rubble. "*That's* what I think of your negotiating!" The Dutch army fought for a little while, but bikes against tanks? Forget it. They surrendered, and the Germans rolled into town. Then everyone is asking themselves, "How should I behave now?"'

'I don't understand, Willa.'

'Is Hitler's way right?'

'*No!*'

'So what are you going to do about it?'

'Fight him!'

She gave me a look of pity. 'Well, that's all very fine to say, but are you prepared to die? Are you going to fight by yourself?'

'With a secret band.'

'Well, your secret band better start inventing things, because the Dutch had no weapons, no leftover resistance tricks from the First World War. With weapons you can strike, otherwise what can you do? Oh, there were a few brave individuals who stole guns from police stations. *They* were the real Resistance. If you were caught with a gun you were shot. All the heroes died. They're all dead. There are no heroes.'

She looked around for a chair but there wasn't one.

'Most people said, "Nothing I can do, I'll just keep

my head down and get on with life as best I can."
Some said, "Let's get with the Germans, it will work
out better for us." A lot of them joined the NSB, which
was like the Dutch Nazi Party.'

We came to a photo of a cinema with a sign on the
door *Boycott de Bioscopen*.

'Boycott the cinema. Oh, that was real hard for me,'
said Willa. 'I *adored* the movies, when you could forget
the war for a little while, but the moff were making
films with the Jews as the bad guys. I can't remember
the name of the film, but two men were fighting on a
cliff when Moeder stood up and shouted, "Propaganda
rubbish!" and dragged me out. After that we didn't go
to the movies anymore. I sulked for three days, but of
course she was right. The moffen were conditioning
us to hate the Jews. So we stayed home and played
charades. At least I no longer had to tell Sara the
whole story of a movie I'd seen and who was in it, and
what they wore.'

Willa tapped a photo of a man in a tin hat. 'He's an
air-raid warden. We had to put up blackout papers
on the windows every night so the English bombers
couldn't see Amsterdam, because that would help the
navigators find Berlin with their load of bombs.'

'*Every* window in Amsterdam?'

'Ja! The city went dark. We lived like moles.' She shrugged. 'It was the new rule, we took it in our stride. Wardens patrolled the streets for a gleam of light.'

She leaned on me and said confidentially, 'An air-raid warden is a real nice job for your secret band, Henni. You can knock on doors and give a message. Of course Jews couldn't be wardens. That was the first rule the moff brought in against them. The moff dished out the rules, conditioning the Jews to obey them, and getting everyone used to being bossed around.

'Some kids loved the war. See, it was exciting – the spying, the games of war. My friend Lodewijk was crazy about the secret radio. I think some humans like war, and rumours and things they find in gutters, but nobody should behave like that to other people.'

Then we came to a photo of a solid, determined-looking woman, wearing a fur, standing like a statue.

'Henni, that's Queen Wilhelmina! Moeder and I thought she was *magnificent*! I was named after her.'

We headed for the next room about the NSB.

'Henni, this is important.'

We turned the corner and Willa froze. She stood staring at a photo of a woman straining as she pushed an old pram loaded with heavy sacks. Willa's bottom lip quivered, then her mouth set hard.

'That's *enough*!' she growled, and headed for the front entrance. Just like that she pulled the plug on the whole museum.

'Was it interesting?' asked the volunteer at the desk.

'I need fresh air,' said Willa.

I told the volunteer we only saw half the museum, but it was too much for Willa. I couldn't resist saying, 'Her family hid a Jewish family.'

'Give me your tickets,' said the woman. She scribbled on them. 'Come back anytime.'

The other volunteer said cheerfully, 'There's a nice cafe over the road near the zoo.'

At the cafe I steered Willa to a table under a big tree. It was warmer now and she began to relax. She summoned the waiter.

'Henni, pick anything on the menu. You have exactly what you want, okay? Anything!'

Anything? Wow, this was *so* un-Willa! It's usually 'No helping yourself from the fridge,' and 'You eat at *mealtimes*,' and 'You've had quite enough, save that for later.' Now she was saying, 'Eat up.'

I looked at the menu for ages. I chose pumpkin soup, and an exotic-looking, mysterious open toasted sandwich, with strange pickled green things and a herring and two little potatoes, all composed like a mini work of art on a big white plate. Willa chose a chicken sandwich. Then I had a large hot chocolate, which was *very* chocolatey. I will never forget that lunch.

'Look at me,' said Willa. 'I got good food when I was little. I grew tall, but Hyacint and Jacob are shorter. They didn't grow so well, they didn't get good food at the right time, like stunted trees in poor soil. That's the war's effect on the body, but up here...' she tapped her head, '...not so easy.'

We caught the trams home. Willa was silent. What was it about that photo of the woman with the pram? The sacks? The woman?

When we got home, Hyacint asked, 'Did you recognise anything of Moeder?'

'Nee,' said Willa, 'but I recognised a lot of things.'

A VERY GOED DAY

I'm not a superstitious person.

Yes I am

No I'm not

Well, to be truthful, I am

a bit

Willa was writing letters. Ja, she still writes letters, and I was thinking about something she said when we were packing, back in Stella Street. 'If you don't risk much you risk a lot.'

I decided I would go to Jacob's friend place, over the water called het IJ, to the land called Noord.

What kind of a word is Ij?

Ij = eye.　　　　　*Ja.*

Het is 'the'.　　　　*Ja.*　(De is also 'the')　*Ja.*

The land Noord. Which direction?　　　*Goed.*

Goed is 'good'.　　*Ja.*

To say goed, get spit in your mouth and make like you're going to spit, like 'Kh...' and add 'ood.'

Goed. *Again.*　Goed　*Again*　Goed　*Very* Goed

To the Friendspot

Amsterdam is *so* confusing because the streets curve around, and the canals are a maze. I have maps on my phone, but they are small and the street names are incredibly long so I draw landmarks on my paper map and try to remember where things are.

If you don't risk much you risk a lot.

Oke. Here goes!

I reached Central Station, and the zillion bikes. I could see het IJ but I couldn't see how to get there, so I headed for the water like a turtle. *Nee! Nee!* Wrong! I stood alone on the edge of the road, with the drivers of cars speeding by, looking at me as if I was a Martian! Finally I made a dash through a gap in the traffic, and got loudly honked. Anyway, I got to the edge of het IJ, and on the other side, floating like a dream origami palace, was a beautiful white building, more graceful than the Sydney Opera House.

Must have been a huge piece of paper.

'The ferry to Noord, please?' I'm growing bold.

A woman in a fluffy coat directed me down the wharf. The ferry had just arrived and a crowd of bikes and motorbikes rolled off, then Tasman and fifty others rolled on. Ja. Free! The ferry set off. Everywhere I looked something was moving, barges slinking through the water, trains sliding into Centraal, bikes on a bridge, cars in the distance, seagulls swooping around, then with a clunk and a jolt, we were in Noord. I wheeled Tasman off, and right in front of me was an Italian flag.

Silvia at al Ponte was was friendly but busy, swamped by people wanting a coffee before the next ferry. I ate my lemon cake and thought of Jacob meeting Floor and buying coffees and time. There was certainly no one there who looked like a potential friend for me.

I went exploring. Noord was boring apartment blocks and suburban streets. I felt stupid roaming around looking for a friend, then a scooter frightened me out of my skin, so I went back to al Ponte. Noord wasn't much fun.

It was peak hour when I rolled back onto the ferry for Centraal. Everyone was on their phones or talking and laughing. I was silly to think something might happen. I watched the world glide by till we reached Centraal and the gangplank clanked down. Lonely and disappointed, I tried to make my way through the sea of bikes and scooters.

'*Henni!*'

What? That's *me*! Who called? Where? I couldn't see anyone. I looked round everywhere. Did I imagine it? No one knows me.

'*Aussie girl!*'

I spun around. Behind me the ferry was pulling away. Above the crowd a hockey stick waved wildly.

'*Henni!*'

It was the girl from the garden cubbies!

'*Carlijn!*'

'*Phone number!*' I couldn't see her.

I was blocking people's way, getting dirty looks. The ferry was clear of the wharf.

I screamed **06 221 456 51**

desperately hoping it was right. I never thought I could yell like that, in public. So much for keeping your private information secret!

The hockey stick waved up high again.

Did I get the number right?

It didn't take long to find out.

Quack! 06 555 206 82

> Where is old lady? Tomorrow k taking stuff fr ma to my bro in antikraak. Want to come?

Henni

> *Ja*

Quack! 06 555 206 82

> Main gate Vondelpark 11:00

Henni

> *Ja*

Quack! 06 555 206 82

> Goed

Henni

> *Ja*

JA! JA! JA! Happiness! Life is goed! When I met Jacob coming out his corner door I was smiling so hard my face nearly fell off.

'Jacob, the friend place *worked!*' I told him about Carlijn.

He laughed. 'You'll be zooming round with the cool guys now. Don't forget, if you hear about Bram, you tell me?'

'Sure. Jacob, what is antikraak, a plaster you put on old walls?'

'Are you going to live in an antikraak? Don't you like the attic anymore?'

'Carlijn's brother's in an antikraak. We're going to visit him.'

Then Floor came out the door with a bunch of flowers.

'Henni's going to an antikraak tomorrow,' said Jacob.

'Well, that's real Amsterdam,' she laughed. 'I lived in a kraak when I was young and poor. I'll tell you about it, but not now, we're late. Doei doei, Henni.' They hurried off to catch the tram. Floor's coat flew back in the wind. It had a lilac lining. I could see why Jacob kept buying coffees.

I suddenly remembered it was Friday. *Oh no!* At my eleven o'clock it was Pizza Night for Stella Street and I had completely forgotten.

Quack!

Zev

Hi Hen

Henni

Zev, I'm so happy to hear you because I TOTALLY FORGOT pizza night.

Danielle

We had fish and chips at the beach. We didn't miss you.

Zev

The tide was incredibly low, and the beach was endless. Danielle invented a game.

Danielle

Eyes-closed running

Zev

She disappeared right down the beach.

Henni

Excellent

Danielle

but I came BACK!

Henni

Dreary me

Zev

Hey Hen, Good news. Lodewijk van der Haag lives at Nieuw Sloten. I found him through his daughter online.

Henni

Whaat? He's ALIVE?!?! Are you SURE he's the one?

Zev

Yep he remembers Willa, and he really wants to see her. His phone number is +31 6 16 61 9362

Henni

ZEV!!! That is FANTASTISCH! OH WOW! This'll spin her windmills!!

Danielle

I have invented a dance

Henni

That's *amazing* Zev. You found him so quickly!

Danielle

my dance is going viral

Henni

REALLY?? How many hits?

Danielle

It's not global yet but it will be.

Henni

You've got my like Danielle. Hey Zev, what's a crystal set? Willa keeps talking about an orange radio.

Danielle

You haven't seen it yet.

Zev

I'll check it out if I get time. I've got heavy homework.

Henni

What's homework?

Danielle

I have 23 likes

Henni

Still earthing?

Zev

Yes, earthing in all sorts of shoes.

Danielle

Frank has a new best friend who doesn't have a trampoline

Henni

Yesterday we went to a museum about Amsterdam in the war, and afterwards – you won't believe this – we went to a stylish cafe and Willa commanded me to order anything I wanted.

Danielle

I don't believe it

Zev

To cheer herself up?

Henni

Ja, and Willa is trying to remember something important called 'the blue dog'. They had a little dog called Dolly but it's not Dolly. It wasn't a toy or an ornament. It was something in this house. What do you think?

Danielle

A kid's drawing in coloured pencil
Socks
a walking stick

Danielle

a cat
a biscuit
one of those getting things out of the oven things

Phases of the Moon

How do I tell the oudes dames about Lodewijk? Hyacint was kind of gleeful he was dead. This will prove her wrong, and sure as eggs, I'll get another black mark. I could just tell Willa and keep it a secret from Hyacint. But Hyacint will find out. She's so suspicious. I'm sick of secrets.

I'll just do it.

Henni

> Hey Zev! Willa is ecstatic! We're going to visit Lodewijk next week. They haven't seen each other for 63 years!!! Wow! Historic! Thanks!!!

I was wrong about Hyacint. She shrugged and said, 'It must have been someone else who died. They're all doing it.'

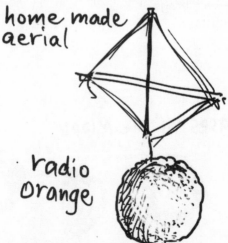

home made aerial

radio Orange

HARTOG + HUNTER

Carlijn rode up wearing a beanie with the world's biggest pompom.

Carlijn said, 'I usually go fast but I'll go slow for you.' She went to push off, but then turned to me, deadly serious. 'The first rule is *Look everywhere all the time*, and the second rule is *Go where you're going*.'

'What?'

'Ride straight. No weird things.' Then she said something that sounded like 'All good?' so I said, 'Ja.' I think she meant don't surprise people.

'Volg mij.' ('Follow me'???)

Ja.

You can go to Disneyland and pay heaps to ride California Screamin'

OR

you can ride with Carlijn.

Briiiing! a tourist!

Carlijn pulled off to the side. Carlijn said, 'Never stop fast or the rider behind you crashes up your bum. Stupid tourists do that all the time.'

O Lordy I don't want to be a stupid tourist.

We're off again down a cob-b-b-b-b-bled lane . . . oops, we broke an Australian law . . . oooh just broke *another* Australian law . . . oooo *third* Australian la-a-a-a-w through an orange light, up over a canal, more cob-b-b-b-b-les, up over another canal, aaaaaahh bike path . . . smooth . . . and *no helmet,* just flying with the wind in my hair!

Riders were swooping in from all directions. I stuck to Carlijn like superglue, going where I was going, wherever that was. No chance to remember landmarks. Where was she taking me? *Oh lucky windmills,* the traffic light is red!

'I don't worry if it's orange, because that's like pale green,' said Carlijn.

'Can you go slower?'

'I *am* going slow,' she said blankly. 'Oke, lowest gear.'

Lowest gear was better.

It seems, when you ride in Amsterdam, if you think something is a good idea, and it won't hurt anybody, you do it.

Now we were in a rough area, away from the quaint streets of bookshelf houses. Rubbish blew around and twisted bikes rusted against a broken fence. Old warehouses, empty factories. Weeds grew in cracks in the road. We turned a corner and there was a river. Het IJ? And a railway line. We stopped outside an imposing old building, with a clever pattern of bricks up near the roof, and huge wooden doors. I followed Carlijn round the corner and we chained up to a metal pipe.

'Is this a warehouse or an old pub?'

'Cigar Factory,' said Carlijn, stabbing a message into her phone.

We stood in front of the door, listening to the sounds inside, then someone came towards us, whistling. A tall blond guy opened the door. He had the same quick eyes as Carlijn, a sort of wise-guy face, and a floppy dog manner.

'Hartog, this is my friend Henni. Henni, this is my brother Hartog.'

'Hallo Henni.' He swooped on Carlijn's bag and took out letters, a packet and a large plastic container. He lifted the lid, sniffed and grinned. 'Dank je Mam.'

The Cigar Factory seemed bigger inside than out, a huge space spanned by strong wooden beams.

It was divided up by smaller random walls, like sets
for different plays, where busy characters buzzed
around to their own soundtrack, a battle of the
sounds. A woman making junk art played jazz,
a sculptor guy in a mess of clay had classical, and
people yakking in a rough cafe in a corner had pop.

Carlijn and I followed Hartog down a passage, up
a wide staircase, and along another passage to the last
room. Wow! This room had class. Well, it had *had*
class. It was lined with wooden panelling, and the big
windows looked down on the street. There was an
interesting faint smell. Tobacco.

'We have the best room,' said Hartog.

Carlijn said proudly, 'Hartog found this building.'

The furniture was a saggy couch covered with
magazines and clothes, a little fridge grumbling in the
corner, a camping stove with a few pots, a green table
and chairs, a desk made from a door across boxes, and
an office chair.

Carlijn said, '*Alles van de straat.*'

I took a guess. 'All from the street?'

'Ja.'

In a corner there were piles of cardboard boxes
neatly stacked, ready for posting.

'Henni's from Australia, with an old lady.'

Hartog wanted to know about me, and Carlijn seemed pleased she'd found someone interesting.

'What do you do, Hartog?' I asked.

'Ceramic hygiene specialist,' said Hartog.

'He washes dishes in a restaurant,' said Carlijn.

At that moment another guy pushed open the door, his arms full of boxes like the ones on the floor. He put them on the pile and slipped off his coat. He was *incredibly* skinny! His shoulders were like a wire coat-hanger, and his clothes hung down from them. You could hang him on a nail on the wall.

Carlijn introduced us. 'Hunter, this is Henni.'

'Hi.' Hunter dropped at the desk and from nowhere produced the skinniest computer I have ever seen. Skinny guy. Skinny computer. He flew into mails, his long fingers pattering on the keys like light rain. He reminded me of Zev, totally focused. I could hear Stella Street saying things like *He's a long drink of water, needs a good feed, beanpole*, etc.

'What's an antikraak?' I asked.

Hartog scratched his head. 'Okay, Henni, you are Rich Lady and you own this building. What will you do with it?'

Ah, the pretending game!

'Make it into an interesting place for artists?'

Hartog laughed. 'Wrong, Rich Lady. Try again.'

'Oh, I want to build luxury apartments?'

'Correct! But first you need permission from the city council and they take a year, maybe longer, to look at your plans, and while you wait some rough guys might like your empty building and move in.'

'Then it's a kraak,' said Carlijn.

'I don't want cracks in my building!'

'No,' said Carlijn 'a kraak is a squat.'

Hartog went on. 'These krakers living in your building, the kraak, might wreck the place and fight you when you want to kick them out, so it's better to rent it out cheap, to nice people.'

'Like Hartog,' Carlijn interrupted proudly. 'Then it's an *anti*kraak.'

'Right, so an antikraak is to prevent a kraak? Oh, it's so hard being rich. How do I find a *nice* person?'

'You didn't even have to,' said Carlijn, 'because Hartog was watching your place and he found your phone number and—'

'And my new gold phone rings! Then I ask, "Are you polite, clean and trustworthy, Mr Hartog? Will you and your friends look after my building?"'

'Guaranteed, Rich Lady.'

'But this area is scary. Who wants to live here?'

'Rich Lady, you ask a low rent, we make a deal. My poor artist friends move in, make stuff, coffee shop, bar. Now it's cool. Artists make places cool.'

'Ah ha! And when it's cool, I tear this building down and build my luxury apartments!'

'No you won't,' said the skinny guy. So he *was* listening. His fingers stopped pattering on the computer. 'Where are you from, Henni?'

'Australia.'

He paused for a second, then went back to the pattering on the keys.

He stopped again. 'Sculpture, sculptor, which is the man?'

'Sculptor,' I said. 'It could be a woman.'

He swivelled round. 'Do you want a job?'

Carlijn jumped in, quick as a flash. 'Paid, right, Hunter?'

'What sort of a job?' I asked.

'Translate instructions for a lamp, from Dutch to English. Do you know good English, Henni?'

'Brilliant,' says Carlijn, 'but she's on a holiday. She doesn't want to work, and translation is like homework. How much?'

'Fifty euros.'

Carlijn beckoned me into a corner and we

whispered. He'd offered me the job but I couldn't understand Dutch. I needed her. We both wanted to do it. Half each.

'Seventy euros,' said Carlijn.

'Sixty-five euros,' said Hunter.

'When do you want it?' said Carlijn.

'In two days. I pay when you deliver.'

'Seventy euros,' said Carlijn with a grin.

'Okay, seventy.' He laughed.

She nodded and the pompom went crazy.

Hunter told us that he had a hundred and thirty old lamps in boxes, with instructions in Dutch. He took one out.

'This is amazing!' I said. 'I know these old lamps! They're from Germany. I was in charge of lamps once, on a holiday in a house without electricity. I know exactly how they work and this is great because my dodgy phone is eating up my euros.'

Carlijn gave me a don't-be-so-keen look as she carefully put the lamp back in its box, then into her bag. 'We gotta go, but where's the toilet?'

'Follow me,' said Hartog, 'it's hard to find.'

The second they left Hunter asked, 'Where are you staying?'

'Eerste Hugo de Grootstraat.'

'Nice area, quiet.'

Then he said, in an offhand way 'If you have trouble with your phone I can help.'

'Thanks.'

It was awkward.

'Show me your mobile,' he said.

I don't like people messing with my phone, especially this dumb one that we'd just got working, but I kind of trusted him.

He tapped around on it and handed it back. 'This thing is old. I've set you up with Gipto. It's good. You don't use any juice. Try it.'

Then Carlijn came back and we left. When we reached a wider strip of the bike lane where we could ride side by side, I asked, 'What does Hunter do?'

'He buys and sells stuff. Two years ago on Koningsdag, King's Day, he found Star Wars merchandise, the first set of characters they ever made, all complete, even in the box. He knew they were gold because when he was a kid they were the aim of his life. He sold them online. I think that's where he started. Now he's hunting for WiiSports for a therapy woman. Last year he searched for old doorknobs for a guy restoring an important house. People ask him to hunt on the internet for crazy stuff.'

'Is that why he's called Hunter?'

'No, that's his gaming name. Hartog met him through gaming.'

'What's his real name?'

'Dunno. He sent two operating tables to Uganda.'

'*Wow*! How old is he?'

'Dunno. Seventeen, eighteen? Why are you so interested? Do you *like* him?' She looked at me in a funny sly way.

'Never seen anyone so skinny.'

Above the last pedestrian crossing button I saw this sticker.

Carlijn likes me because I'm an interesting specimen to show her brother. I don't care. She likes me.

Carlijn is wild but in a different way to Danielle.

Danielle is maddening-fun-fizzy wild.

Carljn is a crazy-daring-fun-sensible wild, if you can understand that.

Sensible wild. I love that wild.

I loved that ride.

OCTON + WEMPLE

A clean lamp shines a bright light.
HENNI OCTON

Carlijn and I met at the library halfway between her place and mine, because she said her place was too noisy. I rode there, proudly zooming along like everyone else, with a useful packet of chocolate biscuits in my bag.

Translating is fun, but it's harder than you think. First we tried Google Translate but it came out all gobbledygook so we googled 'How to translate instructions' and found a teacher who was pure gold. She said be clear and use short sentences.

We invented our own way starting from scratch. Carlijn read out a sentence slowly, translating it from Dutch into her best English, which I typed it into the computer, then I smoothed it into my best English. I wanted to include tips I remembered from that holiday, like putting the lamp on newspaper and using a skewer, but Carlijn said firmly, 'Keep it simple!'

How amazing that I knew this exact kerosene lamp! I added two instructions they had forgotten and a section on larger lamps. It was fun, secretly chomping into the biscuits and thinking of the euros.

We emailed the translation to Hunter. Instantly he emailed back saying it was good and he'd pay us when he saw us next.

'We should go real soon,' said Carlin, 'while he is happy, before he forgets.'

Octon & Wemple

Translators from Dutch to English

Carlijn Wemple
Dutch Language Expert
Business Manager

Henni Octon
English Language Expert
chocolate biscuits

Ja! That'll be us.

Carlijn can't understand why I like reading. 'Books are not life,' she said.

'You can be *in* someone's life in a book,' I said.

'But it's not real things happening.'

'Stories can make things happen in your imagination,' I said. 'Like, if we were somewhere cold and dark, and I lit this lamp and turned it low, then told you a ghost story, it would feel real.'

Then we swapped swear words and I told

Carlijn about Myrte and her friends, and how they'd abandoned me at the bridge.

'What school does she go to?'

'Cartesius College.'

'A kid in my hockey team goes there. I'll ask him about Myrte.'

Then we ate the last two chocolate biscuits.

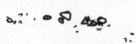

I got an email from Donna. I could hear her voice.

Donna O'Sullivan
Re: A bee
To: Henni Octon

Hi Chicken, it's more than a week since you left and we miss you like crazy. Little Jim keeps saying 'Hen?' and looking for your bag near the door. We love your Bulletins to Stella Street. Keep them coming.

Is there a bee in Willa's bonnet? There was something, wasn't there? I guess we can wait until you two get home to hear about it all, but we're curious.

Why are you so interested in Amsterdam in the war and the Resistance?

Lots of love, D

Henni Octon
Re: A bee and other insects
To: Donna O'Sullivan

Hello Donna! I think of you all the time and wish you were here, so we could zoom around together on bikes, with Little Jim in a seat behind you.

Willa is fine. It's a complicated family. They are nice though. There's a lot of family memories being dug up, and half memories and stuff to sort out after not seeing each other for so long. The war is part of that.

I find the Resistance stuff fascinating. I try to imagine how they lived in the war when Willa was a kid round my age. Scary but thrilling.

Hi to everyone, and tell Danielle I like her dance. It is truly cool! Not as wild as usual. More classy.

X X X X Henni

I got a black mark at breakfast, when I used the sugar bowl to keep a bashy old guidebook open. *Wrong*. And Willa didn't stand up for me when Hyacint told me off. So ungrateful! After I steered her across the world, and put up with her farting. I *do* take care of books.

Hmpf! Hycint is getting black marks of her own! My damn phone didn't save a photo I took this morning.

Quack!

Carlijn

We need €€€ from Hunter before he forgets. k = hockey + homework. You get €€€?

Henni

I don't want to go by myself.

Carlijn

?

Henni

It's scary

Carlijn

@ first. Go early tomor Will be sunny He will be there €€€€. Go♥

Henni

argh

Carlijn

Go! I tell Hartog to tell Hunter u will be there No worries

Henni

o   k

Carlijn

Go

BACK TO THE ANTIKRAAK

It's *not* sunny, it's windy and grey, and I'm b-b-b-b-b-b-bumping over the cobbles into this cold head-wind. Hope the lamp doesn't break. I'm sick of secrets...Willa is Roos...Willa is my grandmother...Myrte is weird......Give me straightforward Stella Street any day...stuff you, Hyacint...stuff you, Myrte...grumble grumble grumble. Jeetje mina, I'm like those dictators who find someone to blame when things aren't right.

I get to the door of the Cigar Factory and *KNOCK KNOCK KNOCK* loudly, and yell that I want to see Hunter, and I wait, and I wait, and I'm *cold*! When the huge door creaks open Hunter looks different. Older. He's had a haircut and he's even skinnier!

'Hi Henni.'

'Was the translation okay?'

'Better than most translations.'

I thought he'd give me the money at the door, and that would be that, but he wanted me to come in.

I locked up Tasman and followed him upstairs out of the cold... well, less cold. I wasn't afraid.

'Godverdomme, it's cold out there!' I said cheerfully.

'Do you say *godverdomme* much?'

'It's a great word. I just heard it yesterday. I'm going to say it all the time.'

'Well, it's like saying *fuck* in Dutch. Don't say it if you don't know how to use it. You'll get a punch on the nose.'

Whoa, that shut me up.

'Do you like writing?' said Hunter.

'Ja.' (Serious now, struggling to get my confidence back.) 'Instructions are like poetry, finding the right words, and using them in the most effective way.'

'*Potverdomme* is a better word.'

'What does it mean?'

'Holy shit.'

'Could it mean good grief?'

'Ja.'

His computer goes *ding!* and he's at it.

'Who are you staying with?' he asks, without looking up.

'My grandmother.' (I like Willa being my

grandmother.) 'And her sister. Actually, I'm staying
in the attic. It's freezing, but it's my own little place.
If I wear all my clothes I'm warm. I use the bathroom
downstairs and have meals with the old ladies and
help my grandmother. She migrated to Australia in
her twenties, and now she's back in Amsterdam for the
first time since she left.'

I'm rattling on, I'm nervous, just ask for the money.

'Is she happy to be back?'

'Yes, very happy to see her relatives, but she's
remembering hard times in the war. We went to the
Resistance Museum.'

'I thought old people forget.'

'Not her, she remembers everything. The war was
traumatic for her.'

'The Hongerwinter?'

'Ja, and other stuff.'

He's easy to talk to, just get the money.

'Is that interesting for you, Henni?'

'Yes. I'm trying to understand how the Resistance
operated, how they used codes like *The goose is on the
nest*, stuff like that, and the danger.'

'Was your grandmother in the Resistance?'

'Gosh no, she was only twelve, but—'

Then Hartog came bustling in.

Phew! What would I have said next...!

Hartog triumphantly dumped a pile of containers in the middle of the floor. They smelled really good.

'G'day Aussie! Not many customers at work. So I scored a heap of food.' He found three clean plates, flipped the tops off the containers, tore open the bags and spread out a feast. *Yum!!*

A mail pinged in on Hunter's computer and he sprang up to answer it. As his fingers patterpattered, lines of Dutch caterpillared across the screen. Zev says one day we'll do things by thinking, using our body's electricity. Hunter and his computer can almost do it now. Patterpatterpatter tap tap *wisssshh*. Mail's gone.

He saw me watching him.

'Clever machine.' He patted his computer. 'It's all in here.' He sat down again.

'Do you know everyone in this place, Hartog?' I said as I reached for my second spring roll.

'Ja, they're friends. I've been in two antikraak with the sculptor near the front door.'

'Is the big door always locked?'

'Always!' He sighed. 'Keys is a problem. There is valuable stuff here.'

'Does the owner visit you?'

'Ja, to check we look after his place and no refugees.'

'Are there refugees here?'

'Are you a nosy reporter from Australia?' said Hunter.

'We had refugees,' said Hartog. 'We held a meeting with everyone here, and some antikrakers said refugees would make problems and they should go back to their country, which was bloody stupid because their country was bombed to shit. The girls in the old workers' dining room were leaving, so we said oke to twenty men. Temporary. All is temporary here.'

'How was it with the refugees?'

Hartog laughed. 'Nice guys. They translated instructions into Arabic and Turkish for Hunter.'

'But there was trouble,' said Hunter.

'What happened?'

'Toilets blocked. Not their fault, old plumbing, but the anti-refugee-ers blamed them.'

'We had a concert for money to fix the plumbing.'

'Do people *always* have to leave an antikraak eventually?'

'Ja,' said Hartog.

'But this building is unusual. They wouldn't tear it down, would they?'

'No,' they said in unison.

'This is history,' said Hunter. 'The cigar industry

was big in Amsterdam. With many tobacco factories.'
He searched in a pile of books. 'See. Like that.'

'To tell the truth, Henni,' said Hartog, 'we expect a
fight for the building.' Then out of the blue he asked,
'Henni, have you been much around Australia?'

'I've been to Sydney with my family to visit my aunt, and to Adelaide, but not to the outback.'

'The outback?'

'Central Australia, the big deserts, Uluru.'

Hartog said, 'My friend went to Australia, bought a van and drove all around. It broke down in the middle, and just when he got it fixed, a kangaroo bounced on it.'

I said I had to go, thanks for lunch. Then I plucked up my courage. 'Hunter, please pay me seventy euros for the translation.'

He gave a slight grin. He had it ready in his pocket and watched as I counted the money on the floor. Ja. Seventy euros. Then he followed me downstairs, past the welder guy who was sending out bursts of sparks from behind a screen.

At the door, as I patted my pocket with the envelope of money, our eyes met for a second. Hunter's face was expressionless, but solemn. Suddenly I had a flash of recognition. It really was a flash. *I knew who he was!*

It must have been like this in the Resistance when you met someone who you thought was also in the Resistance, but how could you be sure?

Hunter let me out. For a moment I thought, *Ask*

him now? but he was standing on the top step, and my bravery had run out. All I said was, 'Dank u.'

'Dag,' said Hunter and the big door closed.

As I rode home, I thought about Hunter's expression. Was that a secretive look? Of course I could be wrong. I didn't *really* know, did I? When the van Veens talked about Bram at the picnic they never said he was skinny. Potverdomme! If I was describing the guy I'd say he was skinny. I could just say, 'Jacob, I met this really interesting skinny bloke?'

Then I thought of the look on Hunter's face.

It's a hunch, just a hunch.

I won't tell Jacob.

If I ever see Hunter again – which I probably won't – I'll just ask straight out, 'Are you Bram?' and then I will tell Jacob. *Any*way, we go home in a few weeks. *Any*way, these days people's information is private. You have to get permission before you tell. How about a form with a tick-box. *Permission to tell grandfather*.

Jacob is kind. He will understand.

I don't know for *sure* it's Bram.

Danielle always says to me. 'You think too much.'

Seventy sweet euros in my pocket. Then I got lost

as usual

Tuesday 7 April

WORK WITH DIRK

Cruising along, sitting up high in Dirk's van (ha ha! Ve are in de van de Dirk van Veen), I noticed all the car drivers watched out for bikes. I guess they all ride bikes themselves.

'Dirk, has every bit of Europe been dug up by humans?'

'Ja, Henni, well, every bit of this place. We say God created the earth but the Dutch made Holland. We have to be clever, because a quarter of this country is below sea level, and the rest is not high.'

At the building site Dirk showed me how they construct a coffer wall to create a dryish man-made hole, then inside it they build the house. I watched them working. *Holy windmills* it was cold.

English
Kofferdam ~ Dutch

Drive in walls.
Brace.

Dig out soil.
Pump out water.

Te dah!

Giant steel pattypan van Henni van van Veen van

The drive home was interesting.

'Dirk, why do the houses have hooks?'

'We use a pulley to lift things in and out of the windows: furniture, building materials, people.'

'People?'

'Or maybe they use the ladder of the fire truck. If you are having a baby at home and things do not go well, and you must go to hospital, do you want them to bump you down the stairs? No, you go out the window.'

Whoa!

'Dirk, why don't the canals rot the foundations of the houses?'

'Because the water stops it rotting. If there is no air, the wood won't rot.'

'Dirk, have you ever had to get people out of a kraak or an antikraak?'

'For a kraak, call the police. I had university friends who lived in a kraak. They thought the world should give them a place to live. Hippy idiots. Scavengers.'

'What about an antikraak?'

'I have prepared an antikraak.'

'How do you do that?'

'This place had dangerous holes in the floors, so we laid wooden sheets over, to make it safe enough.

Antikraak is not so bad, but you get stuck in that kind of life.'

Watch yourself, Hartog and Hunter!

'Dirk, have you ever found a wartime hiding place in a building?'

'Yes, doors in weird places and shelves that don't make sense. Once on a site, I was digging, when my spade goes *clunk*! Hallo! Something metal. Danger! I always think a bomb unexploded, so I go gently, but no, it's a tin of precious things buried by a Jewish family. There were initials round the lip of a silver cup. Bram was the detective, and we contact the family in Boston. They come to collect what is rightfully theirs. They cannot believe it, like a message from the grave. Oh there are a lot of things builders don't declare, can't be bothered.'

'Where would you hide something in Hyacint's place?'

'That blue dog? The attic. Lots of cracks up there.'

'Dirk, why did Willa go to Australia?'

'To get away from her mother. When you choose one side in a war, you take a risk. If you are with the winners and you survive, that might be okay, but if you're with the losers, big trouble.'

'But Willa's mother was on the winner's side.'

'True, but she knew bad things, saw bad things. My grandmother had a hard time. In the Hongerwinter she had two starving babies and no husband to help.'

'She had Willa.'

'Ja. Poor Willa. My grandmother was a tough lady. She had no time for fun.'

I took a chance. 'What about Bram?'

He glared across at me. 'Right. I *tell* you what about Bram! I had a real heavy cupboard to move. I need help. Maybe I ask the wrong way, maybe I smell bad, maybe my hair is not straight, but he should help his father – but he goes to his room. Right? So I am going to call the neighbour to come help me, but then I think *No*, Bram should help me. Why should I call the man next door? Right? And then I'm yelling at the bedroom door! And where did this new computer come from? The sky? Not from me. And why is he out the door so fast? He won't say. He is stubborn, arrogant, no respect, addicted to the computer.'

black mark, black mark, black mark, black mark

Dirk's deep voice boomed. 'Last year I spoke to a friend from work, and he went to a lot of trouble to get a good holiday job for Bram, that would give him experience and contacts, but Bram never showed up.' Dirk's voice boomed even louder. 'Never even showed up! *Eigenwijf!* What do you think of *that*, Henni?'

       I'm not saying

'And I have a question for you, Henni – why do you ask so many questions?'

'To find things out,' I hoped I didn't sound like a smart alec. I was a bit scared of him, this big bear sitting behind the steering wheel, but you know, I also had the feeling of a hurt animal you can't get near.

We drove in silence till we reached a road by a canal close to home. We swung into a side street and stopped. Dirk was cheerful now, and whistled as he climbed out of the van.

'Henni, come and look at this. This is interesting for you.'

I hopped down and followed him to the edge of the canal.

'There will be a carpark under here with two layers of cars, beneath the canal, under the boats. The glass entrance will be over there, so it won't look too heavy in the street.' He waved his arms around like a human windmill. 'And the cars will go down there, and come out there, so people can still have cars, but these streets will be more clear, more beautiful for people.'

'Wow, that's clever!'

'Ja.'

Dirk the Bear stayed for dinner, and beer. Jacob and Floor came up for coffee.

'Willa, what work did your father do before the war?' asked Dirk the Bear. He and the big armchair were one large lump.

Willa answered their questions in a matter-of-fact way. 'Papa had mostly smaller jobs, building cupboards, fixing stairs. People didn't spend much in the Depression, but these little local jobs were enough. I remember Papa telling us about an extraordinary cupboard he was building. Looking back, I reckon he was building a hiding place. He worked for himself, so he never lost his job or had his wages cut, and Moeder's sewing brought in a bit.'

'Where did she sew?'

'In the small bedroom.

there's a big one?

'Remember the Rast & Gasser treadle? Moeder was organised. She used to cut the fabric out on the big table.' Willa sighed. 'It was a lovely comforting time before the war. Moeder never went out without getting dressed up, you know, in a pretty dress, gloves and a handbag to go to the shops, and everything was in Dutch.'

She smiled. 'And after school I used to play in

the street with Lodewijk and the other kids, no cars, no horses either, and in the evenings we sat at the table with a couple of neighbours and played games or coloured in, listening to stories and music on the radio, no television. I was an only child till you two ruined it.'

They laughed and Hyacint poured more coffee.

'So Moeder loved you?' said Jacob.

'Yes.'

They were quiet, thinking about that.

'Did you ever meet Moeder's sister?'

'Oh ja, the rebel! She married a Catholic.'

Jacob grinned. 'What a terrible thing to do!'

'Well, it *was* back then!' Willa was emphatic. 'People marry anybody now. It's all changed, The only thing that hasn't changed is how flat this place is.'

They chattered away in Dutch while I read. Then Willa switched back to English. 'Henni, they want to know what it's like in Stella Street.'

'Oh, it's great!' I shut my book enthusiastically. 'We're friends. We live in different houses, in different ways, but we sometimes go on holidays together. We have Pizza Night on Friday nights. There's more space and the streets are wide for cars. It has big gum trees, and there's a park—'

'I have a garden,' Willa butted in. 'I grow flowers and vegetables. We have four seasons, but it's not so cold in winter, and the summers are hot. Jacob and Hyacint, why didn't you follow me to Australia?'

Jacob crossed his arms. 'What is this, a TV show called *My Life is Better Than Yours*?'

They laughed, but it felt a bit like that.

‑

'How was today with Dirk?' Willa asked when we were alone.

'Okay. I saw the countryside, and rode an electric bike, and coming home Dirk showed me where the car park will go under the canal.'

'Did you talk about Bram?'

'Yes, Bram makes him furious.'

'Goodnight, Henni.'

'Dirk thinks the blue dog's in the attic.'

Henni

Hello everybunny. What's hippyning? Ask me how you build houses in Amsterdam.

Zev

How do you build houses in Amsterdam?

Danielle

I'm not a bunny

Henni

The Netherlands is sand yes SAND and it's wet SAND. To make the new subway line they had to dig through wet sand and the old foundation poles of houses, which took YEARS!

Danielle

The wise man built his house upon a rock

Henni

Ha ha ha! Yes I thought of Mr Nic's old rain song too *The rain came down and the floods came up*

Danielle

*and the house on the sand went **CRASH!***

Zev

How do they build foundations?

Henni

They use piles.

Danielle

Pies?

Henni

PILES !!!
Today I went to work-experience with Willa's nephew Dirk (check that family tree I sent – Jacob and Floor have two adult kids, Wendelien and Dirk.)

Danielle

we know that

Henni

Dirk is about 46, a builder and big. I call him Dirk the Bear.

Danielle

Ggggggrrrr I'm Dirrrrrk de Builderrrrr Strrrrong and Brrrrave

Henni

We went to the country, where he's building a house. It was flat, grey and cold. Dirk taught me how to ride an electric bike and *Weeeeeeeeeee!* I zoomed off to a little town nearby to get coffees for everyone. Danielle don't tell Mum and Dad about the electric bike.

Danielle

Why not?

Henni

They're worrywarts.

Danielle

You don't say! I am the centre of all their worry right now.

Henni

Electric bikes are the future, I do not lie. You can self-power, Zev. What's happening at home?

Danielle

0

Zev

A tree in the park came down just missing Maggs, who was only saved by stopping to pick up rubbish from Macca's. Also Briquette is better after constipation. I am still earthing.

Danielle

I am a toad in the school play

Henni

and real life

Danielle

still not missing you.

Zev

They are taking my blood pressure as part of the experiments now.

Danielle

Dad has been in Sydney and Mum has a cold.

I sent them drawings.

'Amsterdam houses sit on poles driven into soft ground,' says Dirk. It was a swamp.

'The wooden poles under the old houses last for centuries, but if they dry out they rot,' says Dirk.

These days the poles are steel tubes filled with cement. They go deeper into the 2nd layer of hard sand

dry

wet

Bird's eye view

Then a beam is bolted on top, then planks, Then bricks.

dry

wet

'All the wood is in the wet,' says Dirk.

'Poles are bashed down, in pairs,' says Dirk.

LODEWIJK VAN DE HAAG

It took us two trams to get to the suburb of Nieuw Sloten. Sounds like a letterbox. Took ages. Willa cheered up on the second tram, muttering things like 'Why did he move? Wonder if he married? Wonder what happened to his sister?'

We arrived at the front door of a two-storey apartment block. I buzzed the intercom for Number 9. *Bzzzzz* and the door went *click*.

'*Push!*' commanded Willa.

We clomped up the stairs. On the landing outside apartment Number 9, there were wooden crates, stacked to make pigeonholes, all crammed with boots, tools, bags and fishing gear. Hanging on the wall beside them were heavy coats and jackets like two puffy headless, legless waterproof fishing men. A whole winter life.

The door opened and there was Lodewijk van de Haag.

He was old and tall, but stooped and leaning forward a little, with a half smile, so when he walked it was like he was eager for what was going to happen next. His bushy eyebrows were fighting to get out from behind his thick-rimmed glasses and his head sprouted a tousle of strong white hair. Ja man, Lodewijk was bushy.

The old man and the old lady were ecstatic to see each other, amazed they were both still alive. I guess that's what it's like when you're old, when all your mates have dropped off the twig. They didn't hug, just squeezed each other's hands for a long, time, smiling away at each other, not knowing where to start.

'When did you leave Van Oldenbarneveldtstraat?' asked Willa.

'When my wife died, my daughter and her family move here, so I move here too.'

Phew! He speaks good English.

'Then my daughter and her family migrate to Canada! But I am not going there, I have space here, and a balcony. They can visit me here.'

We dumped our winter layers on a chair near the door. He shoved aside a pile of papers and we sat on the couch and he sat on a chair facing us. You could see his habits in the furniture. There's a nice smell of baking.

'Is it strange, Roos, coming back?'

'O ja,' said Willa, 'everything has changed. You pay for everything, even to use the toilet. And the tourists, o mijn God, gawking in your windows.'

'Not here.' Lodewijk grinned. 'You know, Roos, I can still see you standing by the bus, with a couple of old suitcases, and your hair in plaits.'

'Going to the other side of the world, where I didn't know a soul,' laughed Willa.

'Hyacint and Jacob were very upset, When you arrive in Australia, what did you do?'

She frowned. 'You never got my letters, Lodewijk? I'm sorry about that. Well, I went to a migrant hostel for single women. They said, "You can stay here till you find your feet." Friday night was fish and chips, and a kind woman said, "What would you like, love?" She actually called me Love, and I nearly cried. Then

I got so sick with hepatitis from someone on the boat, a Greek girl had to help me to the toilet. I was skinny and yellow. Then a Dutch family helped me get a job in a small shoe factory, then I bought a cheap bike and found a room to rent.'

'Did you speak English?'

'A little. After the war English replaced German but I never paid much attention at school.' She shoved a cushion behind her back. 'I went to English classes on the boat but I couldn't understand the teacher. He was from Ireland. But I wanted to be a nurse, so I studied. Lodewijk, what happened to your sister who was sent to help your aunt with all those kids?'

'Oh Roos, she had a terrible time. My uncle lost his job, imagine, ten kids and no money. My sister hated it – sleeping two in a bed, in sheets that had been wee-ed on the night before. When someone gave them a bag of handed-on clothes, the kids fought like cats. My sister missed a lot of school, because of the snow so high.'

Willa hugged herself. 'So *cold*, Lodewijk. Remember how we skated on the canals? Jacob says the ice hasn't been thick enough to skate for years. How long since you could skate on the canals?'

'Ten, maybe twelve year. Remember making the

frozen path so the moff would hit the black ice?'

Willa and Lodewijk swung cheerfully from misery to fun to misery to fun. It was like stories from the movies.

'Remember the tandem?' goes Willa. 'That bike was stolen *so* many times. We had nowhere to keep it. Remember once it came back by itself? And Lodewijk, your grey army bike!'

'An *army* bike?' I said.

'The army has bikes in the first war,' said Lodewijk, 'even the army band. Look on the computer. Meester De Vink had an army bike. Remember him, Roos?'

'Oh ja, he was a real good teacher. They replaced him with that moody NSB type. Meester De Vink was a gentle man who never got cross, then *boof*, he's gone and we have this guy who hits us and the German lessons get longer.'

'What happened to Meester De Vink?'

'He was murdered. I think he was in the Resistance.'

They were quiet for a moment. 'He never got to live his life.'

Well, these two had a go at life.

Lodewijk sprang up from his chair. 'Oh *Roos*, I *forgot*! I cook *appeltart* for you! Your favourite!'

As he clattered away in the kitchen, I imagined him in an apron carefully measuring out the flour and butter and sugar for the pastry base like Willa does at home, then cooking the apples and putting the tart in the oven, for his long-lost friend. What a dear, tufty old bloke.

'Did you ever make fun of the moff?' I asked Willa.

'Never!' said Willa.

'We *did!*' Lodewijk called from the kitchen. 'That soldiers' marching song, remember, real nice song, "Lili Marlene", and after each line we sang "Plons plons".'

'Oh yes!' Willa launched into it and Lodewijk, carefully carrying the rattling tray, joined in.

'Da de – da de – daaaa daaaa, Da de – da de – daaaaaaaa Plons plons!'

Da de – da de daaaaaaaa, De da – de da de daaaaaaaaaaaa Plons plons!

They roared laughing.

'What's funny about *plons plons*?'

'Splash splash.'

'What's funny about splash splash?'

'Well, the Germans didn't know about water. They confiscated our barges and towed them south, ready for crossing the Channel when they got around to

invading England, but we knew our barges were
hopeless for that.'

'Plons plons is them falling in the water.'

'Now I get it.'

'And Henni, the beaches were *verboden!* Forbidden!
The moff were scared of invasion, so they built
concrete barriers with barbed wire along the beaches.

'It was exciting, Henni. Ja!' Lodewijk made a pistol
with his hand and shoots the light in the ceiling.
'*BAM! BAM!* Goodies and baddies. Line them up
against the wall and shot them. *BAM! BAM!*' He shot
the doorknob.

A big blob of cream landed on Willa's knee. 'Oh,
look what you made me do!' The cream (slagroom!) is
sponged off.

'Lodewijk,' said Willa, 'tell her about the radio.'

'She won't be interested in that.'

'She's the most interested kid on the planet.'

Lodewijk adjusted his glasses and focused his
bushy eyebrows on me. 'Now, Henni, the radio is very
important, because no one knows what de heck is
going on. England is putting up a fight, they are an
island, and their prime minister, Winston Churchill is
strong.' He waved his fist.

Willa chipped in, 'It was the fight for news.'

'*I'm* telling about the radio!'

Willa laughed, and shut up.

'Henni, the Germans made a law. You must hand in your radio so you don't listen to Radio Oranje. But they will *not* get our beautiful Philips model Erres radio! I *refuse*! Big fight with my parents! So I take the radio to pieces and wrap them and put under the stairs, on top of the wardrobe, in the bottom of sewing basket, all hidden round the house.'

'After the war did you put it back together again? Did it work?' I asked.

'Of course!' said Lodewijk proudly.

'Tell Henni about the aerial.'

'Okay. So. Now the beautiful radio is in pieces, and the moff is the new boss of Dutch radio, telling us great deeds and propaganda which we can't hear because they take our radios...'

'The weapon of the mind!' said Willa.

'*Shhhhhh!*...but we know every night there is fifteen minutes broadcast from the Dutch government in London, so we make a rough homemade radio. The reception is bad, but you can hear some—'

'Then the Germans—'

'*Shhhhhh*, Willa, *my* story!'

wish Zev was here

'So Henni, the Allies, the good guys, fly over and drop leaflets on Amsterdam, how to make a directional aerial for better radio reception. I get the bits from my opa, who was a plumber, and I make the aerial.' He made a diamond shape with his hands and held them up in the air. '*Gksshhhhh*hhurrccccc*rr*ru*hurrrrrrrrrrrr* (I guess that was radio crackling noises) "*Nederland, zal de strijd volhouden, zolang tot voor ons een vrije...*" The Queen is speaking to us! *Ja!* Roos, remember?

They both roared a loud, joyous fanfare, which I guessed was the music for Radio Oranje.

Thump! Thump! Thump! There was a loud banging on the floor under our feet.

'Don't worry about her,' laughed Lodewijk. 'That's her broom handle. She's like the NSB downstairs. Ha ha! So Radio Oranje changes the music theme to the start of Beethoven's Fifth, *bum bum bum bummm*...that sound is not music, you know, could be just an engine or something.'

Suddenly he stopped. 'Wait!' Lodewijk hurried into his bedroom and returned proudly carrying a cigar box.

'Open it, Henni.'

It was full of thin, crumpled strips of silver foil.

'O mijn God!' exclaimed Willa. 'It's jam!'

'Ja! Henni, this is jam! The Germans dropped it like

snow, from planes, to jam the radio signals.' Lodewijk grinned, stood up and tossed it high in the air so it fluttered, twisting and glittering down around him. 'And so now the show is over!'

'Bravo!' We cheered the clever ending.

'Now, do you want another piece of appeltart met slagroom?'

When we left the twee oudes hugged, and Willa said, 'Goodbye, Lodewijk. See you again soon.'

'Ja, Roos.' His eyes shone behind his glasses.

On the tram home Willa said 'Lodewijk helped me remember the time I went to Australia to forget, but I can't forget it. Lodewijk doesn't have anyone to remember it with now.'

Maybe she won't return to Stella Street

'In Australia how did you learn English, Willa?'

'I went to classes and I read books. Agatha Christie is good English, and Graham Greene, but he was on the Vatican index of forbidden books, the Prohibitorum or something. Lodewijk made wonderful machines out of Meccano.'

Willa is always surprising.

'Can we go back to the Resistance Museum?'

'Go by yourself.'

MR KUIPERS AT THE LIBRARY

Willa wanted a quiet day after all the excitement of Lodewijk, and to wash the slagroom out of her skirt. I took off for the library to search the net about the wartime but O mijn God, my heart sank into my possum socks. All those gruesome words and acronyms!

A librarian heard my loud sigh. 'What are you looking for?'

'I'm trying to understand about the Netherlands in the Second World War.'

'Oh, there is someone who could help you . . .' she looked around, '. . . but he's not here yet . . . he usually comes in round this time. Can you wait?'

'*Yes!*'

A little while later a quiet voice behind me said, 'You want to know about the war?'

It was a neat retired schoolteacher, Jan Kuipers. His

rimless glasses gave me the impression he was keen to see everything clearly.

'Do you mind if we move to a quiet corner?' he said. 'My hearing is not good.'

We found comfortable chairs and settled down. 'Now, what do you want to know?'

'Mr Kuipers, I'm staying with an old lady who showed me photos of herself when she was a happy girl in a normal family, but just a few years later they were cold and hungry and frightened. How did it get so bad so fast?'

Mr Kuipers frowned slightly and half closed his eyes, as if he was asking himself, *How do I answer this?*

He leaned towards me. 'May I call you Henni?'

'Yes.'

'Henni, the period before the war was chaotic. Rich people stopped spending, because they lost confidence in the economy. Then businesses and farms made over-production, so workers were fired, then they couldn't pay their rent. Workers still with jobs had their wages cut, but they had overspent, so they were in debt. There was unemployment, strikes and riots, and people were starving. It was a terrible, unhappy time. The economy was out of balance. The government didn't know what to do.'

'The country was out of control?'

'Exactly, and people who were okay had no sympathy for the poor. "They should be able to find work!" they said. There was no welfare unless you were desperate and then they made you feel ashamed. Inspectors visited you. You didn't have to pay the bicycle tax, but you had to wear a bicycle tag with a hole and the subsidised clothing was red. Imagine that. No wonder it was called *de Grote Depressie*, the Great Depression. And all the industrialised countries in the world suffered it. Countries closed themselves in, and looked for strong men to fix the problems, and make them proud of their country again.'

'In the Netherlands, was the NSB the strong men?'

'They *wanted* to be the strong men. *Nationaal-Socialistische Beweging*, the Dutch National Socialist Movement. They copied the German Nazi party with their own salute, newspaper, youth club, uniform and all that nonsense. They also wanted a dictator, not democracy. An iron hand to control everything, compulsory military service, control of the press, to ban strikes.'

'Is this before the war?'

'Yes, Henni, and when the Nazis invaded the Netherlands, all groups except the NSB were banned.

"We're with you Germans!" the NSB said. "The monarchy is abolished, and we want our man Anton Mussert to lead the Netherlands.'"

'Did he get the job?'

'No. The Nazis sent their own man, a cruel, hard Austrian, *Reichskommissar* Arthur Seyss-Inquart. The Dutch gave him the nickname Zes-en-een-Kwart, which means six and a quarter. He had a limp from World War One, that was the quarter. His job was to control the Netherlands and round up the Jews.'

'How did he do that?'

'Well, first he wore "the velvet glove" not doing much, then the glove came off. For example, if you did something the Germans didn't like, they'd arrest you, and you'd disappear into prison without a trial. You were a hostage. Then if the Dutch Resistance blew something up, or killed someone they'd take out what they thought was the appropriate number of hostages and shoot them all, for payback.'

'*Jeetje!* Did the NSB do that?'

'No, the SS, which were the German police. There were five thousand SS sent to the Netherlands, more than in all of France. The SS worked with the Gestapo.'

'What's the Gestapo?'

'The secret police. They arrested anyone who challenged authority, and rounded up the Jews and set them to concentration camps. If you wanted to betray someone, you'd tell the Gestapo. They were ruthless, frightening in their long black coats, but at least in uniform you knew who you were dealing with. Often they wore plain clothes.'

'What about the Dutch police?'

'They were generally helpful to the SS and the Gestapo.'

'And the Dutch government?'

'On the day the Netherlands surrendered, the entire government slipped over to London. Queen Wilhelmina went the day before. They became the government-in-exile.'

'What about the people in lower-down government jobs?'

'They went to work as usual, except now they were administering German laws. The Nazis decided not to rule by the army, but through the Dutch systems so the Netherlands could transition smoothly into the German empire. Law and order, if you could call it that, was enforced by the SS and the Gestapo. If Dutch officials didn't like their jobs they resigned. Anyway, one by one they were replaced by NSB men. I believe the NSB had a mean view of human nature and were opportunists using the NSB to get ahead, but they never got many top jobs.'

'Why do you know all this?'

'It is a special interest of mine. My grandfather was the mayor of a large town. During the Occupation he stayed on. Why? Maybe he was afraid he'd be replaced by an NSB type, who'd make it worse for the townspeople. Queen Wilhelmina wanted them to stay on. Maybe he was collaborating with the Germans.'

'Was he?'

'He must have to some extent. Before the war he was respected, but people can act out a role.' He shrugged. 'I was fascinated. I wanted to discover that he was secretly a hero. I collected everything I could find about him and wrote it down. I was surprised when a publisher wanted to publish his story, because the ending was so unresolved.'

'Was he a hero?'

'I don't think so.' He rubbed his eyes behind his glasses. 'Sadly, plenty of Dutch people supported the Nazis and plenty just did nothing. There's a museum about the Resistance.'

'I know, I've been there.'

'Yes, well those museums are quite fashionable.

People want heroes, but there's no museum for people who helped the Nazis or did nothing. Henni, please don't think all the Dutch people were heroes – they weren't. And after the war, when a few Jews straggled home to Amsterdam from the concentration camps, they weren't welcomed, or helped. People said, "We had it tough too, you know." They didn't recognise the much worse hell the Jews had been through.'

It was all so mean. I felt miserable.

'Yes, it's not a nice thought.' Mr Kuipers sighed. 'Everyone wants to be proud of their country and believe their people stand up for what is right.'

'What happened to your grandfather?'

'He had a heart attack just after the war. He was in jail, accused of collaborating, but he didn't flee.'

I wanted to tell him about Cornelia and Willa, but I didn't dare. 'Do you think the only person who can know if they are a good person is the person themselves?'

'Maybe.'

'Does the NSB still exist?'

'No, it ended with the war.'

'What happened to Six-and-a-Quarter?'

'He went on trial at Nürnberg as a war criminal.'

'And then?'

'He was hanged.'

Whoa!

'Yes. Dreadful. But think of the thousands of innocent people he sent to their deaths.'

Mr Kuipers sat for a moment, then he said quietly, 'You should be a reporter, Henni. If you have any more questions, I will be in the newspapers section of the library. I hope I have been helpful.' Then he hoisted himself out of the chair, shook my hand, and slowly walked to the opposite corner of the library.

How depressing it was. Do I still believe Willa's story?

As I was leaving the library I glanced back, and Mr Kuipers saw me and beckoned me over.

'Henni, something I just remembered. The Nazis abolished the bike tax to get in everyone's good books, then later on they confiscated everyone's bikes.'

I pedalled home slowly, thinking how complicated governments were, and I remembered a five thousand-piece jigsaw puzzle my cousin brought on holidays once, 'Map of the Ancient World'. It took hours to turn the pieces the right way up, it covered half the room, and we only got a few edge bits done before it was bedtime. I calculated it would take at least a month to finish.

'Who votes we give up on this puzzle?' said Zev next morning.

Everyone except my cousin held up their hand.

'Four to one. Carried.'

'And me. I had my hand up,' yelled Danielle from outside. She gave up on the puzzle ten minutes after we opened the box.

'I now declare the puzzle closed.'

I like Stella Street democracy.

Mr Kuipers was right, it's better to face the facts.
I cheered up. I would try and face the facts but first I would try and *get* the facts. So I could face them.

'Willa, I just had a great Dutch history lesson.'

'Fine, well, I'm just having a great Dutch cup of coffee. Get out my biscuits.'

Yay! She was in a good mood. I might get some facts.

'Willa, there's something I've wondered about.'

'Oh, you *wonder*, do you?' she said with a grin, winding the handle of the coffee grinder.

'When Sara and Matius moved in with you, bringing nothing with them, did your family pay for their food and everything?'

'Well, that was a problem, Henni. They had a bit of

money, Sara and Matius, but you needed coupons too.'

'Coupons? Like coupon-smuggling-uncle coupons?'

'Yes. We'll get to him. Coupons was how they rationed things to make it fair, so the shops sold their limited supplies in an even-handed way.'

'How did coupons work?'

'Well...' She put the coffee pot on the stove and gazed around. 'Say your kid's grown out of her shoes. You count your coupons to make sure you have enough for shoes...can't remember if there were special coupons for shoes...Anyway, Moeder did all that and she was careful because you didn't get many coupons and they had to last. Then you took the coupons and the money and bought the shoes. You could be a millionaire, no coupons, no shoes.'

'Why wasn't there enough for everyone?'

She waved the oven mitt at me indignantly 'Because the moff were taking everything, *everything* to make things for their war!'

'Where did you get the coupons?'

'From the Distribution Office, but you had to register.'

'But Sara and Matius couldn't register.'

'Of course not.'

'So what did Moeder do?'

'Well, here's where the coupon-smuggling uncle comes in. They *said* he was an uncle. He just popped up. I never knew why and I didn't ask. He would arrive before curfew, sleep on the couch and be gone when we woke up next morning. Moeder always fed him as well as she could. He was very good-natured. Sara and I pestered him about the latest movies, and you know what game we loved to play? Monopoly! Then after the war Moeder told me he was distributing coupons and money to the *onderduikers*.'

'*Jeetje!* He was dealing out *real* money! What's onderduikers?'

'People in hiding, like Sara and Matius. It means "under divers". Food coupons were the most important. You got coupons for bike tyres too, they were scarce as hen's teeth.' She sipped her coffee. 'And you didn't get coffee like this back then.'

'Willa, if you didn't use all your coupons, did you have to give them back?'

'Why would you do *that*? No, you gave them to someone who needed them. Some people sold them, but that was risky, like buying things on the black market. Illegal and expensive.'

'Did the moff get coupons too?'

'Don't know. They had their own money,

Reichskreditkassenscheine, so they could shop in our shops.'

'Jeetje, what a headache for the shopkeepers.'

'Ja. Moeder liked to swap things. She swapped a bottle of grog for a pair of shoes for me. They were too big but they were okay if I wore lots of socks and looked like Minnie Mouse. When Moeder's old friend Wim was dying, he gave her his woollen coat. She cut it up to make coats for a farmer's kids and swapped them for potatoes. Speaking of potatoes, here's a story for you. I once came across an old guy with a sack of potatoes. He said, "Run home and get a big pot," so I did and he filled it up with potatoes, no coupons! I didn't know why and I wasn't going to ask. I was that proud I'd been able to get those potatoes.'

She smiled with pleasure at the memory. 'Henni, make yourself a hot chocolate.'

'Papa used to sharpen Moeder's shears for her.'

BEADS

I wanted to chuck my stupid phone in the canal. It
was driving me *mad*! I wanted to send a photo to
Zev, of a bike seat that was also a lock, but I couldn't.
I tried and tried, then I lost the stupid photo.
Grrrrrrrrrrrr SO frus-*TRAT*-ing!

What happened next was a really bad idea.

I wasn't planning to see Hunter again, but he *had*
said he'd help with phone problems. I couldn't call
him on my stupid phone because he is No Caller ID,
so I just set off for the Cigar Factory. It was afternoon,
don't know what time. I was angry at my phone, and I
forgot the days were short.

I passed the windmill, and found my way to the
side of the Cigar Factory where I locked up Tasman.
I was about to zip round the corner, but the place was
strangely quiet…spooky. I felt alone. Then I heard
bike chains rattling, so instead of charging round the

corner I took a peep. A weird-looking guy in a dark jacket was just slipping in. I ducked back. He hadn't seen me. *Clunk* went the heavy wooden door.

Why was it so quiet? Where was everybody?

I checked out the four bikes by the door. There was one with a crate on the back, and its bike-lock chain was just hanging down, not through a wheel or anything. I looked closer. It had been cut! Lordy lordy. Robbery in progress!

Where are you, antikrakers? I pushed the door. Locked. Hell's bells. Okay. Me outside. Robber inside. Okay okay. I'm scared. What do I do? I should go home right now! *Jeetje mina*, what about Hunter's computer?

Stay calm. I have half an idea. The bike with the crate must be the getaway bike. Quickly I prop it up, then I struggle frantically to derail the bike chain with a stick. Why is it so hard to slip those sprocket things off when it happens in a flash at the wrong time? Phew! I did it! I lean the bike against the wall again.

But I don't have the other half of the idea.

I slip over the road to a deep doorway where I can watch the Cigar Factory. Nothing happening.

What if I'm wrong and he's an antikraker and he lies down and sleeps till tomorrow? It will take me an

hour to get home by the time I get lost a few times.
I should go home now. The oudes will be cross. If he
is a thief…of course he *is* a thief, what will I do? It's
getting dark. Hold on…

A light flashes on in a second-floor window…and
off…another light goes on the same floor…off. He's
going through the building. I watch the top corner,
Hunter and Hartog's window. Stay dark *please*. Stay
dark. Where did Hunter keep his computer?

The light flicks on at the top – oh *no*, he's in there!
It stays on for ages. *Potverdomme!* He's searching. For
goodness sake everyone, come *back*! Hurry *up*! I see
the top of a head, then an arm flashes up and down.
He's not being careful near the window. Oh no. The
light's off.

My heart's pounding. I duck back over the road,
unlock Tasman, prop him just round the corner. Oh
God, where *is* everyone? What do I do? Follow him?
Where to? Then what? Take a photo? Too dark. Stupid
phone. The big door creaks and there are noises at the
bikes. He's outside.

I chance a peep…lucky his back is to me. A bag's
in the crate. He's going. He swings onto the bike and
pushes off. The pedals spin and he tips sideways, hop-
hop-hopping to get balance, swearing blue murder.

Another peep. The bike is upside down. He has his back to me and he's struggling with the chain. The bag is on the ground behind him, in my direction. Grab it? Do I dare? Make a dash before he fixes the bike? Do I? Do it *NOW!*

He's swearing and grunting so loudly he doesn't hear me. Quick as a rat I snatch the bag and swing it on my shoulder. It's not too heavy. *Jeetje mina!* I fly round the corner and rocket off. Don't look back! He's running after me but I'm on a bike. I ride like a bat out of hell. I have a head start. I take a look behind. I can't see him. The road along the train tracks is straight, but I want to hide. Dive down streets? But this is faster. Get a fair way then dive off.

I'm rocketing along, nearly at a good street... have I got away? I look behind. Oh *no!* A flying figure is rounding the corner on another bike. I pedal fast as I can, my head pounding, no idea where I'm going. The bag is bumping on my thigh on the cob-b-b-b-b-b-b-b-b-bles. No one around. Please give up the chase *please!*

I take this turn, that turn, over a canal. Oh no! he's closer! He took a short cut. Oh far out! I need somewhere safe, I need crowds, my gasping breath, my heart pumping, somewhere to duck down and wait. Luck please luck please, down a one-way lane the wrong way, over another. *There's* a street! People and lights. I'm going for it!

Lordy Lord, it's Halloween-crazy! It's a red dream, red windows in a red street, red rooms flashing by, women in bikinis and underwear, slow-moving zombies, Spider-Man, Superman, cavemen. I glance back, stupid on a bike at top speed, in pedestrians. I swerve to miss two priests, struggle to keep balance, I'm screaming, '*HELP!*'

Suddenly, *whooosh!* I'm yanked off my bike. *Oww* my knee hurts! *Slam!* I'm in a red room with a shop window onto the street, and a strong black woman in a miniskirt with ropes of red beads over naked breasts...with whiskers? She's a man? Him...her...this person, they're strong...

'What's he want?' I trust these eyes

'*He stole my friend's computer. Oh God!*'

THUMP!! THUMP!! THUMP!!! on the big window. He's right here, shaking his fist, banging the window, kicking my bike, snarling, pointing at the bag in my hand.

'*Don't break my window!*' Beads whips out the door and blasts Dutch at the thief, close-up like a flame-thrower, then the thief's head's stuck forward, eyes popping, arms waving wildly, yelling at Beads, me, the bag, totally unhinged. Bead's yelling, beads shimmying, there's a crowd now. A man with big muscles and *Strictly Ballroom* T-shirt grabs the thief. Beads is yelling, thief's yelling. Crowd's yelling. Ballroom has thief in a headlock. I watch through the window.

Beads charges back in. 'Keep the computer. Your bike's okay. Give him the bag.'

'He'll grab the computer when I leave.'

'Call your friend to come here.'

'My phone's broken.'

'*Ahhgg!*' Beads thrusts a mobile at me and barges outside again. More yelling. What'd they say? *Smeris?* Is that *cops*? I think it means cops. Nee nee nee please don't call the smeris, not after how Hartog and Hunter talk about them and the antikraak.

I call Carlijn. Jeetje mina, I remember the number!

'Ja?' yells Carlijn. There's an incredible din behind her, people chanting and yelling.

'Carlijn, it's *Henni*!' I scream.

'Wat? Wie is dit?'

'*It's Henni!*'

'What? Who?' yells Carlijn. 'I'm at the demo. Call me later.'

'NO **STOP** Carlijn it's *HENNI!*'

THEN SHE LISTENED!

O Boy, Lord and holy windmills, she listened.

Someone's coming to rescue me. Beads and I bring my bike into the room and wait.

'Where are you from?' asks Beads.

'Australia.'

'Australia? I want to visit Australia!' says Beads. 'I love opals so *much*, they're so magic, that colour. They are rocks, right? Natural rocks?'

'Yep, real rocks out of the ground! You could go to the opal mines in Coober Pedy. They would *love* you in Coober Pedy!'

Beads in Cooper Pedy? Yeah, I reckon that'd work.

'Where are you from?'

Beads grins. 'So you don't think I get this tan in Amsterdam?'

'No.'

'I'm from Suriname.'

'Is that near Vietnam?'

'Hell no, north part of South America.'

Beads is rubbing a sore hand. Must have knocked it when I was grabbed. Beads looks up and down the street.

'He's gone, that crazy guy. I've seen him round. Where's your rescue? Why are they taking so long? This is bad for business.'

Then Carlijn arrives.

'I thought your friend would be a man,' says Beads. 'I guess you'll be okay.'

'No worries,' says Carlijn. 'She can throw a boomerang.'

'Nice beads,' says Carlijn.

'What's your accent?' says Carlijn.

'Dutch, you cheeky girl.' Beads does a shimmy-shimmy and the room is all aflicker-flash with glints and sparkles.

'WOW! Do you do voodoo?' says Carlijn.

'Get out the door!' Beads laughs. 'Or I voodoo you two!'

Very sincerely I say, 'Thank you for saving me and the computer. Otherwise I don't know what would have happened.' And that is *true*.

'I have been chased myself and it's not nice,' says Beads, waving long brown arms, shoo-shoo-ing us out. 'Be away from my room, you two, with that damn computer. I must get back to work.'

What a great person.

Out into the crazy night.

We ride to Hartog's restaurant. Carlijn is asking a million questions but I can't concentrate because I'm petrified the thief will pop up and have another go.

We arrive at the restaurant, which is quite classy, and go down a side lane where Carlijn knocks on a door. Suddenly there's Hartog in a T-shirt, a dirty big apron and bare arms, and behind him, like a ship's engine room a steaming bustle of clatter and voices, and delicious smells.

I deliver the computer into his red-raw knuckly hands.

Hartog looks me square in the eye. 'I have no time to hear it now, Henni, but you saved Hunter's universe! You did real damn *great!*' Then the door bangs shut and the steam-world's gone.

Carlijn rides with me to a canal that looks familiar.

'Thanks for collecting me, Carlijn. You're a legend!'

She pokes out her tongue. The yellow pompom zooms off into the night.

She'll be in trouble. I'll be in trouble, but I'm back on good old Nassaukade. Jaaa, I know where I am. Tired as hell and heading for trouble, but I'm happy happy windmills!

Nine o'clock. The oude dudes had finished dinner ages ago and whipped up a fine slagroom of worry. Jacob was part of the worrygang.

'Where were you? What happened? We couldn't call you. What would we tell your parents?'

'I got lost.' (Which actually wasn't true, for once!)

I was exhausted, but so glad to be home. I spun my story cheerfully, which, in fact, I thought was quite good, about how I saw a crowd at the end of a street where two funny guys were swinging their fridge up into a fourth-floor apartment using the hook at the top of the building and a pulley. One was trying to heave it in through the window (like I saw a couple of days ago). I watched for ages, talking to a man who turned out to be a lady, then I rode off in the wrong direction.

Hyacint simply tuned out. For her it confirmed that I was totally unreliable, and telling a bunch of lies. Willa was angry at first, but glad I was back. She kind of trusted me, even though she didn't believe me, and just wanted to go to bed. But Jacob, canny old Jacob, wasn't convinced one bit and he stayed worried and annoyed and hurt. That's when he started going cool towards me. He said, 'What really happened, Henni?' and I said again, 'I got lost,' maybe a bit too cocky, and he raised an eyebrow and gave me a disappointed look.

'Your dinner is in the oven,' said Willa, popping to the bathroom in her dressing gown.

Carlijn told me later I'd ridden straight into the red-light district. There was a big soccer game the next day and the city was packed with fans. There was no one at the Cigar Factory because all the antikrakers were at a big refugee demo, on one side or the other. Whoa! What an epic day!

Wonder if I could find Beads again?

One thing for sure: this Hunter/Bram business just got more complicated. I shouldn't have been so smartypants with my story.

Two things for sure: I feel horrible lying to Jacob.

Three things for sure: I'm glad the van Veens are techno dinosaurs. If Mum and Dad heard about this, oh boy that would be *bad*!

MOLLI CAFÉ
IN DE PIJP

Back to the Biblical man with my stupid telefoon.
I don't know what he did, but it took a minute, cost
eight euros and he didn't say one word! Jeetje mina, the
euros go fast. Just as I was walking out my phone rang!
I nearly dropped it with shock. My third call.

Mr No Caller ID!

'Come to Molli café in De Pijp today.'

Like a command. *Whoa*! They said the Dutch could
be blunt!

'Okay, I'll try. I have to help my grandmother but I
might be free after that. Where's De Pijp?'

'I'll text you.'

I was annoyed. He should be saying, 'Thanks a
zillion for saving my computer,' and be endlessly
grateful and friendly after all I went through. But I was
curious. Ja man, I was curious.

'Okay.'

click

I took Willa to the chemist, who helped her untangle her bowel problems. She has more energy in the mornings, and usually likes to stay home in the afternoons, but today she wanted to go to the cheese shop and it was hard to get away. I rode like crazy to De Pijp.

Hunter's meeting spot, Molli café, was near a big noisy fruit and veg market that ran along a street. Hunter was sitting at the table right up the back. I didn't recognise him at first. He had a black beanie pulled right down and was wearing a heavy black coat. He still looked like clothes on a coathanger, except draped over a chair. He was still Hunter. He asked lots of questions about the robbery and listened carefully, saying, 'Ah,' and 'Ugh,' and 'Ooh.' Then he said, 'He's crazy, that guy, but he wouldn't kill you.'

Well, that's reassuring!

'You *know* him?'

'Ja, but I didn't know he was into crime.'

'Why did he want your computer?'

'I don't know. I was stupid to leave it there.' He stopped and looked me straight in the eye. 'I don't live at the Cigar Factory now and I don't want anyone to know where I am.' Then he dropped his eyes. 'Thanks for the rescue.'

He rummaged inside his coat, took out a battered

envelope, and shoved it towards me. Money?
Carefully I opened the old envelope. No, not money,
it was...labels? I turned them over. A collection of
beautiful illustrated old Dutch ex-libris.

'Oh Hunter! I *love* them! Where did you find them?'

'Online, not that Spui tourist market.'

'My souvenir of Amsterdam!'

He was pleased. He lightened up. 'How's the
Resistance?'

'My grandmother doesn't want to go back to the Resistance Museum.'

'Why?'

'Something spooked her in a photo of a woman pushing a pram of sacks.'

'Go without her.'

'But it's good with her. She remembers and tells me what it was like.'

'You know, there was a porcelain factory in one of the concentration camps. You can recognise the pieces by a certain mark on the bottom. I have a client who collects it.'

'Jeetje, do they keep their collection secret?'

'No.'

'Do you hunt for any secret collections?'

'I don't ask.' He shrugged. 'I just find things.'

'What are you hunting for now?'

'Space toys, shoes for a cross-dresser, WiiSports for a physiotherapist, Mickey Mouse things. Props for a movie.'

'It's all in the clever machine?' I said.

'Ja.' He looked at me this time. 'Thanks, Henni.'

He wanted to know about Willa. He laughed when I described the twee oudes at breakfast. I told him everything about a wedding coming up, and folding serviettes into swans. Then I told him about Willa's childhood in the war. It all tumbled out, but I was careful to keep the Cornelia story secret. I also told him about a bust-up in the family and the son that shot through, and the dear old grandfather that was worried. I watched his face. Nothing.

'You are really inside this Dutch family,' he said.

Did I imagine a tiny smile?

'Yes, but it's not a happy family...'

'I must go,' he said abruptly, and before I could say another word he stood up, went to the counter and paid.

'*Tot ziens*,' he called back over his shoulder. At the door, he looked carefully both ways before stepping out.

Jeetje mina, we are still in the Resistance.

He's Bram, I'm sure, and I am one hundred per cent sure he doesn't want me to tell!

Potverdomme. Now I have two Amsterdam secrets.

BULLETIN TO STELLA STREET
My Life in Amsterdam
SUNDAY 12 APRIL

I've been in the city of windows for seventeen days. Out my dakvenster I see little video clips, except they're real-life in the windows of the houses opposite. A lady is ironing. Yesterday I saw a couple pashing. Wonder if anyone sees me? I don't care, I'm like them now. When I get into my pyjamas I don't bother to go to the back of mijn zolder anymore, I just change at lightning speed to keep my warmth. I leap into bed *fast*. Get dressed *fast*. Downstairs *fast*. It's freezing, but with my own body heat, in good warm clothes, I'm okay. Your coat is a life-saver, Maggs. I have a collection of odd gloves to choose from now.

People on the ground floor live in a sort of fishbowl and you can see straight in. Sometimes their windowsills are little exhibitions of ornaments or children's artwork or plants. Jacob and Floor have blinds and a wooden dog and a pottery bowl. Tasteful. Ja. A sort of inside–outside thing.

Donna, most houses have a tiny patch of soil beside the door, with a plant, sometimes a rose but usually hollyhocks, which grow tall, like the Dutch. Their flowers open up, bud after bud, up the stem like slow flower

animation till they reach the top. The colours are glorious –
scarlet, cream, purple, or pink. Forget the tulip, for me the
Dutch flower is the hollyhock.

We're settled nicely here now, me op mijn zolder, and the
twee oude dames below. They can double-Dutch to visitors,
and I'm happy up here. I go downstairs anytime I want, and
when they don't need me I zoom off on Tasman. Hipidihip!
(that's hip hip hooray!)

Mum and Dad, you will be pleased to know I'm being
useful. The oude dames do the cooking and cleaning. I
set the table, and wash up while Willa dries, and I do the
shopping, and be Willa's guide dog. Albert Heijn is the
supermarket. It's a chain. I guess Albert started the first one.

Hyacint likes Nizza Kokos biscuits, Delicata chocolate,
Kesbeke gherkins and Chocomel. Willa likes Verkade
chocolate and the little Zaans Huisje biscuits with a
chocolate house stamped on one side. I also take the
bread bag to buy a loaf of *brood* from the baker.

And I take down the bags of rubbish, and plastic and
bottles and papers, and post them in the right bins in the
street. There's no space for every apartment to have a bin.
The communal bins are like stern, stumpy letterboxes. You
pull down the handle and post into its mouth.

I'm reading *The Diary of Anne Frank*. She lived near here, and there's always a long queue to visit the house.
I will go sometime. How weird, that it's a diary by a kid around my age, that explains to the world what it was like, living in hiding. Some people don't believe she could have written it, but I do. Anne Frank liked the bells of Westerkerk, my night-time clock. I think of her sometimes when I hear them. She was so lively and hopeful, but being cramped together in secret drove her nuts. Imagine, Danielle, if you and I had to hide together! IMAGINE *THAT!!!* I can hear you groaning!

When I first arrived, the stairs to mijn zolder felt dangerous, but now I'm used to them. Kids here have to learn to swim, because there are canals everywhere, and the land is below sea level. Wonder if they learn how to fall down stairs?

Briquette, you wouldn't like Amsterdam. I've never see a dog off a lead, except in Vondelpark, which is the long main park, and perfect for bikes. Riding around Vondelpark is a dream.

Doei doei dear Stella Street (that's bye bye)
Tot ziens (see ya later)
Henni

FINDING OUT

'Henni! *Henni!*' The yellow pompom sped towards me and screeched to a halt, triumphant and out of breath. 'I have chocolate…*puff puff*…I know about Myrte…*puff puff*…You have euros…*puff puff*…We go to Westerpark!'

'Ja!'

In Westerpark we split the cash for the translation, then Carlijn wanted the whole hair-raising account of the computer-chase because I left out so much on the ride home that night.

She listened one hundred per cent, polishing off the chocolate fast.

'Okay Carlijn, spill the beans on Myrte and give me that chocolate.'

'Spill the beans?'

'It's what an old guy at home says. It means *tell* about Myrte.'

Carlijn grinned. 'Oke, here's the beans spilled on Myrte. She lives with her mother, her grandpa and his dog, Box. Myrte's mother makes life hell. Myrte's mother kicked out Myrte's father who now lives in Breda and Myrte doesn't see him much. Myrte's grandmother died but Myrte's mother hasn't got rid of Grandpa who has loud opinions, and she hasn't got rid of Box either and he is old and blind and pisses in the corner.'

'Why doesn't Grandpa leave?'

'It's Grandpa's apartment. Myrte's mother should leave. Grandpa cares for Box to annoy her and walks kilometres each day to stay healthy, so he won't give her the pleasure of his funeral.'

'What's this got to do with Willa and me?'

'Myrte's mother is on holiday, so Myrte is looking after Grandpa and Box. Okay, here's some real good beans. Grandpa is haunted by Willa. He commands Myrte to *spy* on you, he remembers Willa and he's scared of her.'

'Wow! *Why?*'

She shrugged.

Jeetje mina! What's so scary about Willa? I'm not raising the subject of Myrte with the twee oudes.

Carlijn jumped on her bike. 'I'm late for

homework. Tot ziens.' As the yellow pompom
disappeared round the corner she shouted back, 'We
must plan King's Day!'

Carlijn likes to cut it fine
She slides in on the bell
as the lights are flashing
and the barrier comes down

Carlijn sails close to the wind
She lives in the chase scene
She would've given that robber
the flick for sure

Henni, hurry up!
The hare waits for the tortoise
Carlijn zooms round the place
as if she owns it
She does

Back home, setting the table (the ouds face each other, I'm at the end), I ask 'What's this King's Day that everyone keeps talking about?'

'No idea,' said Willa.

'It's *Queen's* Day,' said Hyacint.

Willa laughed. 'Of *course* Queen's Day is *King's* Day, there's a king now.'

'But what *is* it?'

'A holiday for the king's birthday,' said Hyacint.

'Are you Dutch crazy about royalty?'

'No, it's an excuse for a street-party.'

Willa was in a jolly mood. 'When Wilhelmina was young, it was Princess's Day. She was the special little princess who had to behave herself and bow nicely. She made her doll bow and bow and bow, till its hair was tangled. "How do you like *that*?" she grumbled. "That's what *I* have to do!" Of course in the war the moff banned Queen's Day in case we got up to patriotic tricks.'

Dinner was Hyacint's *stamppot*, which is mashed potatoes and kale with heaps of butter and spices and smoked sausage. *Yum!* My favourite.

Wendelien and Floor dropped in.

'What will you do on King's Day, Wendelien?'

'Eric and I will sell the worser of everything we

have two of, and I will clean out the cupboard on the landing. Not one spoon is coming inside, and I will not buy a single thing.'

'Floor?'

'Jacob and I will take a walk to see everything, then I will sew my hat for Wendelien's wedding.'

'What will you do, Hyacint?'

'Watch it on TV.'

'What will you Aussies do?' asked Wendelien.

'Depends how I feel,' said Willa.

I said, 'My friend Carlijn will think of something.'

'Tackle the attic, Henni,' said Wendelien. 'I cleaned out a lot, but there are plenty of things left to sell. Just check with the family before you take anything.'

'Help me, Willa?' I leaned towards her. 'We might find *treasure*!'

'Like that blessed animal?' She smiled.

Which reminded me, and before I climbed the stairs, I asked again, 'Willa, when we can go back to the Resistance Museum to finish it?'

'I told you to go by yourself. I don't want to go.'

'But it's more interesting with you.'

'Goodnight, Henni.'

'Please?'

'Oh, stop pestering me! Goedenacht.'

'Goedenacht, Willa.'

I'll ask again in the morning when she's chirpy.
I zoom upstairs, through my little door and leap into
bed. Everyone thinks the dog is here.

Goedenacht, blue dog.

* ☆ · ☆ · ☆ ☆

Before this holiday I thought then was then, and now
is now. But there's a lot of then in the van Veens' now.
The oudes keep scratching at each other about *then*.
What freaked Willa out on the plane? It's something
deep down. Donna would know the questions to
ask. What went on with Moeder and Papa, especially
Moeder? She's at the heart of it somehow.

The Eating Wars

Willa ate her egg at Hyacint
Moved her glass of water pawn to the left
Cutlery down, her knife pointing directly
at her sister's heart
Stalemate
Hyacint moved the salt and pepper left
Willa reached out
And took the butter

DETERMINED RESISTANCE

This morning I got the answer to my question. The washing-up from breakfast was done and Hyacint was busy with bowls and flour. I started to ask, 'Willa...' but I didn't get any further. She said, 'Come into the lounge and let Hyacint cook.'

'Goede,' said Hyacint loudly.

We plonked ourselves near the window overlooking the street. Willa got straight to the point. 'You want to know about the photo of the woman with the pram.'

I nodded.

'If I tell you, and we go to the Resistance Museum, will you leave me in peace?'

'Yes, Willa.'

'About the blue dog and everything?'

'Yes, Willa.'

'And that will be an end to it?'

'Yes, Willa.'

'And no more questions?'

'Yes, Willa.'

'Very well.'

She gripped the arms of the chair and took a deep breath, as if she was about to take a rollercoaster ride.

'This happened when Moeder and I were managing by ourselves. You know Moeder was up to … let's call it uncertain things, right? Well, from time to time she would say to me, "Roos, take the babies for a walk." We'd carry Hyacint and Jacob down to the bottom of the stairs, and squash them into the pram, with all those layers of clothes, then she'd give me directions. It was always something like "take them round the back of the church" or "to the lane behind the baker's" or "to that narrow street by the canal",' always a different place, then I'd set off and bump them around the streets.'

'The pram was heavy and when I reached the spot, a stranger would always appear and say, "What beautiful babies!" even if they were screaming blue murder. Then I would lift out Hyacint, leaving Jacob in the pram, and turn away and show Hyacint leaves floating in the canal, that sort of thing, and when I went to put Hyacint back the person would be gone, and the babies would be cranky but usually the jolting of the pram soothed them.'

'Willa, what happened? I don't understand.'

'There were parcels hidden under the babies.'

'*Jeetje mina!* Did you know that?'

'I knew the pram was lighter after the stranger.'

She sat back and crossed her arms. 'One time I will never forget. Moeder sent me off with the babies to a back street near old Westerpark. It was a rainy afternoon and it started to rain lightly again. I hit a kerb at an angle and the pram tipped over just as a German soldier came round the corner. The babies were half out, and screaming. He helped me get the pram up and straight. He would have felt how heavy it was. He said, "*Wo ist die mutter?*" which means "Where is the mother?" We learnt German at school so I said, "*Die mutter ist krank,*" which means "The mother is sick." I was terrified he would ask where I lived and escort me home. I said, "*Danke*", which is thank you in German and he walked off.

'I was too scared to go home, too scared to go to the place, scared to death they'd follow me home and arrest Moeder. I pushed the screaming babies in the soft rain till it was near curfew and I thought I would go crazy. Finally I went to the church we knew, and the minister sent someone to tell Moeder we were okay. We stayed the night with him and his family. His wife fed the babies with bottles and got us warm again. O mijn God...' She shook her head at the memory.

'Did you know what you were delivering?'

'Underground newspapers. A paper called *Trouw*.'

'What does *trouw* mean?'

'Faithfully.' Willa thought for a moment. 'It was a religious group that published it, when they could get paper, and maybe *Het Parool*. They started in the war, and they're still going. O mijn God, I was terrified.'

She picked at something stuck on her coat. 'Look, to be fair, Henni, there were good Germans too. My father's uncle had his bike stolen, but the moff who stole it felt so bad that after the war he replaced it.

'O mijn God, everyone gets swept up in a war, and the poor young men trapped in the army. Everyone gets trapped on one side or the other. Very well. Let's get this over with.'

234

We went to the Resistance Museum.

coats on
hats on
gloves on
out the door
down to the landing
down to the landing
down
down
down to the door
UP the street
On to the tram
Grumpledcrumpy Willa
Grumpledcrumpy me
DETERMINED

'Henni, come here!' Willa's voice sounded strange and made me hurry. She was peering into a display case.

'My mother made that.' She pointed at a little orange brooch of folded ribbon, about the size of a stamp. 'See how she bent a pin for the catch? I had one of them. Maybe that's the one.'

'Why is it here?'

'It was a sign of solidarity. Are you going to arrest everyone for wearing a brooch or a flower? The Queen said wear a marguerite, which was flowering when the moff invaded.'

She was slipping into one of her dark moods. I listened carefully, hoping to learn something.

'You know, Henni, the Nazis had already murdered thousands of inconvenient people before they got around to the Jews. They practised on the Romanies, homosexuals, the disabled, then they got the system going, the trains and the factories, *factories for killing people*. They wanted to kill every single Jew, as plain and simple as that. If you were a Jew, they wanted you dead. And once they'd worked their way through the Jews, who was next who didn't fit their plan?

'Some people think it never happened.' Willa sighed. 'Well, here's what I say to them. That evil little Hitlerman and his officials had a conference, and their plan was written down and they *all signed the documents!* Make no mistake, Henni. You can go to the place where they met, Wannsee, and there are the documents in glass cases, with their signatures, and if you can't see that as proof you don't deserve a brain.'

'Why did people go along with it?'

'People felt helpless. Their lives were a mess, their hard-earned money worthless, no jobs, no decent politicians, just a choice between the communists and that evil little Hitlerman who shrieked his totalitarian message and once he got the power, with his henchmen attack dogs, well, that was that, you had a dictator who blamed everything on the Jews.

'Watch your leaders, Henni, watch the parliament and the laws they pass. Get good people into parliament, listen to news you can trust, and don't let any strong man get too much power. He starts off nice, oh yes, he starts nice and promises the world, but he changes when he gets that power, oh how he changes. Plenty of examples of that in the world right now.'

'Why didn't the newspapers say what was happening?'

She snorted. 'Girl, the newspapers are the first to go. Report the wrong thing and you disappear quick smart. Then the artists, writers and actors are told to shut up because they're dangerous. It was a different time. The value of life was different. I'll lend you some books to read, but not now, you're too young. We're living in a fool's paradise. It *infuriates* me!'

Oh boy, I'd never seen her so bitter and angry.

I was glad there were no schoolkids in the museum.

In the children's section there were rooms from different houses in the 1940s. We were alone in a lounge room, which felt comfortable and homely, but Willa kept pouring it out.

'I was a good liar,' she said grimly. 'When our doorbell rang, they sent me down to answer it. I'd go down the stairs slowly making a lot of noise, to give everyone time to hide, then I'd spin a story for whoever was at the door. Sometimes I took Hyacint.'

She put on a child's voice. 'Oh no, my father has been away for a long time, and my mother is out shopping, and I have to look after my sister, and she's getting a disease, I think it's infectious.' She chuckled. 'Hyacint always obliged by screaming her head off. But it only takes one mistake…'

The last part of the kids' museum was a shock. We went from a comfortable family room through to a heavy sliding door into a cattle truck. It felt like the museum had tricked us.

'Slide the door shut, Henni,' Willa commanded.

We were standing inside four walls of rough planks. It was frightening and dark. Pale rays of light filtered through slits in the planks. Willa took my hand and held it tight. We could hardly see each other.

'Imagine your mum and dad is here,' she said in a low voice, 'and Danielle, and Donna, and Zev...imagine we are crushed in with a hundred other people and Mr Nic is sick on the floor. No home anymore. Babies, grandparents, locked in, no food, no water, maybe a bucket for a toilet, no idea where we're going or how long we're in this hell. Stopping for hours sometimes. Going again. Stopping. We're sick and starving. We're not people anymore, we're just a nuisance to be got rid of—'

She was interrupted when the heavy door slid open and a family came in.

'This is how they sent them away,' the father explained quietly to the wide-eyed children.

We walked back into the light. Willa was sniffing and searching in her pockets for a tissue.

'A *nightmare*,' said Willa quietly. 'Poor Sara.'

As we went out into the street I said, 'Some people survived. Maybe they didn't come back to Amsterdam because it had such bad memories.'

'Sara would have got in touch with Moeder.' Willa was exhausted. 'Take me home.'

On the second tram she said, 'Our pram was the same as the one in the photo. There now, that's the end of it. I'm not telling you any more.'

Tuesday 14 April

FRITES

Jacob said, 'Come for frites.'

The frites were great, light and long and salty and skinny and just how a frite should be. We were in a cafe a couple of streets away and I wasn't picking up any vibe that Jacob was annoyed with me. It was friendly, and we were chatting about the things people put on their windowsills, and I said it was funny to see three kisses everywhere – XXX – and he said it was the symbol for Amsterdam. We were laughing, and then straight out of the blue he said, 'Have you seen Bram?'

Gulp!

'Oh, I don't know. I've met lots of Carlijn's friends and their friends, but I don't always know their names.' I chattered on brightly. 'People are very friendly etc etc,' but I didn't really believe that, and I hadn't met that many people and I didn't want to talk about it and I couldn't really believe myself.

240

'How was it at the antikraak?'

'Good. Yes. Very interesting. I want to ask Floor about living in a kraak.'

Jacob poured us both a glass of water. He spilled a bit.

'Henni, at the picnic at our garden house when you just arrived, maybe I sounded like I don't care much about Bram, a bit casual? Well, I am not. I'm worried about who are his friends and where he is getting money. Young people can get in a tight group, where money is important, and little by little you get bold, and you don't see what you are doing.'

He was printing wet circles on the table with the bottom of his glass.

'Henni, I know I am the dinosaur generation and that Bram is playing computer games, so he is in that world, which is okay...' He wiped the circles away with his hand. 'But Bram is a healthy outdoor boy, who turned into a skinny boy in his room with the door closed. He doesn't talk to me, to anyone...'

skinny

He waited till a noisy group near us walked past.

'When Bram was a kid, Dirk was always busy on some new project, so Bram stayed with Floor and me a real lot. He was my happy shadow and I love

'"Resistance is not only justified but compulsory!"'
She huffed her most satisfyingly indignant huff. 'They
should have just asked Moeder, and saved the bother.'

Willa looked funny waving frites around with her
fluffed-up hairdo. She was on a roll and normally I
loved her like this, but I still felt miserable.

'*Dictators!*' Willa went on, 'You know the more
totalitarian the leader, the harder it is for a person
to be different. They force everyone to be like them.
They make everyone think like them. What a boring
life they want you to lead.'

With that final blast about dictators we bundled up
in our winter gear and grumped off home.

I went to the library, but I couldn't settle to reading.
I was nervous, thinking, *Hunter will call again. He
wants something.*

Sure enough…

No Caller ID

'What happened?'

'I was talking to Jacob.'

(Hunter didn't say 'Who's Jacob? or 'Sorry'.) 'Come
to the field north of the gas factory in Westerpark in
an hour.'

Click!

And I'm thinking, *Jeetje mina! Am I his slave or something?*

And I'm thinking about what Jacob said

And I'm thinking *he's in trouble*

And I'm thinking *where in hell is north of the gas factory?*

⌒

Two pairs of gloves and my hands are still cold. I feel like I'm in a movie. *That's* what Hunter does, he makes you feel like you're in a movie, a thriller, widescreen.

A deserted park, all grey, no colour. Silence except for the wind through the trees. In a worn patch of dirt someone has made a rough seesaw out of a rock and a plank.

A young man, very thin, in a long black coat, with a hood over his head, is lifting one end of the seesaw with his foot. He has his hands in his pockets. He is a simple dark shape.

From a distance a girl rides towards him across the park. Before she can reach him, he walks away. The girl rides after him, follows him out of the park.

The man goes to a small Turkish cafe where he sits at the back facing the door. In a moment the girl enters and slips into the seat opposite him.

NOW! Before anything else is said *NOW!* before anything happens, before I lose my nerve *NOW NOW NOW*

'Are you Bram?'

He is looking at me, his face absolutely passive. He gazes through me in a stony way, then it becomes a stare.

I look away. *I said the wrong words. I'm playing the part wrong*

I'm embarrassed, determined, shaking but determined and very determined.

'Why did you leave home and not tell Jacob?'

The waiter brings our drinks.

Jeetje mina, what do I do?

'Okay, I'm going now,' I say.

He focuses on me at last. I exist.

'Because my father is an arrogant, forceful, controlling bastard who pisses me off.'

Whoa! It's a different movie now!

'I went to your father's work with him, for a day. He's a bit scary, but—'

'He's the big boss at work, but at home his son will not obey him.'

'Hunter, when we arrived in Amsterdam he told us how to cross the road and...' He snorts. 'No, Hunter, it was good because I was nearly hit by a bike.'

'He thinks he's in charge of the world.'

who's controlling?

silence

The waiter goes out the front door. We sit there.

'Jacob said your mother abandoned you.'

'Abandoned? That's a bit strong.' He slowly stirs in the sugar, then gives me a weary look. 'You're sorting it right out, aren't you.' Then in a jaunty kind of way, 'She left, maybe she saved her own life. I don't remember her.' He licks his spoon, and his thin wrist reminds me of a photo of a Hongerwinter kid.

'How's Jacob?'

'Worried.'

The waiter is back and brings frites.

'Why shouldn't I tell him about you?'

He stares at me for long time, then sighs.

'Jacob wants us to be a family. I don't want to be part of that family. Yeah. I'm sorry about Jacob, but I got myself into a situation and I must get myself out.'

He's in trouble

'You could tell Wendelien.'

'No. She's cool though...'

Then he surprises me. 'What's your family like?'

He's being nice

'Well, there's Mum and Dad, and me, and my younger sister Danielle, who's a pest, but I think we play a game where she aims to annoy me, and I get annoyed.' We sound ordinary. 'We're a family family. We live in a street-family.'

'What does that mean?'

'Everyone in our street knows each other, and we have a good time. They all put in money for my plane ticket. Willa lives in our street.'

'Willa is Roos?'

'Wilhelmina Roos Petronella van Veen.'

'Your grandmother?'

I don't feel inclined to tell the truth.

Then he looks at me. 'There's a parcel to collect tomorrow.'

Ha! I knew it!

'Collect it yourself.'

I can't believe I said that.

'The parcel is at the Cigar Factory, with the welder guy near the door.'

long pause

'If I do collect it, then what?'

'Keep it in the zolder. The attic.'

'Is it big?'

'A shoebox.'

> *long pause*

'What's in it?'

'I don't know.'

> *l o n g pause*

He stands and walks to the toilet. I plot my next negotiation. I sit for ages, but he doesn't come back. I look around.

'Your brother left out the back door,' says the waiter at the counter cleaning glasses. 'He's paid.'

Potverdomme, what a cheek!

Jeetje, do we look like brother and sister?

Back op mijn zolder, in a junky blue dog mood I shoved things around. *Why didn't I say No? Why did I get myself in deeper? I'm not in the Resistance. He's not my operator.* I heaved a suitcase. *Why* am I the one risking my neck? Potverdomme, this is no way to do business, whatever his stupid business is. Then I felt worried for him. *Potverdomme, I will tell Jacob.*

But I knew I wouldn't.

Jeetje Wilhelmina! Honestly. This stupid family.

> *Grrrrrrrrrrrrrrrrrrr*

Then I had this thought. If Roos is my

grandmother, then I'm related to Hunter, and part of his family that he doesn't want to be part of.

HA! Chew on that, Dutch scarecrow!

If I tell Jacob
Hunter will hate me because I told on him
but he's in hiding
Jacob will try to talk to Hunter but nobody can
No Caller ID
Jacob may tell Dirk but I don't think so
Jacob will worry more
Jacob may not tell anybody
Jacob may like me again
but Hunter won't like me at all but he won't know
but when Jacob talks to him, he will
I will feel awful
I feel awful now
I will feel more awful
Hunter has to tell!
What if he doesn't know what's going on?
I don't know what's going on
Jeetje what a mess
Do I trust him?
Why should I?
A hunch

A hunch?

A leap of trust

To trust him, I must trust myself.

If it all goes wrong it's my mistake

Trust is heavy and light as air.

Trust builds trust, I know that.

It makes the next step easier.

Took me ages to get to sleep.

Walls have ears
and stairs can talk
and floorboards
a door hinge
a draught
a chink of light

'Meneer Woortman upstairs
turned a blind eye', said Willa.
'He helped Moeder carry up
heavy things.
In the Hongerwinter
he tried to grow an orchid.'

THE PARCEL

I woke up feeling positive. We would go home in a few weeks, and besides, you can't be angry all the time, plus when I opened my picture-book window it wasn't as cold as usual.

I rode to the Cigar Factory easily and thumped at the door and yelled till Wim the welder heard me. I am bold now.

Wim is incredibly tall, even for a Dutch man, and he is strong, and a giant of giants. His overalls were filthy, his hair stuck out above his goggles and his hands were greasy. He was expecting me. I thought his voice would be loud and booming but it was gentle.

'There's your present, Henni.' He pointed to a parcel under his workbench.

'Where's Hunter?' I asked.

'Don't know,' he dropped his quiet voice to a whisper, 'but there's a guy trying to find him. Looks like he's from the tax department.'

'Is he in trouble?'

'Well, I would say yes. He got in trouble once for buying stolen security cameras.' He laughed. 'The robbers turned off the cameras, and stole them too. He returned the cameras, returned the money. Now he's super careful.'

'Where did the parcel come from?'

'Don't know. Someone left it here. Now you do him a favour too. Well, that's what friends are for.'

I rode home, thinking how weird it was that, instead of being at school, I'm riding around Amsterdam with a mystery parcel, for a guy who's left his family, and disappeared from an antikraak in a cigar factory. Sure beats maths.

I had just chained up my bike when someone yelled, 'Henni! Hi! *Henni*! Quick, come and look at *this*!' It was Myrte, near the street corner, waving hard. How come *she* was here? Why would I want to do anything with Myrte the spy? '*Come, quick, Henni!*'

I was suspicious as hell, but I looked where she was pointing. A large rubbish truck was emptying the bin for the whole street. A crane from the truck had pulled the bin out of the ground, like a giant rectangular metal tooth. From the shoulder of the bin swung a manky worn-out stuffed toy, a floppy dog, while on the footpath a mother in a puffy jacket tried desperately to calm her hysterical little boy who was sobbing so uncontrollably he could hardly breathe.

The operator twiddled his remote controls to lower the bin while an anxious crowd willed him to hurry. The operator was easing the bin down when the dog fell to the ground. The little boy wriggled free, made a dash and snatched it up. The crowd cheered.

'I would have let it fall in the truck,' laughed an old guy nearby.

The operator raised the bin again, dumped the load in the truck then lowered the bin back into its hole. *Clunk!* The End. What a funny little drama.

Myrte and I chatted a bit and that was that.

It wasn't until I was sitting on my bed in the zolder that a bolt of panic shot through me. My *bag*! I left it in the bike basket!

I flew downstairs two at a time and dashed out the door. The bike basket was empty.

Oh *NO! Despair!* My heart sank through my boots. Anguish and fury and...BRAM'S *PARCEL! O mijn God!*

They warned me to *always* chain my bike up, *never* leave anything in the basket. It had my purse (at least they didn't get my keys, I was still holding them from chaining up), my notebook (at least they didn't get my main notebook), my pen, but worst of all they got *my phone* and very worst of all BRAM'S *PARCEL! Misery! Misery!* I was furious with myself and angry and upset. *Oooow!!!*

After a time of wailing, I knew the only thing to do was tell the oude dames and start facing the music...from *both* sides of this stupid damn family. *Potverdomme*, I felt sick! More proof for Hyacint that I was untrustworthy, and who knows what Hunter would do. He was in trouble and he didn't even know what was *in* the damn parcel and I had *lost* it. With feet of lead, I trudged up the stairs to the apartment.

'Are you looking for this?' Hyacint came out of the kitchen holding up my bag.

OH LUCKY WINDMILLS! JOY! JOY! JOY! My body flooded with gratefulness. I took my bag.

'Myrte found it in your bike basket and brought it up.'

Oh THANK YOU, Myrte. Oh thank GOODNESS! Parcel still there? Yes. Purse? Yes. I was so *grateful*. How *fantastic* that Myrte brought it back! I nearly cried with sweet relief.

'You've been lucky this time, Henni.' Hyacint gave me a glare. 'But be more careful. What if your keys were in the bag and it had been stolen? We would have to change the locks, which would be *very* expensive. Your travel allowance certainly wouldn't cover it. You are fortunate Myrte is such a good friend.'

I apologised a hundred and ten per cent and said I'd be extra careful in future. I could just imagine her going on and on to Willa about how unreliable I was and *knowing* it would happen again, endangering them and the whole city, and civilisation as we know it. My biggest black mark by far, but I was so relieved I couldn't care less.

Then I sat on my bed with the parcel

And I started to wonder

Had Myrte been so kind?

…bringing back my bag

Just something about the way she popped up at that moment. Was it a coincidence? Had she been waiting for me? Did she know I was coming back from the factory? But no one could organise that manky dog on the rubbish bin.

One thing's for sure, I'm getting super suspicious.

And why am I doing this? For Hunter? For the van Veens? Explain that to me, Henni? Nope. You can't, can you! You got yourself in a mess. Coincidences. Why do I feel that? Don't ask me. It's mad. But the bin and the dog and the boy *was* amazing though.

Wonder what's in the parcel? Wonder if Myrte looked in my bag? Can't see anything different.

———

I saw Mr Kuipers in the library again this arvo. I told him we'd gone back to the Resistance Museum, and it made more sense now and I've collected the laws the Germans brought against Jews which I've called 'The Funnel'. That's what they call it.

He told me to keep looking on the bright side. He's right, it is so depressing.

The Funnel

1940 *May 10* Germany invades *May 14* Netherlands surrenders *July 2* **Forbidden** Jews can't be air raid wardens *Aug*
Forbidden to hire Jews or promote them **Classified** If your grandpa or grandma is a Jew you are a Jew. All Jewish
businesses must be registered *Sept* **Forbidden** for Jews to be civil servants Everything a business owns must
be registered *October* Every government official must sign a sworn statement he, his wife, fiancé, parents or
grandparents are not Jewish. *(First anti Jewish laws)* **Forbidden** to be promoted or employed in government
jobs *Nov* All Jews in Dutch Civil Service are sacked *Dec* People of German 'blood' are not allowed to
work in Jewish houses. **1941** *January* **Jews must register with German authorities** or prison for 5 years,
or property taken or both. *Feb 21* Amsterdam ghetto established after an attack on old Jewish quarter
by groups of Dutch Nazi sympathizers. Subsequent Counter attacks by Jewish & Dutch youths
brought severe reprisals by Germans. *(The excuse they wanted!)* *Feb 22, 23* **First round up of**
Jews Compulsory ID card marked 'J' **Forbidden** to donate blood **Forbidden** to belong to an
organization **Forbidden** to enter hotels, restaurants, theatres, and the movies **Forbidden** to be
a doctor for non-Jews **Forbidden** to own a farm **Banned** from swimming pools, race tracks
Forbidden from owning pigeons *Feb 25* **February strike**
Dutch workers general strike for several days. Crushed. Leaders taken to the dunes and shot.
Feb 28 **"Duty for the performance of services."** The *Arbeitseinsatz* All Dutch men
18 - 45yr forced employment in Nazi-Germany & occupied territories. *Reichskommissar*
Seyss-Inquart, *March* Germans start to 'Aryanise' Jewish property *(aryanise = steal)*
Jewish Council has authority over all Jewish organisations *(has to do the dirty work)*
Forbidden to travel without special permit **Forbidden** to do stock exchange
business, or work in a gallery, orchestras, theatre etc *April* **German ID cards**
issued to all Dutch *(With photo & fingerprint)* *July* Jews' ID cards are stamped 'J'
Aug Jewish kids forbidden from ordinary & vocational schools. Must go to
separate schools with Jewish teachers. Jewish assets blocked -bank deposits,
250 guilders cash max per month for own use. *(Preparing to steal*
everything!) **1942** *January* Forced labor camps for Jews. Concentration
of Jews in Amsterdam. Jewish actor, director or anything in the movies your
name is removed from credits.**Forbidden** in public places, *March*
confiscation of Jewish bank accounts & property *April 29* **Ordered**
to wear yellow Star. Movies with undiluted anti-Jew propaganda
Jews must register houses & apartments then sell them
May 3 **forbidden** to shop except between 3- 5pm
Forbidden to be in street between 8pm-6am
June **forbidden** to enter homes of non-Jews
forbidden to have a bike
forbidden to use public transport
forbidden to use a telephone
July 5 1,000 Jews to forced labour in Germany.
Deportations began *July 6* Anne Frank family hides
forbidden to enter concert halls, libraries,
sports grounds, art galleries, museums
1943 Jewish hospitals, orphanages &
old folk's homes shut, one by one
April, May Most
Dutch Jews
transported.
Gone
except

those

in

hi-

ding

BULLETIN TO STELLA STREET
Work with Floor
THURSDAY 16 MARCH

Things are going pretty well. It's Wendelien's wedding in two days, and King's Day holiday in eleven days, not that a holiday makes any difference to me!

Today I went to work with Floor. She asked me to dress nicely, and be early because she wanted to show me her favourite view along a canal. Dressing nicely was a bit of a problem, but I tried. Mum, I wore that dress we decided on for the wedding.

Floor works at a fabric shop called Lotus. Maggs, you would *melt* in Lotus. It sells materials from all round the world, mostly India and Pakistan, hand-woven, dyed or printed, with strong patterns (very Maggs), or soft and gentle (very Floor), but they're always top quality, expensive.

I folded samples while Floor sold curtains to a lady from Monaco for *two thousand euros*! For *curtains*! Floor told the woman how much pleasure the curtains would give her through the years. Even I was starting to think the curtains were a good idea. Their conversation was in English with a Dutch accent and with a French accent. Must be a big house, that's all I can say.

Floor took me to lunch in an exclusive department store, de Bijenkorf, which has a great view of the main square of Amsterdam, the Dam. As we walked to our table Floor met a friend, one of her customers, then she fluttered her fingers at a woman on the other side of the room.

At the next table was a little boy's birthday party. Beautiful stylish mothers with sweet well-mannered children ate cake. It was so pretty, with gorgeous flowers and shiny cutlery, the women and children seemed like they were in an unreachable state of grace.

I thought about the poor people in India who made the beautiful fabrics Floor sells. She saw me looking. 'They're nice women,' she said. 'I help them distribute their wealth.'

Floor wanted to know about Willa's life back home. In de Bijenkorf dear old Stella Street sounded like a rough sort of village. Then we talked about the van Veens. Everyone in this family wants to know what I think of the others. I have to be careful.

At the end of my day at Lotus I flew home, hopped into comfy clothes, and zoomed to my friend Carlijn's place to plan for King's Day.

Now Amsterdam houses might all look the same on the outside, the patterns of windows and the little bricks, but let me tell you, inside each one is a different story. Hyacint's is a comfy old person's home.

But my friend Carlijn's place is wild.

The front door is the usual anonymous black, between a jeweller and cafe, then you go up the steep staircase with worn carpet, to their orange door on the first floor.

Carlijn's place is smaller than Hyacint's – but they're both like a long box with windows at both ends. It feels like Carlijn's family is playing a game called The Small Box Family Challenge. Carlijn's dad, Henk, is the Grandmaster of Making (yes, Frank, another Henk!) and he loves inventing a place for something new. He uses wood, magnets, hooks, clips and rails.

Say you think *I need a wooden spoon*, you just have to look around and without having to move your feet there'll be a wooden spoon. Every now and then there's a flop, or a crash when something gets too heavy for its magnet. I won't tell you every clever little thing, but honestly I couldn't stop looking at it all. It's the opposite of the Phonies. Remember how in their house every surface was smooth, like a shiny white skating-rink with no evidence of life? (They don't have much evidence of life now either, in jail. Not many shiny surfaces there.)

Henk is like you, Rob, he loves wood.

Carlijn's family don't own this place. It's social housing, which they rent from the city and the law says the rent can't increase much, so they put up with the small space, and spend most of the summer at their garden cubby. Carlijn's mum and dad split up. Her mum lives in Haarlem, and her dad lives here with Lena and they have a little baby girl, Janneke. Hartog moved out ages ago but they all use the garden cubby and sometimes Carlijn's mum stays there too when she's in Amsterdam. She's good friends with Lena.

They have a yellow budgie called Rocky Two. They used to have a canary called Rocky, but he had a sad accident with the ceiling fan, so now the fan switch has a sticker that says *Rocky zit in de kooi?* which means 'Is Rocky in the cage?' Henk has made little perches for Rocky Two all round the apartment, and Rocky flies freely everywhere. If he does a poo, it's a neat little pellet which doesn't worry them.

I said to Carlijn, 'Your dad is great at woodwork.'

She said, 'Yes, but *you* don't have to listen to him make something. "Shave a bit off there. Jeetje, that's heavy, screw that back in. That will make it straighter. *Potver!!* What's going on? Ah now I see. Hacksaw blade drill and screwdriver. Jeetje, that's screwed that up . . . Now, three of these. Oh that was never even big enough for the stupid thing!"'

Then Carlijn clapped her hands. 'Henni, stop looking! We must plan King's Day.'

She wrote on her notepad KING'S DAY – *Carlijn and Henni do something funny.*

'Like what?'

'Anything!' says Carlijn. 'On King's Day you can sell things – no taxes, no permits – so it is an everything market everywhere in the whole country and a giant party.'

a giant giant party

'We need sunshine!' she said forcefully at the grey clouds out the window. 'People spend more in sunshine. Do we want to get money? Yes, we want to get money. It's useful. Can you do any tricks?'

'No.'

'Can you sing?'

'No.'

'Play a musical instrument?'

'No.'

'Are you *hypermobiel?* What's this in English?' She bent back her thumb till it touched her arm.

'Double-jointed. Me? No.'

'Can you draw?'

'No.'

'You have a good imagination?'

'Ja.'

'Can you act?'

'I'm getting better at that.'

'If you could be anybody, who would you be?'

'Queen Wilhelmina.' That surprised me, and I was the one who said it!

'Goed, you can be Queen Wilhelmina. Last year my little cousin, who was five, after one violin lesson, played two notes all morning, wearing rabbit ears so he couldn't hear himself. *Horrible!* He made twenty euros!

Obviously busking is cool on King's Day. Danielle, if you were here you could do your dance! Then Carlijn showed me her stick insect, then it was time to go home.

I rode back from Carlijn's feeling happy. I love hanging out in Amsterdam.

Wish you were all here on bikes
X X X (that's the symbol for Amsterdam)
Henni

Lady from Monaco

Op mijn zolder that night I thought about my lunchtime chat with Floor. She told me living in a kraak was a good experience, an experiment in living together. It was rough, but everyone was young and they saved a beautiful old school building, which had been closed because there weren't enough kids living in the area. Dirk thinks krakers are lazy, but Floor wasn't. She started her first business in the kraak, selling vegetables. She drew a symbol on her serviette. 'That is the sign for a kraak. Look around the city and you'll see it.'

I recognised it! Where had I seen it?

Then she asked me, 'Henni, you went to an antikraak. Who is living there?'

'Carlijn's brother and his friends.'

'Do you think Bram might live in a place like that?'

Careful

'Well, it would be cheap.'

Floor looked at me for a moment, waiting for more, but I kept my trap shut. They didn't warn me about this back home. I took it front on and asked right back, 'Floor, what's the relationship between Jacob and Dirk and Bram?'

'Oh, it's complicated. They're very different.'

Now I'm *leaving the silence.*

'Dirk is ambitious and wanted to be successful in

business, he did *not* want to be like Jacob. He thinks his father is talented but hopeless. When Dirk and his wife split...no, before that, we looked after Bram all the time. Jacob has been more his father than Dirk has.'

'Floor, what about the fights between Jacob, Hyacint and Willa?'

'The family tensions go back to the war. I would stay right out of it.'

Too late for that!

'Floor, did you know Moeder?'

Floor folded her serviette neatly and smoothed and smoothed the fabric. 'Well, first I will say that after the war people had to remake their lives, and get on with each other. Moeder couldn't do that. She was bitter. Roos was strong-willed. They had shocking arguments. It was a relief when Roos left. Hyacint never annoyed her mother like Roos.'

'What happened to Moeder?'

'She died the day before she turned sixty, from a bad flu. Jacob did most of the caring. He didn't mind, he's a very kind man.'

'Sixty? That's not so old. What about Papa?'

'He died years earlier. Willa went to Australia and never saw her parents again.'

What a miserable family. 'When Willa tells her stories Moeder and Papa feel alive.'

She nodded. 'I think Willa has a lot of business unfinished.'

Floor called the waiter for the bill. While we waited I chattered on.

'Is it hard to be old in Amsterdam? The stairs are so steep and everyone rides bikes.'

'Well, you catch the tram, you move to the ground floor or you don't go out much. Maybe the city keeps us young. How does Willa find it?'

'Okay, but she gets tired. I'm always scared when she goes down the stairs.'

That was my day with Floor. I kept her serviette with the drawing and I remembered where I saw that symbol.

Molli café. It's a squat café!

DE OLIFANT IN DE ROOM

That parcel is glaring at me. I put it under the low table with the bucket. I don't want it here. Come on, No Caller ID, ring!

Sorting for King's Day. *Sneezing! Sneezing! Jeetje mina*, it's dusty! No cannonball, no magic lantern. I think I found a crystal set, no blue dog, just a hundred years of dust. An old leather belt with a big buckle like the giant's in 'Jack and the Beanstalk'. Hey! That's a good belt for round my middle when I'm writing.

There's something wooden in the corner that *might* be Moeder's Rast & Gasser sewing machine, and a beautifully carved picture frame with a faded-to-nothing ghost-picture in it. I can't make it out. Maybe some people? I like the shadowy feeling. It's wedged behind a box of bottles and tins. I'm going to put it up on the chest of drawers. It will look good.

I pull and shove and heave it up. It's incredibly heavy but it's worth it. The frame makes a fine backdrop to the wrecked shipwreck, which I've wrecked a bit more, and the clogs and the toy truck, and other things that I arrange on a cloth on top of the chest of drawers. My Dutch still life looks good! My interior decorating is fun, and the King's Day pile near the door is growing.

Hmm. I look at the sulky parcel, de olifant in mijn zolder.

At the library I read an article in an English magazine. 'Is He Using You?' *Is he an emotional vampire, good at manipulating others, at pushing someone's buttons and making them feel indispensible?*

he's manipulating, but I'm not indispensable

These people are users. You spend your time looking after them. Selfish. Unhappy. Abusive. Mental health issues from which they never get better. Move on. Sometimes the best way to solve a problem is to stop participating in it.

Too late now, the parcel is here. Stupid responsible me.

What's in it?

I pick at the tape till I have a nice little tab.

rrrrrrriiiiiiiiiiiiiiiiiiiiiiiiiiIIIIIIIIIIPPPPPPPPP!!!!!

I crunch the tape into a satisfying sticky ball, and chuck it in the corner. That feels better.

I lift the lid. Not a bomb. Not shoes. There's a sharp pointed medical instrument sealed in a plastic bag, like the tool the dentist uses to twang your teeth. It looks new. A weapon?

What's this in bubblewrap? More tape. A camera! Small, black, used, in good condition. On the front it says *Lumix*. So what do we think of *that*? There must be pictures in it.

I try to take a photo but the button won't click. I slide the switch to ON. Try again. Nothing. It's not working. It's broken. What's this little trapdoor on the bottom? For the battery? Maybe the battery's flat. That's why it won't work. The little flap pops up. *That's* not a battery! A little folded piece of paper. A message? No, it's folded around...a memory chip! So tiny. Wrong size for this camera, that's for sure! *Whoa! 1TB*. One *terabyte*? How can that be possible, so much data on a thing so small I could swallow it? Spy secrets? Murder? Pornography? Evidence? I don't want to know, anyway I can't. Why did they put it in a camera?

No Caller ID

Jeetje! So soon! Now I'm in trouble.

'Do you have the parcel?'

'I opened it. It could have been a bomb.'

       he's thinking

'What's in it?'

'A skinny dental tool.'

He snorts.

'What's funny?'

'Private joke. What else?'

'A small camera. Panasonic DMC-TZ30, Lumix.'

'What's on the chip?'

'It's not the right chip for that camera. It's one terabyte. Is that possible?'

'Put it in a clean envelope. Which library do you go to?'

'How do you know I go to a library?'

'You translated in a library.'

'Spaarndammerbuurt.'

      click

A minute, and the phone rings again.

'Henni, go to the library tomorrow, just before it closes. Take the chip.'

'I can't, it's Wendelien's wedding.'

'Go *now* to the library, *fast*! It closes at half-past

five. Take the chip. At the back of the library is a plant with big leaves. Put the envelope inside the back of the book closest to the top of the plant.'

'What about the parcel?'

'Keep it.'

'Hunter, tell Jacob.'

'Don't take your phone.'

'Hunter, if something bad is happen—'

   click

   Potverdommme!

I make it to the library just before it shuts. The book closest to the top of the pot plant is a book about fish. How appropriate.

I'm the last person out of the library. I feel suspicious-looking.

Who is the enemy? Does Hunter know?

Closed

The welder had the shoebox
The chip is with the fish
The tide is low at Vlissingen
The doctor will marry the sailor
The blue dog lies doggo

V for hope

WENDELIEN'S WEDDING

Even before I opened my eyes I heard the rain thundering down, and the tops of the trees whipping in the wind. The night was so cold I got up and put my coat on my bed.

Downstairs the oude dames were snapping like terriers and Hyacint had swapped her endlessly coordinated wedding outfit for a trusty woollen dress, so she wouldn't freeze. Now she was fussing about her hair. Willa was wearing the lipstick from Dubai, which made her look like she was wearing her lips. At half past eleven a van was coming to collect us all.

'Someone put a curse on this wedding,' said Hyacint.

Bram? me?

We went downstairs to wait with Jacob and Floor. The van was late because of a fallen tree. When it arrived we made a dash and scrambled in, our coats and umbrellas dripping. I sat near the window, away from Jacob. Floor still managed to look elegant somehow. She had her hat in a bag. It was thrilling, this wild wet day!

'Rain on your wedding means a strong marriage,' said Jacob cheerfully. 'A wet knot is harder to undo.'

Willa was happy too. 'The flowers will last.'

I couldn't get used to her in that clown lipstick.

At the reception place there was a wide puddle where the van would normally pull up and the rain was bucketing down, so the driver drove forward and stopped beside a tub of blue umbrellas. Everyone grabbed one and made the dash.

Whoooooeeeee! Eric and Wendelien screeched in the door, under one big umbrella. Wendelien looked fabulously wild-bridey in silver gumboots. *Wendelien and the Silver Boots*! A whimsical Grimm! Her hair had already started to do its own thing. I was loving this wedding!

Eric's brother leapt around taking photos as we laughed and shook and stamped, and fluffed our raggle-taggle wedding feathers, happy half-drowned rats. Wendelien tossed me her silver boots and put on her strappy high heels.

'*Godzijdank* for strong umbrellas. Where are they

from?' said the reception centre host, examining one.
'Property of Wageningen University. Hey, there's even
your white swan in the logo!' he laughed.

More cars pulled up. I pulled on Wendelien's
silver boots and dashed out with umbrellas. Guests
unfolded from their cars like butterflies into the
storm. A lady in red squeezed out of a car. *SNAP!*
Her cheap umbrella blew inside out and was gone.
She grabbed one from me. Her boyfriend yelled in an
English accent, 'Hold on, Gladys, or you'll be blown to
Denmark!'

The storm raged outside and the wedding raged
inside. Oh boy, so many people, so many names!
Some middle-aged woman relative in a pea-green
dress grabbed me. She was drunk and I was *exactly* the
person she *really* wanted to confide in.

'Oh, you will think I'm terrible, but since Roos
has come back, to be honest I fear for my life, Henni.'
(Everyone knew my name.)

What? Did I get that right? Is Willa going to poison
her? Or is it a Dutch expression? She *seemed* okay.
A branch bashed against the window behind her. She
polished her glasses furiously, then looked me straight
in the eye, well, as straight as she could.

'I stayed home and cared for my grandmother till she died, I looked after my mother till she died, now I'm caring for my old mother-in-law and she's not eager to die. I'm so *jealous* of Roos. She went to Australia and had a life of her own. She said she was never coming back…' She pointed a wobbly finger at Willa, laughing on the other side of the room. 'And now she's *back!* If she stays here, who will look after her?'

Whoa! Is Willa going to stay?

She seemed determined to be miserable imagining she would have to look after Willa.

'She's going back to Australia,' I said.

'Are you sure?' The unhappy relative-doormat peered at me desperately. I felt sorry for her, but also annoyed as she was leaning on my arm.

A deep voice interrupted. 'Hallo, Henni, come and talk to me now.'

'*Lodewijk!*'

He steered me through the wedding guests, Eric's friends the sailors and Wendelien's friends the doctors. We sat down at the back.

'Lodewijk, what are you doing here?'

'Roos invited me.'

'I didn't know you could invite a friend to someone else's wedding!'

'It's okay, one of Eric's crew couldn't make it.'

'Lodewijk, the pattern on your bow tie is like a crystal radio aerial.'

He laughed. 'I'm receiving.'

'What are you hearing?'

'Static!'

'Guess what, Lodewijk. I found some crystal set, op mijn zolder – a cylinder with copper wire.'

'Jaaaa!' He was so delighted I thought he would make us go home right then and get it working.

'Lodewijk, there's some connection between Roos and a family that lives in a grey house down the street. Do you know what went on between them?'

He drew in a deep breath, and scratched his chin. 'Henni, that's not a story for today.'

'But something happened, didn't it?'

He ran his fingers through his bushy white hair. 'Henni, tomorrow I will visit Roos. Maybe we can talk then, and I can see the pieces of crystal set.'

A gust of driving rain hit the windows. '*Jeetje!* It's still raining cats and dogs.'

'No, it rains razors here,' said Lodewijk, 'or telegraph wires, or bricks.'

We laughed. Lodewijk saw someone he knew and dived off. I looked around.

Where was Willa? I couldn't see her anywhere. Where *was* Willa?

The sheepdog must stay on the job. I searched through the crowd in the main room. No Willa. Down corridors, nope. Had she shut herself outside in this weather? Possible but unlikely. Kitchen? It was a sea of fruit and cheese platters. A waiter grabbed me. 'Quick, tell the bride to come here to the kitchen about the cake.' A tall cook in a cook's hat gave me a smile.

I shot off and found Wendelien. Who was that cook? He looked kind of familiar. I was worried about Willa now. Locked in a toilet? Not in the Dames. The Heren? I opened the door and said loudly "Scuse me, Herens!' Thank God there was no one in there. Lost in an office? Locked in a storeroom? Door after door after door…where on earth…

HA! Godzijdank!

Willa was sound asleep in the cloakroom, in an armchair behind a palm, half covered in damp coats. Outside the rain pelted down. I pulled a large puffer jacket up under her chin and left her snoozing.

Back at the party Wendelien and Eric were arguing about Willa's wedding present that we'd lugged from Australia. It wasn't present-opening time but Wendelien wanted to open it in front of the relos. Wendelien's friends the doctors were on her side, but Eric had the sailors who wanted to get to the speeches before they forgot them. Doctors won. Hooray! I wanted to see what was in the parcel too.

'Quick, Henni, get Roos!'

I dashed to the cloakroom. Willa was waking up anyway, fighting her way out of the coats. She put on fresh lipstick, and finally made an entrance, crumpled and cheery.

Inside the bubblewrap the wedding present was bound up in a folksy tablecloth with hearts, doves and trees – an heirloom embroidered by some aunt, and never used. Inside, *ta da!* a little wooden chest with six drawers with ivory knobs. It was plain and charming.

'Grootvader made it for Grootmoeder,' said Willa. 'Look inside the drawers.'

She had put something in each drawer. No wonder it was heavy. The most important thing was Moeder's wedding ring, which was a bit late because the bride already had a ring, and the silliest, my favourite, was a little china donkey playing an accordion. He was white, painted with blue flowers, and his accordion was red.

Wendelien and Eric made a big fuss and Willa was tickled pink.

Then came the speeches, in Dutch of course, and funny, even if I couldn't understand a word. I sat on the floor down the front with four babies, two toddlers and a naughty boy of about seven called Ramon.

Dirk the Bear made a speech about his sister, then a doctor friend of Wendelien's told stories about travelling with her. Best were the sudden bits in English, e.g. 'Op schrij harringo pzeem eeri! Nneop melt *Emergency Exit* Instads warpezgeins! Pirjan aa ronderkinderee! Honfk ranto *You can't do that!* Vindtu eenrgan govezijn Ditis een ruwover cht, *return ticket is not possible* Vbezorgen, ophetveld,' etc etc etc.

I think there were also lots of references to body parts. Everyone rocked with laughter and a guy called Hildo, with a purple bow tie, fell off his chair. Eric's friends from all over the world did a combined speech, interrupting each other and finishing with a hearty song. A Dutch sea shanty?

Wendelien said she saw a rainbow just after the speeches.

Dirk the Bear said he wanted to show me something very important about building in the Netherlands, so next week we're going to the Amsterdam City Hall.

Someone said, 'There's a guy in the kitchen who looks like Bram.'

'I don't think it was Bram,' I blurted.

'How would you know, you've never seen him,' said Willa.

'Well... (*quick, brain!*)... if he wanted to be here, why would he be in the kitchen?'

Wendelien grinned broadly and whispered to me, 'Would you like the donkey playing the accordion?'

We all packed into the van. Willa was in a fantastic mood.

'What a *wonderful* wedding! I *am* glad I came. They are well suited. They *loved* the present.' Etc etc etc. When we got home Hyacint went to lie down, but Willa was high on the wedding.

'My life is three different times,' she announced. 'Netherlands, Australia, Netherlands. First part good then very bad, second part very good, third part excellent.'

LODEWIJK COMES TO BREAKFAST

Zondag, ja! De zon *was* shining on this dag!

Goedemorgen was a good morning!

The wedding storm had washed the world sparkling and clean.

Lodewijk arrived, and we all had coffee in the kitchen. The sun streamed in behind him, making him look like a silver bush. They were laughing at a photo Hyacint had found, of Lodewijk and Willa as little kids. Willa was holding up the letter R and Lodewijk triumphantly waved an M above his head.

'What's happening?' I asked.

'Those letters are chocolate,' said Lodewijk. 'On Sinterklaas Eve, we got our initial in solid chocolate, big as your hand.'

'That was before the war,' said Willa.

'But you have the letter M, Lodewijk.'

He chuckled. 'My letter L was disappointing.

It was milk chocolate which is for sissies, also
not much chocolate with L. My friend Millie got
dark chocolate but she liked milk chocolate, so we
swapped.'

'Did they call you Modewijk?'

'Probably.'

'H is good, Henni,' said Hyacint, giving me a wink.

'R was okay,' said Willa. 'Remember how
disappointing the letters were after the war? We
imagined they were enormous and the chocolate
divine. They had become a heavenly chocolate myth.'

'Ja, they were ordinary chocolate and only half as
big. Coffee didn't live up to the myth either.'

'Like peace,' said Willa.

'*What?* You don't mean that,' said Lodewijk.

'Moeder actually said that.' Willa nodded. 'She said,
"Life is dull now."'

Lodewijk looked at her in disbelief. '*Potverdomme*
your mother was fierce.'

There was silence for a moment, then Lodewijk
sighed. 'Ah, the cold was colder, the distances further,
mothers were beautiful . . . and the older I get the better
I used to be.'

Willa laughed. 'Moderately brave fathers were
heroes, and those who did nothing were cowards, and

if you acted against something you were a traitor...'

'And cauliflower tasted more awful.' Lodewijk chuckled. 'You know what was my favourite meal, Henni? Stewed pears on mashed potatoes.'

Hyacint went to church and Willa shooed me off so she and Lodewijk could talk.

I got back just as they were saying goodbye.

'Till soon, Roos,' said Lodewijk. 'Henni and I will sit downstairs for a little while.'

Lodewijk and I settled on the bench by the door, and like most of Amsterdam that day, we soaked up the sun. I showed him the pieces of crystal set and he explained how it worked.

'Now will you tell me about Roos and the house down the street?' I asked.

'I hoped you forgot.' Lodewijk took a deep breath. 'You know the van Veens had onderduikers?'

'The people in hiding, Sara and Matius?'

'Ja. Well, when Sara and Matius "escaped", their apartment was not empty long because Roos's cousin Cornelia and her family moved in. They pull some fast strings in the NSB and get the apartment. Like cuckoos they move into the nest.' Lodewijk shook his head sadly. 'Cruel. But it did not bother them.'

'Did you ever meet Sara and Matius?'

'Yes. Sara was slight, and high-spirited. I liked
her straight off. Matius was the opposite, clever and
serious. I saw them in hiding at the van Veens'. My
father was minister of the local church and they
trusted us. I remember Roos's mother just come back
from delivering a special dress to a very anti-Jew lady
who loved her new dress, and we laughed because
Sara had sewn the dress. Then Sara says, "I left all the
pins in!" We gasped. "Imaginary pins," she jokes.'
Lodewijk sighed. 'My father regretted taking me that
day. He told me to forget it.'

'Secrets.'

'Secrets and lies,' he said. 'They go hand in hand.'

'Willa was a good liar.'

Lodewijk laughed. 'Oh, the *best*! She wanted to be
an actress.'

'After the war, what happened to the NSB families?

'Most went to Germany where they weren't
so hated. Some were murdered officially, some
unofficially. Oh, many paybacks. Some were sent to
the camps where the Jews had been held. Cornelia and
her husband went to Germany, and relatives moved
into their apartment. They took a risk. To answer your
question, sometime after the war, the van Veens have
a mighty fight, and Roos, who is a fierce teenager,

gets mad as hell and storms down to the relatives'
place and tells them what she thinks about them and
Cornelia and her husband.'

'What happened?'

'They shove her out the door, very roughly.
Probably made Roos feel better, but a month later the
father hangs himself.'

'*No!*'

'Ja. Terrible, but remember what everyone had been
through. He was in the NSB too, but not so deep.'

'Did they blame Roos? For the father...'

'What do you think?'

'So, Lodewijk, the people who live there now are
distantly related to Willa?'

'Distantly, ja, maybe three generations back.'

'Can you remember any more about Sara?'

'No. After the war people don't want to talk about
horror, they just get on with life. Today what have
we learned?' He looked at his phone, stood up and
stretched. 'Time to catch my tram.'

'What will you do on King's Day, Lodewijk?'

'I will sing with my choir in front of our church.'

'In orange?'

'Ja, orange jacket, orange hat. Doei doei, Henni.' He
bent down and gave me a hug.

'Doei doei, Lodewijk.'

He had a nice smell of...nutmeg?

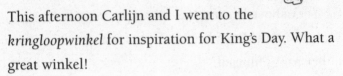

This afternoon Carlijn and I went to the
kringloopwinkel for inspiration for King's Day. What a
great winkel!

kring = cycle *loop* = course *winkel* = shop Op shop!

Carlijn found an orange blow-up windmill for a hat,
a huge orange T-shirt and orange glasses.

'Henni, you will be Queen Wilhelmina and we dress
up super amazing and charge a euro for a selfie with us.
Or we decorate a frame so amazing that people want to
take a selfie in that frame...'

'Carlijn, what are these?'

'*Perfect!* Tarot cards for telling fortunes.'

'How much.'

'Twee euros. Some cards missing.'

'That's interesting!' I thought a fortune-teller on
King's Day might give me a clue about Willa's secret, or
at least a hint about the blue dog.

Carlijn misunderstood. '*O mijn God!* Queen
Wilhelmina will tell *fortunes!* I persuade the customers,
you read the cards to tell the fortunes!'

'Oh fine, I just tell the fortunes, the easy part!

What if I tell the wrong fortune and they jump in the canal?'

'No,' said Carlijn, 'they won't think you are serious.' She was so pleased she did a little dance. 'I predict in the future very soon you will buy tarot cards.'

'Carlijn, who's telling the fortunes?'

'You.'

I put them in my bag then we wandered around till Carlijn said, 'We must dress Queen Wilhelmina.'

'I need glasses, those old lady shoes, and a fox fur.'

'A coat?'

'I'll wear the one I brought with me.'

'Hat?'

'There's one op mijn zolder.'

The shoes were easy, and the glasses, cheap dark glasses that we could pop the lenses out of, but the fur was difficult. All the fur things were expensive and not right. We checked out anything that looked foxy, fluffy scarfs, and hats till a woman assistant asked what we were looking for.

'Oh, I just threw something out.' She disappeared into *Alleen Personeel* which I guess is Staff Only and came back holding a long tatty fur thing between her finger and thumb.

'What do you think, Carlijn? That stuff on it looks

like porridge. It's ripped. It's pretty manky.'

Carlijn whispered, 'Perfect!'

'How much?'

'*Urgh!* I cannot sell that,' said the woman. 'Disgusting!' and she dropped it in a plastic bag as if it was poisonous. We paid for our other stuff and skipped out of the kringloopwinkel before we saw another thing. Willa will know how to clean it. We must mark our spot for King's Day, said Carlijn. It's many days away, but people are taping out their territory. It was a city-wide Game of Zones. Carlijn knew a good corner in the Jordaan and it was still free! We taped it out, then in the middle we taped *Car + Hen*. Carlijn loved the name. She laughed and the pompom bobbed.

Plan B: If I chicken out of fortunes, Queen Wilhelmina will read a speech in English, for Radio Oranje. I'll find out what she said.

I WANT TO TALK TO ROOS

After the weird parcel manoeuvre, I didn't want to
hear from Hunter again. I guess he got the chip.
I hoped he was in hiding, couch-surfing at a friend's
place while he tried to find who was after him. If he
was scared, he never showed it. It didn't seem real.
Maybe crime is like that, unreal like in the movies.
Strangely, since the waiter called Hunter 'your
brother', I did sort of think of him as a moody big
brother. Hey, how's that – he's my brother and Willa's
my grandmother!

When my phone rang in the dairy section of the
supermarket I nearly dropped the milk.

    No Caller ID

    'When do you fly home?'

            silence

          will I hang up?

    'Twelve days.'

'I want to talk to Roos.'

'You're *kidding*!'

'Arrange me a meeting.'

'Hunter, you don't like your family, remember?
Jeetje mina, Jacob thinks I'm lying, which I *am*, he
doesn't *trust* me, he doesn't *like* me anymore,
I don't look forward to seeing him, I get nervous, and
now…'

        silence

                more silence

'You still there, Henni?'

'*NO.*'

'Does Roos remember the wartime?'

'Matter of fact, she does.'

    understatement of the year

'Was anyone in that apartment smuggling
coupons?'

    this changes things

'Coupons?'

'Henni, in the war you need money and coupons to
buy food, clothing.'

'What do you know, Hunter?'

'I found two informations, separate from each

other, that could mark it as a place of coupons.'

'From the chip?'

'No.'

'Willa told me about her coupon-smuggling uncle. He would arrive just before curfew, sleep on the couch and be gone when they woke up next morning.'

'Is Willa still clear-thinking?'

'Oh she's sharp, but that doesn't mean she will answer your questions. If she doesn't want to talk, she won't. At the Resistance Museum something upset her, and she walked out.'

'Arrange me a meeting. She doesn't know me.'

'What do you want to find out? Do you know about the van Veens in the war?'

'No. Do you?'

'A bit.'

'Were they religious?'

'No, but they went to church.'

'I have an old Bible with that address, and with coupons in it.'

'Hunter, the van Veens are at war with each other right now. First reason, *you*. Second reason, some deep family thing. Willa and I leave soon.'

'Arrange me a meeting.'

'Okay Hunter, it's a deal if you find something for

me. It's called the Blue Dog. It's something important that Willa remembers from her childhood. It was in their house, but that's all she remembers.'

'Impossible.'

'So is a meeting with Willa, unless you talk to Jacob.'

Click!

(*My* click!)

Jeetje mina! They were at it again as I went op mijn zolder. O mijn God. This was the worst fight yet. I know Danielle and I yell at each other, but when adults fight it's *horrible*, plus in Dutch! I was desperate to go to the toilet.

It wasn't about Bram. I would have recognised his name. What should I do? Pretend everything was normal? If I was rich I'd get Donna to fly over and bang their heads together. I *hate* it!

I heard Wendelien's bike chain. Good! She'd sort it out. I heard her go into the apartment and I listened, but sadly she didn't seem to make much difference. Okay, there was one thing I could try.

I went downstairs, treading loudly, then took a deep breath, coughed, opened the door and walked into the room.

silence.

Everyone was standing, except Hyacint who was sitting by the window. It reminded me of a game we play at home called Hawks Overhead, where everyone is an animal and you freeze when the hawks are overhead.

Instantly Willa switched to English.

'Get your things Henni, we're not welcome here.'

What?

'Don't be *stupid*,' said Jacob.

Willa was in a rage. 'I shouldn't have come!'

'True,' snapped Hyacint. 'Fly back to Australia!'

I stood there.

Hyacint glared at me.

'*No, Tante Hyacint!*' said Wendelien.

Hyacint pointed at me. 'It wouldn't have happened without her. I hate this fight.'

'Ignore her,' said Wendelien. 'It's not true you caused it, Henni, and personally I think Hyacint *loves* the fighting.'

Jacob growled, 'God's *naam*, Roos, tell us what happened.'

Willa is a closed book. I know that stubborn look.

'Roos, you are a selfish, difficult woman.' Jacob grabbed his coat. 'No wonder Floor is keeping her distance from us as a family.'

'I resent that.'

'Well, resent as much as you like. It's true.'

'You have no idea,' snapped Willa.

'No we *don't*,' snapped Jacob, 'because you won't *tell* us.'

Jacob went to the bathroom, and everyone moved around, and Jacob came back. He shot a glance at each of us and said, 'I'm going for a walk.' And that was the end of that... for now...

I rode Tasman to Vondelpark. I know Hyacint is going downhill, but still, I felt hurt. I felt like an outsider, an intruder, a servant. Had I caused this? I did what everyone wanted me to. *Not* lucky duck. *Not* lucky pig. Maybe it would have been better if we hadn't come. I know a lot of what Jacob wants to know but I can't tell, it's not my story. I also know Willa can drive you *nuts!* And then there's Hunter...

When I got back it was dark and I was plodding quietly up the stairs, wondering if I should just have some biscuits in the attic for my dinner, when Willa popped out of the apartment. She shut the door behind her, climbed a few stairs, then sat down and patted the step beside her for me to sit. She put her arm round my shoulders and leaned her head on mine.

'Henni, I lost my temper this afternoon. I'm sorry. We won't move out. Please don't feel I'm taking you for granted. You're my anchor, up there in the attic. You are. And thank you for bringing me. It's just that they're hounding me and I'm afraid if they stir up too much it will...be difficult.'

I wanted to say, '*What* will be difficult?'

'Will we go to the naval museum tomorrow afternoon?' she said.

'I wish Donna was here.'

'Ja, I think about them all back home too.' She patted my arm. 'Henni, don't be too upset, this will blow over. Hyacint is Hyacint. Come down in half an hour and we will have dinner.'

Dinner was a bit forced, but we sort of returned to normal. Hyacint didn't say sorry, but she gave me an enormous helping of mashed potato. I brought down the plastic bag with the manky fur and chucked it in the bin. Stupid thing. When Hyacint had gone to watch her favourite TV show (which is called *Good Times Bad Times*, funnily enough) and we were cleaning up, Willa was about to scrape something off a plate into the bin when she exclaimed, 'Henni, what's this dead *animal*?' She pulled out the bag.

'It's rubbish. We tried to find a fox fur for my Queen Wilhelmina costume for King's Day.'

'Dis*gusting*!' she said, but I noticed she put it beside the bin.

Godzijdank I have my own space.

Henni Octon
Re: This is a Whinge
To: Donna O'Sullivan

Oh Donna, I'm having a grizzle. It's bad manners to have a conversation that the guest can't understand, because the guest feels left out. If the van Veens get steamed up, good manners fly out the window, and it's back to Dutch, where they have more ammunition, or if you're Willa, you might use your good English in an *I'm-smarter-than-you* way to get a superior edge, which makes her even more forceful. Sometimes I can hear in their voices how happy they are to slip back into Dutch.

Now they don't care what they say in front of me. Sometimes I feel part of the family, and sometimes I feel like I don't matter. Fortunately I've had plenty of practice with Danielle, so it doesn't worry me, unless they're fighting. We don't have the language thing.

I like Dutch swear words. They're satisfying. Obviously I have to know what they mean. Jacob, Willa and Wendelien swear a bit. Hyacint and Floor never.

Today I read a whole book in Dutch by a Dutch writer. Dick Bruna. The pictures helped.

XX Henni van Amsterdam

And another thing to whinge about, the stairs.

Jeetje! It's upstairs!
Domme! It's downstairs!
Dash down in my pyjamas?
Clomp... clomp... clomp
'That's Raoul,' say Hyacint, from above.
De-dup, de-dup, de-dup
'Now who's that going down?'
People pop out of doors.
'OH! Sorry I thought it was...'
Carlijn's a mountain goat
tadup-tadup-tadup-tadup-tadup
We know each others' treads
And the landings?
Well, everyone knows you by
your junk.

POTVERDOMME!

It was just after lunch. I had posted a letter for Willa and I was chaining up when a voice behind me barked, 'Henni!' I jumped.

It was Jacob and he was angry, and his voice was hard like I had never heard it before. 'I want to talk.'

I felt a cold prickle at the back of my neck. O mijn God, the shit is about to hit the fan. We went into their place and sat down at the table.

'Henni, I asked you to tell me if you heard about Bram. Well, a friend's son saw him at the airport last night running to catch a plane. My friend's son yelled, 'Hey Bram, what's up?' and Bram yelled back, 'Ask the Aussie girl!'

Holy jeetje mina!

'You're the only Aussie girl I know. If he's in trouble, leaving the country, that's serious. What's going on, Henni?'

I couldn't think.

Jacob fired on. 'I liked you, Henni, and I trusted you, but when you came in late with those stupid excuses I knew you weren't being honest. We are worried. Now, tell the truth. Where is he? What's going on?'

'I don't know.'

I will NOT cry.

'I am disappointed and angry, Henni! I thought you were my friend and you betrayed us. Well, that trust is gone. Maybe you don't understand about trust!'

I sat there copping it, then I stood up and walked out.

Damn you, Hunter!

There was no one to put it right. At home Donna would get to the bottom of it, but this felt bottomless. It was too much.

When Mr Nic feels bad he chops wood. Danielle bashes a tennis ball. Well, I got on my bike and I rode and I rode. I rode through Vondelpark and I rode. I rode in any direction, down this path, that path, wherever it went I didn't care, then I was out of the city with the cows and sheep, riding over little canals along roads between flat green paddocks. *So I kept a secret for Hunter. It felt like a bigger promise than to*

Jacob, who was nice. I thought it wouldn't matter that much. He was older and would understand, and I didn't know Hunter's history then. Things changed.

I rode over a bridge over a canal, and turned onto a path and I rode straight on.

Why did I side with Hunter? Because Dirk was so against him? Willa said Hunter and Dirk deserved each other, they were both pig-headed, but Dirk was older and he was the dad, so he should know better. But I could have told Wendelien. I felt bad about not telling, and the longer you keep a secret, the more guilty you are of not telling.

I came to a river. It was wide and strong, and I rode beside it with the wind in my face, talking aloud to myself. *To be honest, Henni, you got smug, and let's face it, the Cigar Factory, the antikraak is cool, knowing Hartog and Hunter, and the translation and earning money, and the computer chase, no, that was terrifying…that mad guy scared me to death. But I hate Jacob being against me. I knew he didn't believe me. I won't tell Carlijn. It's not her stupid family. It's not my stupid family either. O mijn God, all that advice from home about not offending anyone, well, I have offended everyone.*

Then my phone goes **Quack**.

No caller ID

Henni

Henni

I'm not talking to you

?

Henni

You really dropped me in it

?

Henni

Someone saw you catching a plane at Schiphol and it got back to Jacob. Ask the Aussie girl.

Henni

Thanks A LOT! Jacob is mad at me.

Watch the news tonight

Henni

Tell your family what's going on.

The news

Henni

HUNTER YOU OWE ME BIG TIME

Watch the news tonight then you can say anything you want

Henni

I'm not telling ANYBODY ANYTHING

The pension story

Henni

TELL YOUR OWN FAMILY

Potverdomme you, Hunter!

I'm with the cows, on a path by a river. It's getting dark, I am totally lost and Hunter wants me to watch the news. Yeah sure! I don't even know what news he's talking about. I rode on slowly, trying to think it out. Finally I stopped and got out my phone.

'Wendelien?'

'Henni, how are you?'

'Fine. No I'm *NOT* fine, I'm out in the country somewhere with cows. Wendelien, can you do me a favour? Watch the news tonight. Get Jacob, Dirk, Roos, Hyacint and Floor to watch it, a story about pensions.'

'Pensions? Why, what's going on?'

'I don't know, but it's important.'

'Can you tell me more?'

'No. Would you please ask them to watch?'

'Sure. Jacob and Floor watch the news every night anyway. Pensions.'

'Yes, pensions. I'm lost, beside a big river.'

'Oh the Amstel. Henni, it's late. Can you get home?'

'I think so. Can you give me a clue?'

'Make sure you're pointing the way the river's flowing. Stick to the river and you'll be okay. Let me know when you get home. I'll tell them you'll be late.'

'Thanks, Wendelien. The story about the pensions.'

'Sure.'

I felt *so* much better.

~~~~~

When I got home Hyacint had gone to bed but Willa was waiting.

'What happened to you?'

'I rode into the country and got lost. Did you watch the news? Was there a story about pensions?'

'Yes. Where did you go?'

'Along the Amstel. What's all this about pensions?'

'A man in the pension department has been stealing a tiny amount from every pensioner's payment for twenty years. From Hyacint.'

'Did they show pictures?'

'Yes, they caught him at the airport. He was very fit for a man in his sixties.'

I tucked into Hyacint's gluey stewy *suddervlees*. It was *so* good.

'Wendelien said you followed the river back.'

'Ja. It's easy to get to the country. I saw cows.'

She laughed. 'You *like* getting lost.' Obviously Jacob hadn't told on me. 'Go to bed now. Jacob wants to talk to you in the morning. Goedenacht, Henni.'

'Goedenacht, Willa.'

Jeetje mina, what's going to happen now?

LIKE IN THE MOVIES

I knock on the corner black door.

'Good morning, Henni.' Jacob is formal but he looks like an old grandfather, in a soft shirt and a worn brown jacket, his glasses at a slight angle. For the first time I see him as an old man with lines on his forehead. We sit where we sat yesterday. The table has a beautiful vase of roses, but Floor is out.

'Bram is coming later this morning, at ten o'clock, and he wants you to be here. He's not overseas.' Jacob looks down at his hands. 'Sorry I was angry yesterday, without giving you a good chance to reply. Will you come back at ten?'

'Yes. See you then, Jacob.'

———

Op mijn zolder, I'm nervous. I try to write but my mind is flickering and my legs are jigging. Jeetje mina, Hunter is coming to see Jacob. Jeetje mina, that is goede! What will he say? In my *How to Be a Writer* book, it says a lot of information told in a lump is called an info-dump. Jeetje mina, Hunter, you owe me an info-dump, and not a quick hello from Bram the clam. Jeetje mina, I've got to stop saying Jeetje mina.

I'm cold. It's King's Day in a few days. I'll sort some junk to warm me up. On with the layers. I tie a scarf over my nose for the dust. That never lasts long, it's so annoying. I shove things into the corner to make space, I find a box of hats, and it's ten o'clock.

Jacob and I wait. We don't talk. Jacob sits in his chair with a sheepskin on it, drumming the fingers of his right hand on the table, ever so lightly, like he's playing a very quiet piano piece. He looks vulnerable. He gets up and wanders out to the kitchen. It's after ten o'clock. It's like in the movies, a scene where they're waiting for the doctor to come out, and say what happened in the operation.

Knock knock!

We both jump.

Hunter stands in the doorway, tall and dark against the light, ja, like in the movies, except for the paper bag in his hand. He hesitates, like he's not too sure about coming in.

'Dag, Jacob.'

'Dag, Bram.'

They shake hands. No 'nice to see you again', no hugs or kisses. I think Jacob is really glad to see him, but he's scared to do anything. Hunter gazes around the apartment, very cool.

'Hello, Henni.'

'Hello, Hunter.'

'Hunter?' says Jacob.

'To her I am Hunter.'

He hands Jacob the paper bag. It's apple tart. Smells delicious.

He takes off his black coat and drops it on the couch. I see Jacob wince at how skinny he is.

He pulls a chair up to the table, and turns to Jacob. 'Are you good?'

'Okay,' says Jacob. 'I get one day older every day.' He makes coffee, and a hot chocolate for me. It's awkward.

Jacob begins the conversation in an ordinary voice. 'We watched the news last night, about the pension thief. What was so important that Wendelien had to tell us?'

Hunter stares into his coffee as if it's a potion that will reveal the answer.

Jacob continues, 'My friend's son thought you were catching a plane. Why did you say, "Ask the Aussie girl?"'

Hunter gazes into his coffee and continues to stir. Reminds me of Danielle when there's explaining to be done. A bit of the truth? Just enough of the truth?

He looks up. 'Jacob, I have a business. I hunt on the internet.'

Godzijdank! The info-dump!

'My clients have no time to search, some can't, some have secrets. Whatever. They ask me to find things. I am careful. They pay me.'

'Did you do this business before you moved out?'

'Ja. Paps thought it was video games.'

'He thought it was drugs. You had a new computer, remember.'

Hunter stops stirring. He's thinking. We wait, Jacob and I and the apple cake. Hunter's getting his story in order, like one of my teachers at school who teaches slowly. She's good, she's clear.

'A businessman calls me. Another client has recommended me. This guy wants particular documents from the war. These are hard to find. Museums want this stuff too, and they are expensive. So I need to know if this guy can pay me. I check on him. He works at the pension office for twenty years, which is like a voluntary prison sentence!'

Jacob nods, doesn't interrupt.

'This guy is dedicated, makes sure things are done right, but he's not a boss, not earning big bucks. Where is his money from? He says his aunt died, left him money, so I take a chance. I get lucky. I find a whole file of top-level Administration of Rationing Order with signatures, which makes this guy super happy. He pays me, no trouble. I am glad, I tell you, but I am still wondering about this guy. He is sharp. Why is he still so long in that pension job? He wants me to find more documents. Collectors cannot stop, they have the collection disease.'

Jacob and I listen. The coffee's getting cold.

'Then I hear the pension office is upgrading computers. A friend is in the team doing the work, so I ask my friend to check out my Pension Man, not a big deal, just see what he finds.'

'Then...?' says Jacob.

'My computer is stolen.'

'*What?*' Jacob nearly falls off the chair.

Hunter grins. 'It's okay. Henni gets it back.'

Jacob looks at me, astounded.

'Then my bike is gone,' says Hunter.

this is news

'Who is after me? All I can think is Pension Man. Then I get a message. A parcel is at the Cigar Factory. Well, I'm not going back there.'

'The Cigar Factory is the antikraak, right?' Jacob looks at me.

'Ja.'

'Is the parcel still there?'

'Op mijn zolder,' I say. 'It was a camera with a chip inside with *masses* of data.'

'Who from?' says Jacob.

'It's pension data,' says Hunter. 'I think this is from a whistleblower who smelled a fish, but doesn't know how to find the fish. Or blow the whistle. Maybe the answer is on the chip...'

'Then...?'

'I have a systems friend. A girl who is good at this code stuff. She looks at it, goes back and back in the programming, finds nothing. Back to before the euro, finds nothing. Programming is hell, you know. Can you imagine? Pensions? She can't sleep. She goes back past one decimal point. She finds nothing. Two decimal points, rounding off, and...*bingo!*'

'Bingo *what?*'

'A hidden account.'

'*Verduistering!*' Jacob's eyes are wide behind his glasses.

'I don't understand.'

Hunter looks up the definition on his phone and reads slowly. '*Em-bezz-le, in charge of money and trusted, but steals some for personal use.* When Hyacint gets her pension, Pension Man gets point nought nought something euro cents. Every pensioner, every payment. The program hides the trail.'

'*Wow,* that's *clever!*'

'So he gets two dollars every month?'

'Don't ask me. You figure it out.'

'Why did the whistleblower give you the information, and not the police?'

'The whistleblower gave the information to my friend upgrading the computers, who sent it to me, and I sent it to my systems friend who *found* the fish.'

'Were you at Schiphol?'

'Ja, and when I see him start to run we *knew* it was Pension Man. Jeetje mina, he can run! There is security guys, emergency guys, travellers, Marcel's son, police, cameras, I thought for sure you will see me on TV, so I yell to ask the Aussie. Sorry, Henni.' Hunter takes a sip of his coffee. 'I was right near him. Did you see me?'

'No.' Jacob laughs. 'You are not famous.'

Something happened in that moment, like the sun came out. Everything felt easier. Hunter grinned.

'Will you get back the documents you sold Pension Man?' I ask.

'Maybe.'

'Did you go to the wedding?'

'Ja, I saw you in the kitchen.'

'Blue umbrellas?'

'Ja, borrowed them from a university friend.'

'Did you see Wendelien?'

'Ja.'

'Sell the lamps?'

'Four left. Want one?'

'Ja.'

Jacob listens in amazement.

When I finish my cold hot chocolate, Jacob asks me to go, so they can talk family stuff. Fine by me. Not my family. Not my business. But potverdomme, I tell you that is the best apple cake I ever tasted and p o t v e r d o m m e, the best info-dump I ever heard!

Op mijn zolder I wrote what just happened, page after page, so engrossed that the knock on the door nearly shot me through the roof!

It was Hunter in his long black coat. He stood taking it all in.

'Ah the ship. I wrecked it,' he grinned. 'This place was magic when I was a kid.'

'It's magic to me now.' I felt self-conscious, him looking around my place.

He saw the parcel.

'I'll take that. Jacob's coming to the Cigar Factory. Want to come?'

Hunter left before us to get keys.

Riding to the Cigar Factory with Jacob was the opposite of going with Carlijn. I cruised along slow and steady, following Jacob's brown jacket. He took us a new way, beside canals, and when we reached a bridge, the barriers were coming down. Us riders watched with our toes to the ground as the bridge split apart and rose up in front of our eyes, until the road pointed to the sky.

Jacob smiled at me. 'My favourite bridge is putting on a show for you, Henni.'

I smiled back and it felt so good.

We watched two barges and a yacht slide by. Was this where Myrte lost me? Who cares.

Jacob knew the Cigar Factory, but he'd never been

inside. He inspected the building with his expert architect eye. Hartog now shared the top room with his girlfriend, Lotte, and her five thousand pot plants. Hunter showed us the room he's moving into. It's big and dark and empty. He's going to take the paint off the windows. Why would anyone paint over windows? It's not wartime.

Hunter gave me one of the lamps that we did the translation for, and, how's this for luck? A friend of his wants to buy Tasman! Hunter paid me right then, ten more euros than the fietswinkel! I must deliver Tasman before I go.

We had a drink at the cafe downstairs, playing jazzy music now. Hartog went into serious business-business with Jacob. 'What do you think, Jacob, a tobacco museum?'

'Keep it like this,' said Jacob, 'with artists and small businesses in every corner. You pay more rent, but you don't have to move. Talk to the owner. Do a deal. You can manage the place.'

They got deeper into the future of the Cigar Factory, but Hunter wanted to talk with me about Willa.

'Arrange me a meeting, Henni?'

'Why are you so desperate to meet her?'

'The war economy is interesting to me. I want to hear it from someone who remembers. How was it with Dutch gilders, coupons, and *Reichskreditkassenscheine,* that German money? And I want to know about the coupon-smuggling uncle. Also I like black markets.'

Willa would meet him, for sure. Here's our plan. I organise a meeting with her, while Hunter gets his questions ready, then we meet up after King's Day.

Whistle blower!
One of my best flat things.
Can't believe it!

AFTER CORNELIA

I heard a huffing and puffing coming up the stairs, then a loud familiar fart. I jumped to the door before she could knock.

'Willa!'

'*Jaaa, ooooh* . . . how are you going . . . *Oooh* . . . *aaahhh* it's a long way up those stairs. *Oooh* . . . *ooooff* . . . *Jaaah* . . .' She sits down. 'That's better. Put the heater on.'

She got her breath back and cheerfully settled in. 'Pass me that rug for my knees.'

'Willa, guess who was up here yesterday?'

'*Sinterklaas.*'

'Bram!'

She smoothed out the rug. 'I know. News travels fast.'

'He wants to meet you, to find out about the black market in the war.'

She let out a weary sigh. 'Good for him. Now, Henni, what have you found?'

WATERSNOOD IN GELDERLAND,
den 8: Maart 1784.

J.E. Grave del et sculp.

'Toys, books, a coffee grinder, walking sticks,
a picture of a flood bursting in...'

'Oh, I remember that. It terrified me when I was a
kid. That is why I was a good swimmer.'

'...a pile of stuff that we can't sell, a box of letters.'

Willa looked around. 'Jacob and Hyacint made
houses and caves up here. Have you found Moeder's
Rast & Gasser?'

'I think it's in that corner, see the flower fabric? The
box on top is heavy.'

'Oh, too much bother.' She was disappointed. She pointed to some material in a drawer. 'We'll take that home for Maggs.'

Then something caught her eye. 'Henni, pass me that little book.'

Slowly she turned the pages. 'This was a present from my coupon-smuggling uncle, my birthday book.'

She found what she was looking for. She gazed out the window, remembering something.

'Is it from the wartime?'

My question brought her back. She nodded. 'Henni, never forget that nations are just lines drawn on a map.'

'But nations have customs and a language, and history and...'

'Nations are lines drawn on a map by the man with the most power.' She said it in a strange dreamy way. 'If a strong man has enough power he can redraw the lines, simple as that.'

She was in a funny mood, calm and thoughtful.

'What happened on that night, Willa? When Cornelia came?'

'Meneer Woortman lived under here.' She tapped the floor. 'He was an older man, discreet. Moeder trusted him. He went to his sister's in the country.'

She was talking in her slow story voice, which I love. I slipped under the doona.

'The moff had taken his bike,' she continued, 'but he got another one on the black market. He must have known what was going on in our place, with all the voices and the babies, especially Hyacint's shrieking, but he turned a blind eye. Before Meneer Woortman left he gave Moeder the key to his apartment, so she could water his precious orchid plant. God knows how he kept it alive. He must have ridden off early in the morning.

'This was the most horrible time for us, because baby Jacob had a very high fever, and it stayed up. For two days Moeder and Sara tried all the remedies, cool baths, sponging him in vinegar and I don't know what else. Oh the poor little soul, it was horrible. The long nights were the worst. I fell asleep at school. I prayed to any god that would listen, "Please please let Jacob live, if you let baby Jacob live, I will…" But what could I promise? What could I sacrifice? Nothing would make a speck of difference.

'The fever went on and on, till he was hardly breathing. They were so desperate that in the end they took a big risk and called the doctor, but it was too late. The doctor was a brave man, and gentle, but he had no words of comfort. He pronounced the baby dead. "There's nothing you can do, my dears. Put him up in the attic till morning." It was just before dusk.'

'That was *Jacob*?'

'It was soon after that, there was the knock on the door. "Roos, are you okay? It's Cornelia." It had been a terrible day. I didn't know what I was doing. I opened the door to Cornelia and she saw a strange woman at the stove.'

'The *same* evening?'

'Right on curfew. Cornelia had seen the doctor leave the building and before the downstairs door closed she slipped in. She said she wanted to know if we were all right. Moeder gave an excuse and dispatched her quick smart, but the second she was gone, Moeder was in a fury. "Cornelia's husband is an NSBer. They are *poison*! They'll come for Sara and Matius. Sara, you must go *now*! Quickly, take your things."

'Moeder sent me out with a message, to a man a couple of blocks away. I was terrified. It was curfew. I had to give it to him and no one else. I had never been so scared. After curfew they could shoot you on sight. I found the place, but I couldn't deliver the message. They said the man had been away for two days. When I got back home it was strangely quiet and empty. "Where did they go?" I asked. "Where's Jacob?"

'"Go to bed!" said Moeder. I went to bed confused, exhausted, but my nerves so jangled I didn't think I could ever fall asleep. Suddenly we were woken by a banging on the door downstairs. *Bang! Bang! Bang!*

'I heard Moeder get up. She bustled down the stairs. "I'm coming, I'm *coming*!" she called like any offended Dutch woman woken roughly in the night. "No need to knock the house down!" Then men's voices at the door, and Moeder protesting, then she said clearly, "All right, come and see for yourself." Heavy footsteps clomped up the stairs. It sounded like a dozen men.

'What a frightening scene in our living room, a Nazi SS man in uniform and three other men in ordinary clothes, two of them with guns. Papa in his dark coat by the table, me in my threadbare coat over my nightgown, and Moeder in her dressing gown.

'"Tell them to come out," said the SS officer.

'Hyacint sent up a wail from the bedroom.

'"Baby," said one of the men.

'"That's our daughter," said Papa, staring hard at Moeder, scared of what she might do.

'They searched the place and found nothing, in fact Papa thought they were about to leave. Then one said, "They are in this building."

'"Who lives upstairs?" said the SS officer.

'Moeder shrugged. "A neighbour."

'"You stay here," the officer barked at Papa and me. "You come!" he snapped at Moeder.

'Clomp clomp clomp, up the stairs. *Bang bang bang* on the door.

'Moeder didn't see everything, but one of the men opened the door, or maybe it was already open. She said when the light flicked on they jumped. Two figures stood in the middle of the room. Sara and Matius hadn't even bothered to hide. What we had feared for so long, was happening.

'When they filed into our apartment Sara wouldn't look up.

'"Where is this one?"' said the NSBer, peering at a list. "Another baby?"'

'Nobody spoke.

'"Where is this one?" the SS officer repeated loudly.

'"For *God's sake*, have a heart," Moeder said quietly.

'Then a baby cried. Papa had put Hyacint back in her cot.

'"Ha!" growled the NSB man. "*There's* the baby."

'"No, no, that's the baby girl."

'"Are you sure? Check where that cry came from."

'The other man went to the bedroom, and the cries grew suddenly louder.

'"It's the girl."

'"She said she saw baby stuff for two. Is there another baby?"

'"He died yesterday," Moeder said quietly.

'"It was never reported."

'"For God's sake, man, have pity."

'In that split second I thought the SS officer would insist on seeing the body. He wrote something down. "You're coming with us too," he said to Papa. "Get your things."

'The farewells were quiet. Papa and I were terrified that Moeder would explode. Papa begged her with his eyes. *Please don't get angry!* Moeder stayed calm, but you could never tell with her. Papa was afraid for us because of her anger, and because he was leaving us with little food and it was cold. We said goodbye to Sara and Matius. Moeder hugged Sara. Papa kissed Moeder, then down the stairs they went.

'Sara drifted down like a ghost,' said Willa, 'a sad whispering spirit, no fight left in her, it was like her soul had already floated away. And then the doors shut, and the cars drove off and it was just Moeder and me. I asked Moeder, '"Will Matius and Sara be all right?"

'Moeder said bluntly, "Matius, maybe."

'"And Papa?"

'"They'll take him to a work camp. The moff are hunting out our men to be slaves in their factories. All the German men are away fighting, so they force our men to build their war machines, guns, planes, bullets."

'She fed Hyacint and put her back in her cot. "Nothing we can do tonight," she said.

'I crawled into bed beside Moeder, still a bit warm from Papa. I cried and she told me to shut up, but I did cry, then she hugged me. I don't think she could cry.

'Then, it must have been in the early morning, I was woken by a faint sound, a faint mewing like a cat. I woke Moeder and she heard it too. The sound was coming from upstairs. Up we went. Not from Meneer Woortman's, no, it was coming from the attic, from the wooden drawer that was Jacob's cot. Jacob was *alive*! The cold of the attic had broken his fever!'

Willa turned her face away, it was so painful to remember.

'Moeder gently lifted him up and carried him down, and from that moment Hyacint had a twin.'

'What? But they were twins already.'

Willa was quiet.

'*Whoa!* Jacob was Sara and Matius's baby?'

'Ja, but Moeder never for one second behaved as if he wasn't hers. She'd helped care for him when Sara was sick, but oh, that tiny boy, just because the cold of the attic broke the fever it didn't mean he was well again. Poor pale little thing, with skinny legs sticking out of his sad little potato body, too weak to even cry. Moeder would massage his little stick legs. The doctor said, "That's not a baby, that's a hare."' Willa turned to me. 'But you know something, Henni, he always had bright eyes.' She blew her nose hard.

'Willa, when we were in the Resistance Museum, it said every person needed papers. How did Jacob get papers?'

'Oh, Moeder got him papers, all right, Jacob Matius van Veen. Look at his passport, same birthday as Hyacint. There was only ten days between them anyway. Moeder fed them both. She made me swear never to tell a soul.' Willa tipped back her head and closed her eyes. 'Sorry, Moeder. Now you know too, Henni. Don't tell a soul.'

'I won't.'

The attic felt like a small dark church.

'Does Jacob know?'

She shook her head. 'He was a baby. Nobody talked.'

Her chair creaked as she changed position.

'Did they survive?'

Willa gazed out the window.

Finally she said, 'Papa came home.' She was in such a sad dreamy mood. 'He turned up after two years, with a suitcase of cigarettes. They were like money back then. He was skinny as a rake and if anyone ever spoke about the work camp he walked out.'

I longed to ask what happened to Sara and Matius but I didn't dare.

'Will you tell Jacob?'

'I don't know.' Her finger still marked the page.

'How was it with Moeder after that night?'

'That's enough, Henni.'

'Oh Willa, I have so many questions.'

'I bet you have.'

'Tomorrow?'

'That's enough.'

'Willa, one last thing, what's in the book?'

She opened it and then slowly read aloud.

> *Als dit bladje is versleten*
>
> *ben jij mij dan ook vergeten.*

'What does it say?'

> *'If this page is faded and worn*
>
> *Will you also have forgotten me.'*

'Sara wrote that.'

'You haven't forgotten her, Willa.'

OLD DUTCH LAMP

I was dreaming that Zev had invented an electric swing that hung from the hook out my window and we were going up and down from the ground, and people were running up and down the stairs, and Briquette was barking and doors slamming and then I heard doors in real life and someone was slowly climbing the stairs to the attic.

tap tap tap

Who was visiting so early in the morning, puffing out of breath on the other side of the door? I was wide awake.

'Henni?'

'Wendelien?'

'Can I come in?' Her smiley face was serious.

No! No! Something's wrong! Mum has died. Dad has

died. Danielle has died. Briquette has died. Zev has died.
Someone has died. I feel sick. I don't want to hear.

She sat on the chair. 'It's *freezing* up here!' She
grabbed my coat and put it on. 'Get back in bed, Hen.'

Zev has died. Mr Nic has died. Donna has died.
I pulled the doona tight, terrified. *I don't want to hear.*

'Willa died last night.'

I knew it. Boom! Just like that ...

'Hyacint found her when she didn't come for
breakfast.'

My eyes were open but I wasn't seeing.

'Hyacint's doctor just left. He said a stroke, which
was my diagnosis too.'

I vacantly thought, *So this is how it happens ... some-*
one knocks on the door and tells you.

'Was she sick, Henni?'

No sense keeping the pills a secret now. 'A couple
of weeks ago we went to the chemist, but Willa
couldn't get the pills she wanted unless she went to a
doctor. She didn't want to do that, she said she'd wait
to see her own doctor at home. She didn't want a fuss.'

'Oh.' Wendelien sighed. 'A common story. Two days
ago she complained to Jacob she felt dizzy. Was she
stressed about anything, besides staying with Hyacint
and their arguing?'

What could I say? The tears spilled out. 'Flying here was stressful and remembering her childhood...'

Wendelien put her arms around me, then the tears really flowed.

'We'll call your folks...when you're ready.'

I cried even more when I thought of dear Stella Street, and how sad they would be that Willa wasn't coming home.

'Her body was worn out,' said Wendelien. 'She was old, Henni. No one lives forever.'

'But there was *lots* of life left in Willa.'

'I know.' She sighed. 'We're so glad you brought her here. We'll always remember her at our wedding. She had a wonderful time.'

'And the wedding present.'

We laughed and cried and rocked.

'Danielle said she was an old elephant going home to die.'

'Old elephant? I saw her more as a cow.'

'For me she was a dear old horse.'

'Let's go downstairs.'

Jacob was there, and everyone else. Floor, Wendelien's Eric, Dirk the Bear and another couple whose names I couldn't remember, and Hyacint's son and daughter.

Not Hunter. Everyone went a bit quiet when we entered, then the talk about Willa continued.

They decided she had a good death, not like the neighbour, Mevrouw Sprokkelmaan, who struggled for breath for months, and o mijn God, what a way to die, drugged to the eyeballs, and did you know her front teeth were on a brace? At least that's what I think they said, as it was mostly in Dutch. Anyway, they started to laugh and polish off a scrappy breakfast.

I sat in the corner, in a daze. I thought about Willa in her garden, standing there with the hose, talking to Mr Nic about what Parliament was doing wrong, and going into the house for a little treat for Briquette. (I had to fight the tears, but I managed). The Dutch voices were all weaving into one sound, then the tone changed to that realistic-sad sound of *it was for the best*, and I imagined they were saying her coming to Amsterdam was a happy ending to her story, judging by their voices. All things considered, it was turning into a wonderful death. I recognised a few words, *vliegtuig*, which is plane, and *huis*, house, and *Henni*.

What did I think? Was she ready to die?

No she was *not* ready to die and *yes* she had a problem, which she may have sorted out (or solved by dying)! Was she happy in Stella Street? *Yes!* Did she have a good life? *Yes*! Nobody knew anything about her son and they were astonished by this new relative. They wanted to know how to contact him, but I couldn't help, I knew as much as they did. To tell the truth I thought the van Veen family took the whole event very matter-of-factly, although not Hyacint. She kept wiping the table looking anxious and confused, blinking a lot at all the new information. Plenty of that lately. She would miss her sister to fight with.

How would they get Willa down the stairs? Swing her out the window like a fridge? In Stella Street, Old Auntie Lillie was carried out the front door to a van.

Then Hyacint said something, and everyone went quiet and looked at me.

'What did she say?' I whispered to Wendelien, but she didn't want to translate it.

'Come on, tell me what she said.'

'She said Willa brought trouble back to us, and she's somehow worked it round in her head that her death was your fault.'

'Oh *gosh*!'

'It's all right. Jacob has headed her off that track. Poor Hyacint.'

I didn't feel 'poor Hyacint'.

'What about your honeymoon?'

'We postponed it till after the funeral.' Wendelien leaned over to me. 'Do you want to see her?'

I wasn't sure.

'Come with me,' said Wendelien. 'She's just in her bed.'

We went into the little bedroom, with the morning light seeping in through the curtains. There was Willa, lying straight in pale blue sheets, still and cold and grey, with her eyes shut and her mouth open slightly.

I didn't say, 'Goodbye dear Willa, I grew to love you very much.' Know what I said? 'Goodbye, you stubborn old Dutch lamp.'

I talked to home for two hours easy. First it was sniffing and deep breaths, and blowing, and terribly sad, then it grew lighter, and bit by bit we cheered up. I was glad the internet connection was poor, so it was just our voices, no video. People dropped in at home, and it was like Pizza Night without the pizzas. We said all the things we remembered about Willa and the things we would miss her for. Mr Nic would miss the political lectures, Donna would miss the list of seedlings to get from the nursery, I would miss the books to go back to the library, Dad would miss the washers in her kitchen taps, Briquette would miss the treats and bones. We remembered when Briquette buried a bone in Willa's African marigolds, and the incident of the Botfids' dog.

Willa *was*…Willa *was*…Her 'is' time has stopped, and the 'was' time has begun.

Donna told us that the day after we left for Amsterdam, she went to Willa's and when she opened the front door it was like entering a model house, absolutely spick-and-span.

'It's a Stella Street tradition,' said Dad. 'First Old Auntie Lillie and now Willa. If you're an old lady here, you die suddenly, lying out straight, leaving a spotlessly clean house.'

Maggs laughed. 'I'll break the tradition!'

Donna said, 'On the kitchen table Willa had laid out instructions for everything, bank account, photocopy of her passport, healthcare card, list of contacts for the phone and electricity, when to water the plants, bills to be paid, *everything*, like she'd laid the table of her life. It did cross my mind that Willa thought she might not be coming back. The blue-and-white tiles by her sink gleamed, and the tins with names like *kletskoppen* were all perfectly lined up. Now there are two lots of sad folk, on either side of the world.'

'That's what happens when your life is split between countries.'

I told them how mellow Willa was in Amsterdam, and how happy she was to see her family, especially Jacob.

'And how are you, Henni?'

'Okay. Sometimes I feel angry, but there's no one to be angry at.'

'Be angry at me,' said Danielle. 'You always are, so that can be normal.'

'Oh, don't be kind, it just starts me crying again. It feels like a school project that was *terribly* important and *had* to be handed in exactly on time, then *boof*! It's *cancelled*! And I don't have to finish it *ever*. But she wasn't a school project...'

Donna said, 'You will be all of Stella Street at the funeral.'

Well

that will be a task.

Six days from going home. We decided that I would fly home as planned, as normally as could be expected in the circumstances, and I would buy a black liquid gel pen and write.

And just when we'd said our goodbyes Mr Nic chipped in, 'Oh and don't waste time thinking about dying, Henni. We're all young. It won't happen for a long long time.'

'Bye bye. Love you all. Love you all.'

Bip

That's when I started to howl. I'll be all right. I just want to cry.

Willa
Wilhelmina Roos Petronella van Veen
Willa

I'm angry
you crafty old horse
you solved that one neatly didn't you!
You didn't take it to the grave
You handed it on to me.
Not fair!
You said we'd go to the naval museum.
What a lot of crap everyone talks.
Oh it's plain straight out dumb
sad
oh Willa

Your old horsey bigness
Smelling of roses hand cream
your crabbiness
making the air warm around you
breathing down on me
I got to know you
your story
everything you told me
your voice was familiar
you became dear to me

Jacob said, 'Ask if Carlijn can come and stay.' Jacob understood.

Carlijn was quiet and respectful and brought us a sunk-in-the-middle cake she had just baked. We carried her sleeping bag and air mattress op mijn zolder and juggled it through the little door. Carlijn stood up straight and looked around.

'I know why you like this place, it's like a secret story.'

She doesn't know how true that is! I was glad she felt the mystery. I showed her the bucket and how to do a wee, which she *did*, right then! Jeetje mina, she is bold!

'No worries,' said Carlijn.

I told her how terrified I was at first, of meeting someone on the stairs with the bucket in my hand. Then we shoved things around and made up her bed.

That night op mijn zolder, talking in the dark, I told her about the turbulence on the plane, breath by breath, the fear, the prayers, the smells, the imagining. It came pouring out, even the embarrassing trips to the toilet in Dubai. It was the first time I'd told anyone.

'I will have nightmares,' she said. 'Do you have nightmares?'

'No, but since I've been here I've cried an awful lot.'

'Are you homesick?'

'Sometimes.'

I would have cried again except Carlijn started doing funny imitations of people crying, especially her baby sister who takes an enormous deep breath and in that long pause everyone dashes out of the room, or blocks their ears, before the ear-piercing wail. Then I had to explain ear piercing, both sorts, and then I wasn't crying.

'When some people cry it makes you feel like crying too.'

'Not Marienke, this kid at school!' said Carlijn. 'When she fell off her bike and cried I wanted to slap her.'

We talked about things that are alive and things that are dead. How we only eat things that are dead. What about fresh oysters? Or are plants alive when we eat them? If we just picked a cherry and ate it right then, was it dead? And what about seeds? They have life in them.

We talked about secrets.

I said, 'I don't like secrets.'

Carlijn said, 'What about good secrets, like presents and surprise birthday parties? What about secrets we need to keep, like keeping part of yourself unknown, your secret self that protects you?'

I told Carlijn about my friend Leo, in Berlin, who hid a friend so he wouldn't be deported from Germany, and how the emails between Leo and me were a secret from everyone. She was really interested in Leo, but I had to tell her Leo is a mystery now too, because I've lost contact with him. Does my family have secrets? Nope. If they have secrets they're well kept. Well actually, who knows? I guess a secret is something that nobody knows.

We talked about everything. People we liked, people we didn't like. She told me about her friends at school, and the music they liked. I told her how I'm not very good at friends. I told her once, when I rode to school after a swim, my bike helmet moulded a circle in my wet hair and some girls posted a picture of my hair, saying my halo was getting heavy. I told her how I tried to make them like me but it didn't work, and I decided there was no point in being somebody I'm not, and if riding a bike isn't cool, who cares?

'They're nuts,' said Carlijn. 'What's uncool about riding a bike? Everyone rides a bike here.'

Then she asked, 'Is it hard being in a place where you don't know anyone?'

'Ja. Once, as I walked past some kids my age, they laughed, and I felt they were laughing at me. They probably weren't, but I felt lonely. In Stella Street there's always someone around who I know. I only have to go outside and there's a friend. But here...well, I guess I did get hit by a lucky boomerang.'

Jaaaaaaaa. Carlijn told me about her funny relatives, especially her forgetful uncle who's lost his wallet four times. I told her about the Stella Street mob, and she said was coming to stay and I said YES! She told me about her family holidays, camping in Croatia and Norway, and how long it takes to pack, and I told her how we were camping in wild bushland, cut off by a flood, when little Jim was born, and I felt homesick and had another sad pang thinking that Willa wasn't going home.

'She was an old lady. That's what happens, you get old and die. Think of good things.'

'Carlijn,' I said, 'if I say the words "the blue dog", what do you think of?'

'Having a cold, jumping, a hound, wet shoes… why, what's the blue dog?'

'Something Willa remembered from childhood, which was important but she couldn't remember what it was.'

'Oh well, it's not important now.'

TO FALL WITH THE DOOR INTO THE HOUSE

Next morning I lay wondering if Carlijn was awake, then came a whisper: 'This is a cold place.'

'A *small* cold place,' I whispered back.

A small cold *junk* place.

A small cold *high-up* inside place.

A small cold high-up inside *full-up* place etc etc etc etc etc etc.

Then we talked about how you collect expressions from other people, like Willa says…said: 'You make a better door than a window.'

Carlijn said 'to fall with the door into the house' in Dutch means getting straight to the point.

Carlijn likes 'no worries'.

I told Carlijn some of Mr Nic's sayings, and she echoed me.

Samfu.

Samfu?

A self adjusting military fuck-up. It's an acronym.

Same in Dutch! Acroniem.

It ain't illegal if you don't get caught.

It ain't illegal if you don't get caught.

Bugger that for a joke!

Bugger that for a joke.

As crooked as a dog's hind leg.

As crooked as a dog's hind leg.

What time does the balloon go up? That means
'when does the party start?'

What time does the balloon go up?

Get a wriggle on.

Get a wriggle on. That's because of all your snakes.

My sister Danielle says 'cool bananas'.

'Cool bananas' is cool.

I like *Plons plons*.

We went down for breakfast with Hyacint, then
Carlijn went to hockey, and I looked at the tarot cards
for King's Day.

Donna O'Sullivan
Re: Willa's contacts
To: Henni Octon

Dearest Henni,

I went through more of Willa's stuff today. What a mystery she was. She donated thousands to Red Cross and Amnesty International. It annoyed me that she gave away money, then cried poor when it came to the trip. There was also a list of medical details, and prescriptions for painkillers. Was she upset or hurting? Did she complain?

She was passionate about democracy and freedom of speech, which we knew, and corresponded with politicians and activists. She'd left all her affairs in order, written lists and given us jobs. Wish she'd told us when she was alive, but anyway, she's easier to wrap up than old Auntie Lillie.

I found two addresses of friends in Amsterdam. Please contact them.

Another surprise, there was a note about her son in Canada. I contact him. So strange that Willa never mentioned him. I'll tell you how that goes when you're home.

Bye Chicken. Sorry we can't be there. Thinking of you all the time.

X D

One of the two addresses Donna sent was Lodewijk's old address, and the other is now the Albert Heijn supermarket.

Wonder what job Willa gave me? Bet the secret I have now is not on the lists!

It's all happening fast. Jacob was on the phone to Donna, making arrangements. They were laughing and enjoying it. Didn't sound like organising a funeral. Donna has spoken to Willa's son. He sounded like an American businessman. He can't make it to the funeral. Dad sometimes helped Willa with money stuff, and he and Jacob have decided that the funeral will be a plain affair, but the coffee and cake will be good, and any money left over will go to Amnesty International and Red Cross.

Rob will sell her house in the spring. He will get it painted first. Donna asked if anyone in Amsterdam would like to stay in Willa's place and have a holiday in Stella Street?

MISERY

I won't open my eyes.

I won't get up

The sun won't rise it will just get less dark until it's the usual grey

There are no tears left in my swollen eyes

My nose is blocked, my mouth is dry

I can't go downstairs

Tomorrow at seven o'clock Carlijn will ring the bell.

Oh God, she will ring it again.

She will message me. She will message me again.

She thought my idea was great, she helped me find my costume.

But it's silly. I've wasted my euros.

Carlijn will be disappointed but she doesn't need me.

She'll have a good time. She always does.

Quack

Carlijn

Dag Queen Wilhelmina?

Carlijn

Dag Queen Wilhelmina.

Henni

Carlijn, I can't do King's Day

Carlijn

WHY?

Henni

I don't want to.

Carlijn

What will you do?

Carlijn

Hen, what will you do?

Carlijn

HENNI, WHAT WILL YOU DO??

Henni

Stay in bed.

Carlijn

Bugger that for a joke.

Carlijn

Be miserable or be not miserable. If you have fun that doesn't mean you aren't sad. What would Willa say if you lie in bed on King's Day?

Carlijn

What would Willa say?

Henni

Wipe that crummy look off your face.

Carlijn

Ha ha. Come on Hen. It's Car + Hen remember! King's Day will be good. I need you.

Carlijn

Hey Queen Wilhelmina, don't let the Netherlands down.

My stomach rumbled. Oh well. I suppose I have to
eat. I will go down and make breakfast for myself.
Hyacint has probably gone to church.

I carried the bucket downstairs, washed my face, and
stepped into the kitchen. I jumped in fright. Hyacint
was sitting there, alone in the dark. She looked
pathetic and so sad.

Suddenly I felt achingly sorry for her and ashamed
of thinking only of myself.

'Can I turn on the light, Hyacint?'

'Ja,' she said in a flat voice.

'You want coffee, Hyacint?'

'Ja.'

'Will I make breakfast for you?'

'Ja.'

I had seen the oude dames make coffee a dozen
times, but it's different when you have to do it
yourself. I thought Hyacint might get up and boss me
away, but she didn't. I had to ask lots of questions, but
eventually she had her coffee.

'Hyacint, I want to make those egg bread things
you cook in the frying pan.'

'*Wentelteefjes.*'

'How many eggs?' Then I asked two dozen

more questions, until at last we had a plate of two
funny-looking blobs of fried bread each, and some
strawberries I found in the fridge. Finally Hyacint got
out of the chair. She went to the cupboard, and what
did she get? *Chocolate sprinkles!*

'*Hagelslag.* Do you want them?'

'Ja.' I scattered on a polite sprinkle.

'More,' said Hyacint, tipping on a snow of
chocolate.

With my strong milky tea, it was good.

Poor Hyacint.

Poor me.

Oh Willa, we miss you.

'I have to get ready for tomorrow,' I sighed as I
cleaned up.

'What will you do?' asked Hyacint.

'I will be Queen Wilhelmina,' I said, resigned.
'I have a hat and glasses.'

'The Queen wore a fur.'

'I had a bit of fur but it was dirty.'

'Oh, I found a fur in Roos's room.' For the third
time the fur was fished out of the bin, but this time
the fur was furry! Somehow Willa had cleaned it.

'Do you have a coat?'

'My black puffer coat.'

Hyacint went to her bedroom and returned with a brown woman's coat.

I tried it on. 'What do you think?'

'It's big.' She put the fur round the collar. 'Good.'

'Can I borrow it?'

'Yes. I don't wear it. It was my mother's.'

Moeder's! Hyacint found something else, a little orange folded-ribbon brooch. I stood while she pinned it on as if it was a medal. 'Moeder made them.'

'I know. We saw one at the museum.'

'Ja.'

Op mijn zolder, I hung the coat on a beam, but it was too human. Was it Moeder telling me to keep the secret? I took it down and dropped it over a case, then I buckled the big belt around my middle and sat down to write, but all I could think of to say was *The past keeps busting in* . . .

I thought of how Willa remembered Sara sitting on the ironing table swinging her legs, smoking like a Hollywood movie star – except it was a pencil instead of a cigarette – and laughing about the evil little Hitlerman having his moustache trimmed.

I wondered where they lived, before it all turned bad? Myrte's place. I'd never even seen it. Willa said it was easy to find. 'It's the grey one,' she said. This grey day was as good as any. I would go and look at Sara's house.

I walked on the other side of the street, praying I wouldn't see Myrte. *Potverdomme!* I should have walked on the close side. *Potverdomme!* I should have gone on a school day. I found the house easily – a couple of weeds grew by the door. Then dread of dreads, I was looking up at it when there at a second-floor window staring straight back at me was Myrte! *POT VER DOMME!!!*

We stared at each other for ages, then she waved. After a moment I waved back. *Arggh!*

Why did I do that?

Myrte vanished from the window and I ran. I didn't want anything to do with her.

'Henni! Come and look at this!' she yelled in an angry voice, just as I reached the corner. I shouldn't have turned around. *Bloody hell!* She was standing on the footpath out the front of her place, pointing down at her feet, as if I'd left dog shit or something.

Damn you, Myrte! My blood boiled. I spun round and marched back.

'Whatever's biting you, don't take it out on *me*!' I snapped.

'*Look!*' said Myrte. She was pointing at the cobbles. 'Every time I come out the door I see this. It's not *me* who did this. I *hate* it.'

'What are you talking about?'

'*Look!*'

There were two engraved metal squares in the footpath. 'Are they graves?' Then, with horror I realised what they were. They were memorial plaques.

'They are like graves to me,' said Myrte. 'Those two people lived in our apartment, back then...' she flicked her hand, 'and since you arrived, my grandfather won't shut up. He says you will make us leave, and things taken in the war must be given back.' Then Myrte recites, like something from the Bible, '"One day they will come to claim what is rightfully theirs." Will you do that?'

'Why are you asking me?'

'Why are you looking at our house?'

I didn't know what to say.

Myrte said, 'We are related somehow. My grandfather met Hyacint in the cheese shop and set me up. He says to me, "Make friends with that girl. Go and find out about them. Go and see her again." He says, "What did that girl say? Are they going back to Australia? Find out about the old lady. Go this afternoon!" *Jezus*, I thought, I will be a bitch, and you will hate me.'

'You did that pretty darn well.'

'I told Opa you wouldn't talk to me.' She was being honest now, but I still didn't like her.

'Myrte, when you called me to see that toy dog on the bin, was that an accident?'

'The toy was, but riding past your house, maybe not...'

'Did you look in my bag?'

'Yes, you had a parcel. I gave your bag to Hyacint. I felt better after that.'

'The old lady, Roos, is not my grandmother.'

'You said she *was*!'

'No, you *assumed* that.'

'Hyacint said she was. You're *lying*.'

'She died two days ago.'

'I don't believe you.'

'Believe what you like.'

I walked off.

I bought an orange at Albert Heijn. I practised my tarot card reading, then Hyacint and I watched *The Bold and the Beautiful*.

QUEEN WILHELMINA TELLS YOUR FORTUNE

King's Day

I am dawning

And what kind of a day am I today?

I am a sunny day

And what day is it today?

It is King's Day.

And who am I today?

Queen Wilhelmina

And what must I do today?

Speak to my people on Radio Oranje.

Which reminds me I must remember my orange.

And what else will I do today?

Look for a sign.

What sort of a sign?

About the secret of Jacob.

And who will ring me very soon?

Carlijn

So what do I need to do now?

Get up.

I look out my window. Yep. It's going good and crazy out there. A woman in an orange feather headdress is setting up a stall outside her front door. She's eating a sandwich as she drags out boxes of plastic stuff, piles of plates, toys, a lamp. Today I feel unpredictable, powerful. I am a potent brew.

I am Queen Wilhelmina.

Ja! For my people.

Carlijn comes and we load our bikes with the bags of stuff to sell, and then we wobble off carefully to Car + Hen. It's chilly but Moeder's coat is keeping me warm. The streets are bustling with people setting up stalls, laughing and chatting and not a single car, except the car of Car + Hen ha ha ha! A flock of rugged-up bargain hunters rides past determinedly, with empty bags hooked on their handlebars.

Orange! Orange crowns. Orange feathers. Orange wigs. Jeetje mina! Orange everything. Orange jewels, dresses, bow ties, overalls, space suits, the more orange the better. Dogs in orange hats, and sunglasses. If it's orange, whack it on. Hallelujah! In fact, you kind of stand out if you don't look a bit orange-crazy.

Oh my lucky constellations! A fortune-teller!

'Carlijn, I'm coming back here to see what she does.' I check the landmarks.

We set up our stall, then I dash back and watch the fortune-teller from the other side of the crowded street. The middle-aged woman – somehow she looks like a teacher – is arranging things on a kids' mat with a hopscotch pattern. She puts out a buddha's head, books on Yin and Yang, long cushions with tassels on the end, other cushions with strange writing, and two small chunky books, *JA* and *NEE*, and now her sign, which is in English. Maybe foreigners want to know their future more than locals.

Your Fortune €1

Her wig is long and curly. Orangelocks. Her orange T-shirt, under her orange and brown striped jacket, has a silver heart. She wears orange jeans and enormous dark glasses, the ones that go lighter at the bottom so you can still see the eyes a bit. She kneels on two cushions.

A young woman plomps down confidently on a cushion in front of her. I move closer. 'Do you speak English?' she asks with an American accent.

'Of course!' Orangelocks gives a big smile. 'Your name?'

'Megan.'

Orangelocks explains she can have her fortune

told by tarot cards, or by the Ja, Nee books, or by
something called the fortune box. Megan picks the
fortune box.

Orangelocks rings a little bell. Another middle-
aged woman (her sister?) in an orange jumpsuit and
a monster afro, pops out the door behind her, holding
out a delicate wooden box. *Woo*, now it's eyes-closed
chanting, with swirling-hands over the box. Big
flourish. Orangelocks opens it and offers it to Megan.

It looks like honeycomb, but it's hundreds of tiny
paper scrolls. Megan picks one out. Orangelocks
unrolls it, glances at Megan, then looks into the
distance with her head on one side and pronounces in
a mystic way, 'You have come far to learn your fortune
. . .' and other stuff which you can guess by looking at
Megan. Not rocket science. I'm disappointed.

But still, I kneel to have my fortune told. I too pick
a tiny scroll from the fortune box, and as I unroll it,
thinking about Jacob, a wave of desperate hope flows
through me, and it's not funny anymore.

Ask the way even if you know it.

'What does it mean?'

'Ask the way even if it is familiar to you,' says Orangelocks. 'Be surprised, do things freshly.'

I sit there trying to figure it out. Ask, even if in my heart of hearts I know the answer? I want so badly to know what to do. I don't *know* in my heart of hearts.

Orangelocks doesn't laugh at my bewildered face. She says kindly, 'Be there in the moment. Be young. Be curious. Do things for the first time, although you already do it a dozen times.'

I don't understand. 'Am I asking the way now?'

'Yes, *mijn beste*. You have a problem,' she says gently, 'and you are the only one who can solve it.'

I know that. I'm afraid I will cry. 'Should I tell?'

Another woman wants her fortune told but Orangelocks asks her to wait.

'Don't worry.' She pats my hand, and hers is warm. 'What is past is past. You will know when the time comes.'

Feeling stupid and miserable and sorry for myself I slowly weave my way back to our stall. Two people are strolling towards me, and the one with a cool walk catches my attention. This person is immaculate, in a black hat and an orange jacket so sharp and perfect they could be a character from a comic. Then I look at the face and I say to myself I *know* that face, and the person looks at me as if to say I *know* that face, then they put their hands up to their face and on every finger is a ring and on every ring is an opal, and the person says, 'Computer Girl!' and I say, 'My saviour!' and we laugh like crazy.

'Did you get home okay?' asks Beads.

'Yes, fine. How *amazing*! I'm so glad to see you because I wanted to say thank you again for saving me.'

'Hey, I'm coming to Australia next year, so you better get your opals ready.'

'No worries. You must visit us.' I had a pen but no paper, so I write *Henni* and my email address on their palm. 'Our street will have a party for you!'

'Ooo I am definitely gonna be there,' and Beads gives that excited little shimmy-shimmy except without the glitter.

They pat the fur. 'Why do you have the animal?'

'I'm the Dutch Queen Wilhelmina back in World War Two, telling fortunes. What are you doing today?'

'Looking for jewels.'

Then a woman wants to take a photo of us together. We must have looked pretty crazy because some others do too.

'I must catch up to my friend,' Beads says.

'I must get back to my people,' I say.

Beads points at me. 'I will see *you* in Australia!'

'What happened?' asks Carlijn.

'The fortune-telling was disappointing, but remember the amazing person who saved me that night of the computer chase? I saw them! I saw Beads!'

A kid a bit older than me is selling newspapers, yelling, 'News! News! News! Buy stuff. News News News! More bad news. *Warpzegeins! Pirjaan aan ronderkinderee! Honfk jonk!* Floods. Crocodiles. Murder. Buy more stuff. News News News! Kids trapped. Earthquake. *Op schrij haarringo scheem jonk!* Buy stuff. Gunfight. Gorilla. Attacks. News News News! Buy more stuff.' And just near us, at an open second-floor window, an old guy dances in his trousers and singlet, flinging his arms wide as if he's dancing with everybody in the street.

'He's a brain surgeon,' says Carlijn.

'*Really?*'

'Probably. Come on, Queen Wilhelmina!' goes Carlijn.

Meeting Beads makes me bold. I've never done

fortune-telling before, and my tarot pack has cards missing. I don't know what they mean anyway, but I'll give it a shot. Okay.

We set the box up with the sign and the customer's stool, and I put on the hat and glasses. Carlijn adjusts me and laughs like mad, and starts yelling, 'Fortunes! Fortunes! Have your fortune told in English by Queen Wilhelmina for two euros.'

'Carlijn, that's too much!'

'Very good fortune three euros, to know the future in English, and other things in Dutch extra for *free!*'

What's this Dutch extras business? A spotty guy with a dragon tattoo is watching us.

'Will I get the girl I love?'

Of course I want to say yes, but this guy is a bit smelly. I hesitate.

'Guaranteed. Completely guaranteed,' says Carlijn, and he sits down on the stool and gives her two euros.

I deal the first card. It's a knight in armour, with a pale face. In Queen Wilhelmina's voice I say, '*Strength!* You must be determined, yet when you take off your armour be your sweetest-smelling self. You will go on a journey...' I was off, and I had only a little moment of panic after about five minutes because I don't know how to end it, so I just said, 'The card is fading now,' which was ridiculous but he didn't seem unhappy.

The tarot pack fires my imagination. I start to see more in the pictures, and in the people who sit down. I'm very pleased when I predict romance for a girl and her boyfriend turns up and gives her a big smoochy kiss! A crowd gathers. I'm getting into this fortune-telling biz.

'All your future, guaranteed by law,' yells Carlijn. 'All true as the day is long, and the sea is deep and the mountains are high.' Jeetje mina, what next? Then Carlijn's singing 'River Deep, Mountain High' with someone, a boy's voice, and I turn around and it's Eyebrow Boy! He's all in black except for tatty orange feather wings flopping from his shoulders and orange devil horns in his curly black hair. He looks ragged and cool.

I introduce him to Carlijn, but he still won't say his name. He asks the price of every single thing on our stall, and starts selling it and woohoo!! He's got selling charisma! He came from Noord on the ferry where the passengers are dancing to music. He gives a demo. He's a good dancer. We have pancakes from the girls opposite, who are cooking them on the second floor and lowering them down in baskets.

Carlijn goes for a wander, and comes flying back.

'Henni! Quick! *Come!*'

We leave Eyebrow Boy in charge while we dash to a crowd around some organ music. We wriggle to the front.

I'll explain this, so you know how clever it is. In the Netherlands there are decorated wooden street organs, where the organ grinder turns the handle, and the organ plays, and carved ornamental figures tap bells in time to the music. It's a very romantic music-boxy thing. Well, this is what we see!

Hartog is squashed sideways in the barrow of
Hunter's cargo bike, in a frame roughly painted like an
organ. Hartog is an expressionless wooden figure in a
curly wig, and with mechanical movements he dings
a little bell in time with the music. Hunter turns the
organ handle, holding the music player in the other.
He sees us and cranks the handle faster, making Hartog
ding the bell like crazy. It is so *clever*! Carlijn grabs
the cap they have lying on the ground for money and
shoves it under people's noses, and the coins jingle in.

Back to the future.

My next fortune-telling customer is an old woman
who doesn't want her fortune told, she wants to give
Queen Wilhelmina a piece of her mind.

'You shouldn't have gone to England in the war! You
should have stayed with your people!'

In my best Wilhelmina voice I reply, 'The Nazis
would have parked me in a farmhouse under guard,
and I would have been worse than useless, a hostage.
In London with the Dutch government-in-exile...'

Then, amazingly, a young woman leaps in. 'They
kept the oil coming from Indonesia to the Allies. Learn
your history, *mevrouw*!'

'I know my history, *jonge dame*! Know why she left?
Class and privilege. They always get safe.'

I let them argue. She's paid for an argument.

'My turn to roam,' I say to Carlijn.

The canals are packed with boats. Each boat is a drinking party, grooving to music, shouting conversations. There are Red Cross people at main corners, but I haven't seen any police. Probably so much dodgy stuff going on they don't bother.

On a stall near Westerkerk I find a little brass pig with a leg missing. I pluck up some courage and try my Dutch.

'*Hoeveel kost het?*' (How much does it cost?)

'*Drie.*' (three)

'*Vier.*' (four) Oh gosh, I'm going up! Everyone is laughing.

'Drie.'

I say 'Vier' boldly this time. It's funny.

A boy at the next stall says, '*Twee.*' (two) He laughs and chants, 'Twee! Twee! Twee!'

'Oke, twee,' says the guy, acting devastated, as he hands me the pig.

I'm busting to go to the toilet. There's a house with a sign: *Toilet €1*. I'm happy to pay! It's a tiny space under the stairs where I sit with my knees touching the door, and my head on one side because there's not enough room to sit up straight. Would we rent out a toilet to strangers back home? Phew, that's better!

There's another fortune-teller, basing her predictions on animal auras, but she's just plain straight-out wacky.

I come to a stall that's totally different. The seller is an old man in a thick worn coat, tall and stooped, with one eye half closed. He's made no effort to arrange his stall. It's a shambles of picked-over junk, dinted, rusty, cracked, falling out of piles of torn boxes, the opposite to the lively, cheerful stuff going on around him, but in this jumble I find something that stops me in my tracks. It's the saddest thing.

'Do you know what it is?' the old man asks.

'It's a home-made shoe for a little kid.'

'Ja, I think the wood is from a boat.'

'My grandmother told me how terrible it was in the war.'

He wraps the shoe in crumpled newspaper. 'What will you do with it?'

'Remember my grandmother.'

He hands it to me. He hasn't even said a price.

He tips his head to one side. 'Are you Queen Wilhelmina?'

I say, 'I hope that many countrymen, wherever they are, will be loyal listeners of the patriotic thoughts that will reach them via this long road.'

'Very good, ja, and the fox fur and the hat.' He nods seriously. 'Well, you better take these too.'

He rummages around in a pile of old papers. After a search he finds what he was looking for and hands it to me.

'Coupons! What can I buy with them?'

'Clothing. Nobody knows what coupons are now.'

We talk about rationing, and the Hongerwinter. He's a gentle quiet old soul like Jacob, but sad. Suddenly I ask him, 'If, tomorrow, someone told you that you were adopted, would you be glad to know that?'

He isn't alarmed by the question. 'No, I wouldn't

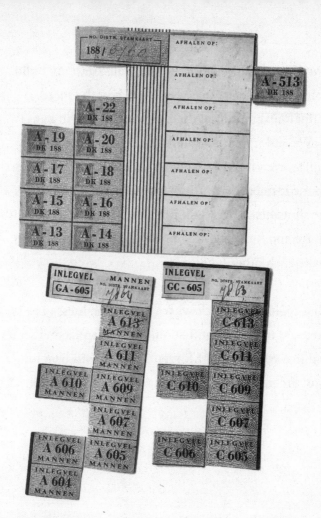

want to know. I'm too old for disturbing news. I have lived my life.'

He looks so sad on this happy day. We chat a bit more. I pay him eight euros, which seems okay, then I head back to Car + Hen. I've been away for ages.

I tell more fortunes, but I've lost the spark, so I

give Wilhelmina's speech a few times, into my radio orange. A lot of people want to talk with Queen Wilhelmina and have their photo taken with her.

We end up with a small pile of junk that nobody wants, even if we pay them to take it away. We swap phone numbers with Eyebrow Boy, who still refuses to tell us his name. I ask him if he's really friends with Myrte and he says only on Tuesdays. He and Carlijn make each other laugh.

That night, I'm struck with a sudden sadness. The tired old man is right. I should just keep Jacob's secret and live with it until I forget it, which will be a long long time. Moeder's coat was telling me to keep it. Oh, it's hard.

Tuesday 28 April

TWO MEN WENT TO MOW

This morning Hyacint said, 'My scissors are missing. Henni, where have you taken my scissors?' Well, that was news to me, but it didn't feel like a black mark, more a kind of sad grey one.

King's Day is cleaned up. The coat is back in the wardrobe. The streets are open for business and the traffic is normal, except us bike riders are watching out for broken glass. Carlijn said there are always punctures after King's Day. Some people don't ride their bikes for a few days.

Today I'm going with Dirk the Bear to the Amsterdam City Hall. He is most particular about showing me something. Tonight there's a family dinner at Jacob and Floor's to talk about Willa's funeral, and me going home. Hunter might come later. I hope so.

Riding behind Dirk was like riding behind a grizzly bear with pedalling legs. How could that bike hold such a heavy man?

Amsterdam City Hall wasn't a crusty old building, it was modern, with posters for the opera and ballet. What did he want to show me? We walked down long corridors and Dirk translated signs about official things like marriage, birth and death certificates.

'Was Roos still Dutch?' he asked.

'Yes, but also Australian.'

We came to a long 3D mural, a cross-section of the city. It was clever and showed clearly the long piles the buildings rested on, going down into the different strata of sand.

Dirk stood in front of me like a tour guide.

'Henni, you know the word *nether* means low,' (I didn't, but I nodded) 'and this country is the Netherlands, which means lowlands,' (another nod)

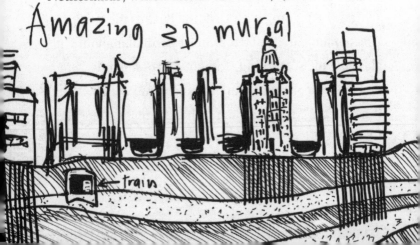

Amazing 3D mural

← train

'so the Dutch is always struggling against the water.

'My friend Joanne lives in Lisse, the centre of the tulip fields, and one of the lowest parts of the Netherlands. In her house there is a monitoring station where the water authorities check the level of the ground water. The trapdoor is right behind the front door in her hall. Ja, when you step into her house, your first step is onto the trapdoor.'

'If you lift the trapdoor, what do you see?'

'Water.'

'Wow! Dirk, I found a picture of floodwater pouring into a house with people in it, like a nightmare. Do you worry because you are living lower than the sea?'

'No, I don't have a boat in my kitchen. It would take something very very catastrophic. In the Netherlands the water authorities are powerful. They can even tell the army what to do. If the water level is

about water levels

airport   canal   dyke   Sea

hard sand

rising too much, they pump the water from the polders into the sea, to keep the water at the right level.

'When I build something I am carefully measuring the right level to construct the building, so I must know the right water level. We have the Normal Amsterdam Level, the city's official level, we call it the NAP. And here it is.' He pointed to a tall glass column like a huge rain gauge going up through the ceiling. 'And this is the exact zero level.'

I sort of understood. Was this what he wanted to tell me?

We were blocking the way of some people pushing trolleys of stuff for an exhibition, so we moved into a corridor at the side. Dirk still wanted to tell me something.

'Henni, I have spent my life building things, getting the level straight and right.' Then he got serious, not that you'd ever call him light-hearted in a million years. He stood in front of me, with his hands behind his back like a kid in grade three who's been asked to thank the guest for visiting the class.

'The weekend after you leave, Jacob, Bram and me, we will go to Vlissingen where the big boats come in. They have been many times, and this time I will go too.'

He looked down at his feet, then back up.

'Henni, maybe someone in my family already has done this, but I will do it for myself, and the family again. Thank you for bringing Willa. Your compass for what is right is better than ours. And your fresh interference has put us on a good course again. I know it was hard for you. I thank you. Really.'

He had thought about the words, and his expression was so sincere, and his desire to thank me so unexpected, that in a sudden rush I was on the brink of tears.

Then he put his hand on my shoulder and gave me a solemn kiss on the top of my head. It was like a ceremony.

'Thank you, Dirk. I'm happy for the van Veens and myself.'

Then he smiled and we both felt ridiculous.

I said, 'I feel like singing.'

'Sing, then.'

I launched into *One man went to mow, went to mow a meadow, One man and his dog, went to mow a meadow*, which really *was* ridiculous, but Dirk listened.

'Sing it again,' he said.

He joined in with *went to mow a meadow*, and he had a beautiful deep bear voice, and it sounded great in that corridor, and when we got to three men he sang it all with me.

When we got up to seven men he said, 'Is that enough mowing? I would like some coffee.'

Jeetje mina, crazy eh?

Strong furniture
Strong barges
Strong trucks
Strong bikes
Heavy bike chains
Tall parents
lift their kids off their bikes like cranes

I can make things
I can live in a small space
I can climb stairs
I can pump water
I can make tunnels through wet sand
but just in case,
I can swim with my clothes on
and
I can speak your language

Wednesday 29 April

O MIJN GOD!

Out the picture-book window the sky was gloomy.
Only a couple of days till I go home. I had nothing
to do after breakfast so I decided to write whatever
popped into my head.

It was cold. I piled on all my warm layers and
grabbed the belt to bind them. It was flopped over the
chest of drawers and I didn't notice that the buckle
was caught by the corner of the big faded ghost-
picture. I gave the belt a yank, and the fabric on top
of the chest of drawers slipped and the heavy frame
slid forward, pushing everything in front of it. In slow
motion my Dutch still life toppled over the front of
the chest of drawers. Trying to stop the avalanche
I lunged and knocked the picture sideways. With a
mighty *CRASH!* it hit the floor on its corner and the
frame split apart, spraying glass everywhere, along
with all the other smashed stuff.

O mijn God! Jeetje mina! What have I *done*? I am as careless as Hyacint says. Someone would be here in a flash. *Oh Lordy Lordy! I've really wrecked the shipwreck now.*

But nobody came.

I felt fragile. I sat on my bed miserable as all hell. The mess was a big fat metaphor. Me in the Netherlands. I wished I was home. I didn't cry, I just felt crushed and mighty sorry for myself.

I remembered that Hyacint wanted to sell all this stuff on King's Day, which made me feel a bit better, but Wendelien liked that carved wooden frame. Too bad about it now.

As I lifted up a large splintered edge, a corner of something slipped back under the paper that was glued to the board behind the picture. I fumbled but I just poked it back in. I tried to get it out with the bookmark from my diary, but that didn't work either.

Look, I told myself, Hyacint wanted to chuck this picture out, and it's shoved up here in the attic, and it sure ain't a priceless treasure now.

I ripped the paper off the bottom of the board and tipped it sideways. A thin yellowed envelope slid out. No writing. The paper was flimsy, and the glue was unlicked and cracked. It felt brittle in my hand.

In the envelope I found a black-and-white photo, very small, but clear: a couple with their baby, the adoring mother gazing down at the baby she cradled in her arms. On the back of the photo there were names written faintly in pencil. I couldn't read them. Matius? and Sara…Sara…Jacob…

Jacob.

I just looked and looked at it. The way she gazed at her baby.

I put the photo in the envelope on the floor, left everything as it was, and slowly, deliberately went down the stairs to the ground floor, out the front door, round to the corner door and knocked.

'Would you come to the attic, please?'

Maybe it was my serious voice, but Jacob called out to Floor, swung on his coat, grabbed his keys and trudged behind me up the stairs.

'Oh, a little crash,' he said, unconcerned by the chaos and glass everywhere.

I handed him the envelope.

He opened it, and took out the photo.

'Looks like the nineteen forties.' He looked at it closely. 'Oh, doesn't she love her baby.'

Then he turned the photo over and read the names. He peered at them. The seconds stretched and stretched. He looked out the window then back to the photo.

'Is it me?'

I nodded, trying not to cry.

Jacob stepped through the wreckage to the chair. He sat and studied the photo. He put it on his knee, and leaned back with his hands behind his head. He picked up the photo again. His life was shifting. Could you take in something so big that fast?

'Where did you find it? Did Willa give you this? My parents? Who are they?'

'Willa told me what happened in the war, how her family hid their friends, and they were taken. It was the saddest thing I've ever heard.'

I started to sob, which was not how I wanted to be, I was not the one whose life had changed, but I couldn't stop myself. I got up and put my arm around his shoulders.

Jacob pulled a big handkerchief from his pocket and I snivelled into it.

'How can people be like that? How can they do that to each other?' Then he took the handkerchief from me and blew his own nose. The two of us, there in the attic, sharing a handkerchief, feeling so sad.

'Who am I?' He sat, still staring at the photo, only

moving with his breathing, then he sort of came back in focus. He gave a huge sigh, scratched his head and, sliding his hands over his knees, sat forward.

'Is there anything else behind the painting, Henni?'

'I think there is.'

We peeled the paper off the old cardboard and remaining corner of the frame. Wrapped in yellowed newspaper was a small splodgy oil painting about the size of a shoebox lid.

'Slapdash,' I said.

'Slapdash,' Jacob echoed.

'Maybe a kid did it.'

'Who'd give a kid oil paints, especially in my day?'

'Nice colours. Do you think it's meant to be anything?'

'Put it over by the door. Turn it up the other way.'

We sat back and looked at the painting.

'It's looking out a window into a garden.'

'The colours are wild. The trees are red!'

'What do you think about that blue blob in the corner?'

'A *dog*!' we said in unison.

'We need to walk,' said Jacob. 'Put your gloves on. It's cold. Leave this mess. We'll go to Westerpark. We need the wind.'

Trouw

VRIJ !

WE zijn vrij.

Waar we om gebeden hebben, waar we voor gestreden hebben, waar we op gehoopt hebben, waar we aan gewanhoopt hebben, maar waar we door alle duisternis en ellende heen toch steeds aan geloofd hebben, dat is werkelijkheid geworden.

We zijn vrij!

De Duitscher is weg.

De heerscher van gisteren is geworden wat beter bij hem past, wat beter voor hem is, de overwonnene van vandaag.

De spanning is weg.

De vrees is weg.

De terreur is weg.

Het onrecht wijkt.

Vrijheid, dat is vandaag voor ons in de allereerste plaats: opluchting.

De loodzware last van vijf jaren bezetting, vijf jaren roof, vijf jaren cultuurafbraak, vijf jaren onschuldig vergoten bloed, vijf jaren verbeten, voortdurenden strijd, is van ons weggenomen.

Vrijheid, dat is vandaag, dat dit alles anders is, dat het niet meer zoo gaat als gisteren en eergisteren.

Vrijheid, dat is vandaag geen zwaar geladen begrip, geen politiek probleem, dat te moeten oplossen, geen taak, die ons op de schouders gelegd wordt.

Vrijheid is vandaag, dat we weer menschen zijn, gewone menschen, die zichzelf mogen zijn, niet meer geremd door wat ons vijf jaren lang in een keurslijf wrong, schichtig deed zijn en ons den weg van bloedig verzet opjoeg.

Vrijheid, dat is, dat Nederland weer Nederland is en niet langer meer "de bezette Nederlandsche …"

Die twee verdragen elkaar. Daarom zullen wij dien rouw niet wegdrukken, ook vandaag niet. De vrijheid, onze vreugde, is duur gekocht.

Zoo gedenken wij in dankbaarheid allen, die vielen, de het slachtoffer werden van den oorlog.

En zeer in het bijzonder al die onbekende kameraden, bekend en onbekend, die in den vrijheidsstrijd bewust hun leven gaven.

Aan ons oog trekken voorbij de mannen en vrouwen van de vuurpelotons, de dooden uit de …

> Looft, gij volken, onzen God, en laat hooren de stem Zijns roems.
> Die onze zielen in het leven stelt en niet toelaat, dat onze voet wankele.
> Want Gij hebt ons beproefd, o God! Gij hebt ons gelouterd, gelijk men het zilver loutert.
> Gij hadt ons gebracht in het net; Gij hadt eenen engen band om onze lenden gelegd.
> Gij hadt den mensch op ons hoofd doen rijden; wij waren in het vuur en in het water gekomen; maar Gij hebt ons uitgevoerd in eene overvloeiende verversching.
> Ik zal met brandoffers in Uw huis gaan; ik zal U mijne geloften betalen.
> Die mijne lippen hebben geuit en mijn mond heeft uitgesproken, als mij bange was.
> Psalm 66 : 8 tot 14.

… concentratiekampen en gevangenissen, al de repres…
… in stad en land.

… de toekomst heeft opnieuw een … doodweekten bodem.

… in het een gave, vandaag mag … Maar morgen is het een opgave.

En het zal spoedig morgen zijn. Eigenlijk is het dat vandaag al.

Wat dan?

Wij staan met onze vrijheid in een naakt land.

Maak er wat van. Maak er wat moois van. Het oude is voorbij gegaan. Ook het oude van voor 1940.

Maak er nu wat beters van. Trek de les uit het verleden. We staan daar nu cynisch tegenover. We hebben er afstand van moeten doen en er nu ook afstand van genomen.

We zien er het goede van, het vertrouwde, het gezellige.

Maar ook het slechte, het scheve, het zondige.

Een nieuwe tijd wacht ons. We gaan aan den slag. Er moet nieuws gebouwd worden.

Er zal een nieuwe Nederland uit den grond gestampt moeten worden. Huizen, fabrieken, verkeersmiddelen enz.

Er zal van ons uitgescheurde, ontwrichte en bloedende volk een nieuwe samenleving, een betere samenleving dan voorheen moeten worden …

Dat is de taak der vrijheid.

Die opbouw moet degelijk en rechtvaardig zijn. Geen revolutiebouw.

De oud-vaderlandsche soliditeit moet zich paren aan een door lijden gelouterd en door strijd gestaald rechtsbesef.

Dan gaan wij naar een Nederlandsche maatschappij, waarin sociale gerechtigheid heerscht.

Dat is de weg der vrijheid.

Die weg der vrijheid zal moeilijk zijn.

Er zullen vele materieele belemmeringen zijn. Geen geld, geen goederen, geen menschen op de goede plaatsen.

Dat alles is te overwinnen en betrekkelijk gemakkelijk.

Het moeilijkste van den weg der vrijheid zal de overwinning aan onszelf, zal de zelfverloochening zijn.

De weg der vrijheid is de weg van het niet zoeken van ons eigen belang en eigen eer en het allereerst handhaven van eigen posities.

Een ieder zie niet op het zijne, maar op hetgeen des anderen is.

De weg der vrijheid is de weg van het Evangelie.

Alleen als Nederland, als de Nederlanden zich met hand en hoofd en hart, gevonden geven aan den Heere Jezus Christus, die de eenige levensvernieuwer is, en doen wat Hij van ons vraagt …

Almachtigen God … … zuiverder doen dan met de woorden van den zes en zestigsten psalm?

Daar danken wij vervolgens onze bondgenooten voor. In de allereerste plaats Engeland, dat niet versaagde, toen in den herfst van 1940 alles verloren scheen, en daarnaast ook de Vereenigde Staten en Rusland.

Vrij zijn we vandaag en dankbaarheid vervult ons hart.

De vrijheidsvreugde kan geen feestroes zijn. Naast de vrijheidsvreugde is er rouw in ons hart …

IN WILLA'S SHOES

Today was Willa's funeral, a small, sad event. They did lift Willa out the window, and the fire brigade ladder took her to the ground. The service was very matter-of-fact. My speech was about Willa in Stella Street and how she looked after us kids, and I read out the emails they'd sent from home. There was tea and coffee and the cakes were good.

Jacob said, 'When Willa left for Australia she deserted us. She wanted us to follow her when we were older, but it didn't work out that way.'

Lodewijk brought flowers. He said Willa was beautiful when she was young and wanted to be an actress. She could have been, he said. Floor took the flowers, for Hyacint.

I saw Hunter put his arm around Jacob, who turned towards him and they hugged, and I nearly cried remembering the hugs when we first arrived.

Hunter wanted to talk to me. 'I'm sorry I never met Roos. I heard about her all my life.' He was sombre. Even though they'd never met, Willa had melted some of Hunter's cool. 'Roos always went her own way. I admire that. *Potverdomme*! I was so close to meeting her.'

'She was like you,' I said. 'If she wanted to do something she'd find a way to do it.'

'Can't find a way this time.' His long face was regretful.

'Hunter, do you know anything about apartments being returned to the Jews after the war?'

He shook his head. 'I will find out.'

Then Lodewijk appeared.

'Ah, Lodewijk, this is Hunter, Willa's nephew. He had questions he was going to ask Willa about the wartime. You remember the war clearly, Lodewijk, will you answer them?'

I left them digging into Lodewijk's childhood and went to find Jacob.

'Henni, tonight, will you please tell my family what you told me? I will bring the handkerchiefs.'

Oh gosh. Big heavy sighs. Big heavy earth-moving sighs.

It was after dinner in Hyacint's apartment that evening that Jacob called the family to attention.

'I've asked Henni to answer some questions. Sit here, Henni, so everyone can see you.'

Not sure where to begin, I described Willa's pestering in Stella Street, and they listened and it unfolded from there. I told them everything I knew.

They got a magnifying glass and peered at the photo. They found the windowsill where the photo was taken. They talked about the shock from every angle. And Jacob, whose life had changed dramatically, was sort of dealing with it as if it was someone else it had happened to.

'Did anyone think Jacob was adopted?'

Hyacint said she was sure *she* was adopted.

'Did anybody ever say anything to him?'

'A lot of funny things happened to families in the war.'

'Did you know the story about your fever?'

'No.'

'Did you ever think you might be adopted?'

'Well, to tell the truth, I always thought our family was strange.'

Wendelien laughed. 'You're strange, but I'm all right.'

'No, seriously,' said Jacob, 'when I was a kid I imagined a whole other life.'

'Is that why we have those adventure books on the bottom shelf of the bookcase?' said Floor.

'Well, just look at my hands,' said Jaocb. 'They're different.'

They compared hands. They remembered Willa's hands, strong and capable. Hyacint's hands are pale but they are work-hands too. Jacob's fingers are longer. I was sorry Hunter wasn't there, his hands are beautiful. They fly over the computer keys.

And so we talked.

It was funny because everything had changed but nothing had changed.

'How do we know these aren't false memories?' said Dirk the Bear.

'Yes, I thought about that,' I said. 'It was a long long time ago, but all my life we trusted Willa, and the truth and the facts were always important to her. I often returned her library books and they were mostly about politics and serious stuff. Maybe she made up stories when she was a kid, but she never made up stories in Stella Street.'

Wendelien said, 'Why would she make up Jacob's story?'

Hyacint said, 'What if Sara is holding me? They were all living together.'

'No,' said Wendelien, 'the names are on the back. It's a portrait, and the painting was hidden in the same place. The two pieces belong together.'

Silence.

Floor asked, 'Henni, what if you didn't find the photo?'

'Willa told me about Jacob the night before she died, and I promised I wouldn't tell. I hoped King's Day would give me a sign... I wore Moeder's coat...'

'I need time to think about this,' said Jacob, standing up. 'Anyone want a jenever?'

Instead of a *jenever* (which is a strong drink) they had coffee with Hyacint's *kletskoppen* (my favourite biscuits, crunchy with peanuts), and looked at the painting, which was a lot easier than the photo. Nobody knew anything about it, so it remained a mystery, but it seemed fair to think it was the blue dog. Wendelien, Jacob and I liked it, Floor thought the colours were too loud, Dirk thought it was childish.

I told them about the pram. How in the war Moeder loaded bundles of Resistance leaflets into the false bottom of the pram, squashed Hyacint and Jacob on top, and sent Willa off to deliver them. And once, a pistol. How terrified Willa was, with only her wits and Hyacint's piercing cry to protect her. How Moeder was always tired and angry. How in the Hongerwinter Moeder pushed the pram into the country to ask the farmers for food, leaving Willa with the babies, afraid her mother would never return.

Dirk said, 'Henni, I have a question for you. Willa was round your age. What do you think of Moeder expecting her to do those things?'

I didn't want to answer.

'Tell me, Henni, what do you think?'

I stared at my feet. 'I think it was cruel, but Willa always said it was a different time...so I'm not sure I can judge.'

'I think her anger was more than her love for Willa,' said Dirk.

'Moeder was doing anything she could against the Germans,' said Jacob. 'Sara was Moeder's best friend, remember.'

'I don't think we can put ourselves in their shoes,' said Wendelien.

'Moeder found Willa some shoes, and if she wore two pairs of socks they fitted,' I added.

———

'Do you want to move down into Roos' room?'
Hyacint asked me. O mijn God, *no*.

Last two nights op mijn zolder.

On Saturday Dirk the Bear will carry my case down
at nine o'clock in the morning, then Jacob will take
me to the airport. Wendelien and Eric said goodbye.
They're leaving on their honeymoon tomorrow.

Eric and Dirk have never been to the Resistance
Museum.

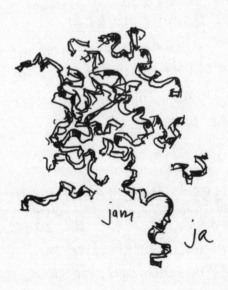

Willa said she was two-in-one

We only knew what we were told
  saw what we were allowed to see
  and the less the better.
I didn't know what I was doing half the time
but I always felt guilty
  and scared.
Things were unpredictable
People were disposable.
They could vanish.

    And me?
How could I be invisible with two babies?
Women wanted to look at them.
Jacob's gaunt little head.
  Honestly his eyes were half his face
peering out from under his blue knitted hat.
And china-doll Hyacint, alert and coy
  in her orange bonnet.

    And me?
Oh yes! That jaunty girl.
I played the bold-as-brass big sister
but inside the terrified me
  stepping carefully, watching out.
But instinctively I opened the door
to a familiar voice.

GOODBYE TASMAN

I wasn't a guide dog anymore, sadly, my time was my own.

'I would like to take you to our art gallery, the Rijksmuseum,' said Jacob, 'to see in real life the "ghost picture", as you call it, that hid my story.'

As we pedalled along side by side, Jacob said, 'that print in its fancy frame hung in my parents' room for years till the light stole the image. You will be amazed, Henni.'

We rode across a park towards a grand palace I'd ridden past lots of times on the canal side. With a flock of other riders we pedalled straight through the centre archway.

Into a magnificent stone passage we rode; stone pillars holding up a ceiling of arches, music from a string quartet echoing around, and through huge glass walls you could look down into the art gallery.

We glided through. Oh, my goodness, it was *beautiful*! Jeetje, this ride was a dream. And anybody is free to enjoy it going to work, or while they're out shopping, or just for fun if they please! It sure pleased me, and I wanted to ride through it again and again, but Jacob chained up, so I did too.

Now the Rembrandt painting. In a word. E*nor*mous! Breathtaking. Dark. Stagey. Historic.

'Gosh, is this *really* the picture?'

'Yes,' said Jacob with a smile. 'What's happening in it, Henni?'

I studied the characters. 'Well…it's…about a play, and some important actors should be rehearsing a battle scene, but the director, a conceited Spaniard, is hopeless and no one knows what to do. A troupe of wandering performers have just arrived in town and one of them, a golden girl, scuttles through unnoticed, her pet hen dangling from her belt, but she knows how to create a ruckus and . . . in a moment she will let loose her hen, and the troubadours will come flying in.'

Jacob laughed. 'That would be something to see! It's called *De Nachtwacht*, or *The Night Watch*. It's a portrait of important men.'

'You're right, Jacob, I *am* amazed, but I don't like it much.'

'Well,' said Jacob, 'let's find something you do like.'

We found a wintery scene of a whole town of ice skaters on a frozen canal. It reminded me of Willa and Lodewijk's skating stories. It must have been fun. Yes, that painting was my favourite.

Just before we left, Jacob hunted through the prints in the shop and found the ice skaters for me. *The Night Watch* was out of stock.

After lunch I packed my trusty familiar clothes. Soon they can all have a good flap on the clothesline at home, instead of hanging limply off drying racks in the lounge. Boy I'll be glad when I don't need to pile on so many layers. I chose a pair of mittens and a pair of gloves from my collected collection. *The Diary of Anne Frank* went in the case. I didn't finish it. I never saw the Anne Frank house either. The queue was always too long, and it was expensive. I was *living* in an Anne Frank house. I can't read her story now. Another time.

Carefully I wrapped my souvenirs in the fabric for Maggs, plus the lamp, the little donkey and my presents. I'm going home! I'm so happy. Jeetje mina, if I stayed any longer I might become a *tourist*!

I lugged the vacuum cleaner op mijn zolder, and

sucked up more bits of picture frame and glass.
I arranged the double-wrecked shipwreck on the
chest of drawers, doing my best to leave the part of
mijn zolder that I inhabited shipshape. My mood kept
changing – one minute I was happy and the next I was
sitting at the table feeling mournful. I wished Carlijn
was there but she was at school. I will be too, soon.

———

My last ride – to the Cigar Factory to deliver Tasman.
What did that fortune-teller lady say? 'Do things as if
you do them for the first time.' How scared I was on
that first ride.

Carlijn came straight to the Cigar Factory from
school. We were in Hunter's room. All the paint
had been cleaned off the windows, which made an
amazing difference. It was a big open space now, not
as nice as Hartog's, but with loads of room to store
Hunter's findings. Plus with a strong door. Hunter and
Hartog were taking measurements to make shelves out
of some planks Hartog had found.

Hunter tossed me a notebook. 'Henni, you are a
writer, write the measurements.'

They were in a lazy crazy mood, which was
unusual, and fun to be around. They are surprising,

those guys. I'll never forget them on King's Day.

'Hoogte, twee metres,' said Hunter.

I guessed 'height', because Hartog was standing on a chair with the tape measure dangling down.

'Carlijn, *hold* it. I want them real big,' said Hunter, standing back by the windows. 'Show me drie metres. Hey Carlijn, hold it straight.'

'How long are you in Amsterdam, Henni?' asked Hartog.

'A month.'

'She goes home tomorrow,' said Carlijn.

'Hey, that went quick,' said Hunter.

'Ja, but it feels like two months at least.'

'Will you have to catch up schoolwork?'

I pulled a grim face.

'How did you get out of school?' Hunter asked.

'My parents asked the principal, and she said it was okay.'

'Did they give you work to do while you were away?'

I nodded.

'Have you done it?'

'Nee.'

Hunter grinned. 'In the Netherlands parents are fined a hundred euros for every day the kid misses school. It's the law.'

'Jeetje, that's harsh!'

'School,' he snorted. 'I have exams, and soon I'm done.'

Well this was news. He must be under eighteen because I know you have to be over eighteen to leave school, or sixteen if you're in another sort of school. He's older than sixteen.

'Why are they so fierce here, about kids going to school?'

Hartog stepped down from the chair. 'Because this place depends on our brains being educated. We got to be clever, Henni. Not like Australia. We can't dig stuff out of the ground, and pour orange juice for tourists.'

I wanted to argue with that but Hunter said, 'Now we measure the planks.'

'How long are the planks? Breedte, two planks wide?'

'Is *breedte* width?'

'Jaaaaaaaaaaaa, real wide like Australia.'

'In Australia is it expensive to shop at the supermarket?' asked Hunter.

'Nee, the Netherlands is more expensive.'

'You can live on eggs,' said Carlijn, 'and bananas are nutritious.'

'Henni, what was the most difficult thing for you in Amsterdam?' said Hunter.

'Willa. Willa's secret, and…' I didn't look at him, 'Jacob not trusting me. Getting lost. My stupid phone. The cold. Ja, locking up my bike in the cold.'

'How do you buy a car in Australia?' said Hartog. 'Do you need a special driver's licence?'

'I don't know. Are you going to visit us? Oh *wow*!' I could see them climbing out of a petrol-guzzling bomb, all covered in dust, with everyone in Stella Street crowding round. I grinned just thinking about it.

'I will come too,' said Carlijn. 'She's *my* friend.'

Hartog produced a paper bag from behind the door. (I thought there was a nice smell.)

I put down the notebook. 'Yum, a snack!'

'A snake?'

'Did you say snake?'

'Is that what you eat in Australia?'

'A *snack*.'

'Jaaa, we know what a snake is.'

'Okay, in the interests of international relationships, a snake.'

Anyway, it was fresh *poffertjes*, puffy little round pancakes, which was funny because when I first heard *poffertjes* I thought it was 'poor features', which I thought was weird because they were delicious.

I gave Hunter the keys for Tasman, then those two tall funny Dutch guys saluted me like an army general. We shook hands in a businesslike way,

'Doei doei Hunter and Hartog. See you in Stella Street.'

Last closing of the big wooden door.

'Doei doei antikrakers. Carlijn, can you give me a dink home?'

'What?'

'A ride on the back of your bike.'

'No worries! Spring achterop.'

I spring op and we wobble off laughing.

Last ride with Carlijn.

'Doei doei Cigar Factory. Have a good life, whatever you become.'

Last ride past Vondelpark.

'Doei doei Vondelpark!'

Last ride over cobbles.

'Doei doei cobbles!'

Last tourist. *Dring dring!*

'Good riddance tourist!'

Last canal.

'Doei doei canal!'

Outside the black door in Eerste Hugo de Grootstraat I hopped off, and Carlijn propped the bike against the little bench.

'Last Henni,' she said.

'Doei doei Carlijn.'

That was a hard one. We hugged each other in a tight bear hug, in all our winter clothes, and felt the strength of each other, but Carlijn's not a person for sorrowfulness. She jumped back on her bike.

'Doei doei Henni. Doei doei. Bye bye. Bye bye Henni. Doei doei...' until the big yellow pompom had turned the corner and I couldn't hear her anymore.

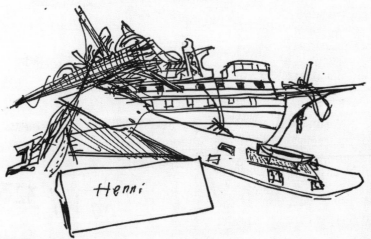

Henni

Hunter had put an envelope in my bag.

Jacob has a good life. No financial hardship or physical disability.
Time for compensation — loss of parents, money, property, insurance
— over long ago

Reward for each Jew = 7.5 guilders
Sara and Matius = 15 guilders to Cornelia and NSBer husband

Money Resistances pays to people hiding onderdujkers – ? to find out

Compulsory Star of David : 4¢ for star + clothing ration coupon
(old Dutch money 100 cents = 1 guilder)

75–80% of Jews in Netherlands murdered or suicide.
Highest rate in Europe, much more than Belgium or France

Why?
Dutch organisation. Good official list of citizens names with religion
Amsterdam map showing houses, according to religion.
SS in charge of Netherlands worse than ordinary army
No hiding places — forests mountains etc
Next door to Germany and occupied Belgium   excuses, excuses

What is a fair view of how the Dutch behave?
Truth is bent with what we want to believe   history is screwed
Present bias

Many things I'm not proud of, but this I am:
The Dutch were the only people who went on strike after first
deportation of Jews. Shops shut, factories close, they protest in the streets. . .
No other country did that. The leaders of the strike they catch and murder,
but that did happen.

06 167 323 8

I stared at the number.

No Caller ID ?!

Did he want me to call?

He gave the information like dried leaves on old newspaper. Bare facts. Why was he so blunt? I tried to nut it out. Is this how he thinks? Don't get involved with the client, get what they want, deliver it?!

I was confused, angry, sorrowful. This wasn't Mickey Mouse toys, or a pair of fancy shoes, this was *Jacob's parents*!

I will be subtle and brief.

'Hi Hunter.'

'Henni.'

'Thanks for finding that information. I thought the property deadline would be over.'

'Ja, took me a while. How is Jacob coping with the big news?'

He's flippant!

'Struggling, I would say. I wish Willa was here for him to talk to.'

'Ja, must be strange learning your parents were Jews.'

'You can't just say "Jews"! It was Sara and Matius. When you say Jews it's like this lump word. *Stamp!* Branded. Label on. Sara was funny lovable Sara, Willa's friend, her mother's *best* friend. She was a character, she made their lives bright. Oh I'm sorry, but they were real people.'

    silence

'Yeah well, you know about them, Henni, I don't. They aren't real to me like they are to you.'

'She was your great-grandmother, Jacob's birth mother. Your life came through her.'

    silence

'See you in Australia, Henni.'

'It's your story too, Bram.'

He didn't hang up, neither did I, for   l o n g l o n g seconds.

I hit the red button.

So much for subtle and brief.

I used to think that THEN was THEN
And **now** is **now**
And **now** is what matters
because THEN was back THEN
but **now** I know
that **now** grows out of THEN
like a plant from the soil
and you can't just weed THEN out of **now**
and when we peer at THEN
we look through **now** glasses.
And what about Yet to come?
Ja, what about Yet to come?

Quack!

> Danielle
>
> Come home now Henni

> Henni
>
> What! Danielle, did I read that right? Are you missing me?

> Danielle
>
> I'm sick of being blamed for everything

> Henni
>
> But you are the one to blame always

> Danielle
>
> well you should come home.

> Henni
>
> You sound like Dad. Actually I am ready to come home

> Zev
>
> Enjoy your last night in Amsterdam Henni

Henni

Hi Zev! Yeah, like they say in the movies 'My work here is done.' How's earthing?

Zev

Now the uni wants to study me. They are testing me: moving, being still, in sunlight, darkness, watching different things on TV.

Danielle

Sitting on the toilet.

Henni

Has she got even worse while I'm away?

Zev

That is not scientifically possible.

Danielle

What is not scientifically possible is that Zev can not be not scientifically possible.

Henni

Hahaha that's good Danielle! How's the Praying Mantis?

Danielle

I will check my famousness   506

Henni

Hey that's more than friends and relatives. Maybe you ARE going viral!

Zev

Have a good trip home Henni.

Henni

Doei doei Zev. Doei doei Danielle. See you in Stella Street.

Zev

Soon

Danielle

don't expect special treatment from me

Henni

Business as usual Nijntje

GOING HOME

Last wake-up in my doona cocoon. Willa said in the Hongerwinter they went to bed early, because in bed you could be warm.

I gaze around this dark wooden place. At home my ceiling is smooth and white, straight lines and right angles, but here it's mystical, the strong beams and baby bear's shelf where I put Willa's ghost. Oh, Sara, you tragic ghost. This is a sad place for me. But I was happy here too. I wrote a lot. Westerkerk, my night-time clock, says it's seven o'clock, and I hear the *clink clank* of bike chains.

Out my picture-book window, the first rays of sun are shining under the clouds, catching the terracotta roofs, and the hooks. The faces of the buildings are dark. No cat, he's curled up somewhere. The sun is catching the small bright leaves at the top of the tree. Have a good spring, tree.

Goodbye mijn zolder.

Okay dust, over to you.

Nine o'clock on the dot, Dirk carried my case down the Stairs of Dread. I gave Hyacint my keys, and she gave me a present, a huge chocolate letter H, like the ones Willa and Lodewijk had in the photo. Oh gosh…

save the tears for the dark of the plane

We had breakfast then Jacob came. Saying goodbye to Hyacint was another wave of sadness. Poor jumbled old lady. When we hugged she was just bones. She gave me a sweet puzzled look as if to say *What? You leaving me too?* Who will do her shopping? Jacob, I guess.

We caught a taxi to Centraal, Jacob and I, with just my case and my bag, then the train to Schiphol. Out the window we watched city buildings fly by, a canal, a dome. I was in a wistful going-away mood. There was something I wanted to ask Jacob, but I wasn't sure how.

'Are you happy that I showed you the photo, Jacob? Did I do the right thing?'

'Do *you* think you did the right thing?'

I thought hard. We passed a grim building that looked like a jail.

'Well, the way it happened, the crash, Willa gone…it felt like the right thing to do. It was spur of the moment.'

'Spur of the moment,' Jacob repeated.

'Ja, spur of the moment,' I said quietly.

In the distance a cow wandered towards a bridge.

'Did you worry that it would make me unhappy?' said Jacob.

I nodded. 'Keeping the secret of Bram didn't work either.'

'Well,' said Jacob, 'I think that one turned out okay in the end.'

'But it made us both miserable.'

'Were you miserable, Henni?'

'Ja.'

'Me too.' We looked at each other and laughed.

'One thing I am happy about,' said Jacob, 'us three van Veen boys are going together to Vlissingen.'

Fine raindrops splattered along the windows.

'You could have swept the envelope into the rubbish,' said Jacob.

'True. And I could have kept the secret. You know for four days I told myself to go home and forget all about it.'

'Would you forget?'

'No.'

A woman's voice announced that we'd soon be arriving at Schiphol. We went into a tunnel.

Jacob was matter-of-fact about Willa. 'She wanted to come to Amsterdam,' he said.

I couldn't talk about Willa right then. I told him about Danielle inventing a dance called the Praying Mantis and it looks like it *is* going viral. Mum and Dad are meeting me. It will be autumn when I get home, etc etc etc.

As we got off the train Jacob said, 'Henni, I can't tell if you did the right thing yet. Maybe in a year or two I can give you an answer.'

The last hug was sad. We were both being brave.

'Goodbye Henni.'

'Goodbye Jacob.'

And then I was stepping into the plane, which I did not wish to think about, so I sat and bit the serifs off my H, and let them dissolve in my mouth without chewing. And then I was in a dream, looking down on the parallels of farm patchwork and canals, and a big river winding its own sweet way.

Goodbye getting lost

I'm going home.

Goodbye eight hours behind, I'm going in front now

Goodbye playful Amsterdam

Goodbye Doei doei.

not forever goodbye

you will see me again

Jacob van Veen

Re: GREETINGS FROM BLUE DOG

To: Henni Octon

Hello Henni,

How is it back in Australia? I imagine everyone is sad for Roos not returning with you.

I want to tell you about life here. I did find a way of thinking about myself, of the kind of emotional boat that I am. I stop it rocking mostly. Sometimes it tips, but I will not let it sink. I am reading and finding out, yes, the saddest piece of research proved our great fear for Sara and Matius. For a time I was sadder than I ever have been in my life, but now I think I am okay and we count blessings. You know us Dutch, we must see the practical side. I have received good family love and care all my life, especially from Moeder, who now I know had a great heart under her thick crust, and who cared so much for my first mother.

It is hard when I think of that other life I never lived, like a story which can go this way or that. I am thinking my story would have stopped, as it did for Sara and Matius, so my life is a gift.

Read this article which I think you will find fascinating, as I did.

The wealthy businessman, Bruno Kreitz, was a Jew, homosexual, and outspoken. He collected modernist paintings, regarded by the Nazis as degenerate. In 1936, at the time of the Olympic Games in Berlin, at the age of forty-four, with anti-Semitism rising and war a certainty, he disappeared, but before his disappearance he distributed his collection of paintings among trusted friends.

This has caused a stir in the

He gave *Blue Dog*, yes it is our blue dog, to my father. Kreitz liked colour and now I know my father did too. Through Kreitz I am learning about my parents.

You won't believe this. I am finding friends, with many other people with paintings from this mystery man. More than eighty paintings so far. Now I have friends in Berlin, and other places. A man called Sevun (Fishing Boats) has done much research and each painting is a story. What happened to Kreitz? Floor and I will stay with Sevun in two weeks.

I don't know what twist or turn my life will take next. To tell the truth I don't like to belong to clubs, but these people are fascinating to me, all different, discovered by coincidence, some old, some young, discovered from their parents. We have two in Australia, one I know, a woman with *Symphony 3* in Brisbane.

Blue Dog is from the school of Fauves, which means 'wild' in French. You will agree the painting is wild, but the artist was not a child as we thought – it was the French painter Derain. Hitler hated that stuff.

Some give their painting to a big art gallery, sell for new car, sell for charity, add to their collection. I keep *Blue Dog*. It is from my parents. I enjoy its colour and life.

From the Kreitz group there is much talk, ideas and stories are coming together. Sevun wants to make a book, but some say a website is cheaper and more can see it, any time. We all tell our attitude and philosophy, also to life, and war.

Floor and I have long walks which always end by saying we are lucky, and having a good coffee, yesterday to al Ponte.

Bram is good. He is doing fine detective work with the painting. There is still some battle with Dirk but no longer warfare. Bram is still thinking he knows everything. But that is not possible because Dirk knows everything. Anyway, there is small-scale peace outbreak and we laugh together.

Do you believe in God, Henni? I cannot believe in a god. But I know when leaders describe people like animals, watch out and speak out.

My German parents gave me the first gift of life, then my Dutch parents gave me the second gift of life. Roos and you brought them together. My English is no good, but my desire to say is strong. I am trying to learn the German language, the language I might have talked, if it so happened that I was talking. My Dutch parents always lived in each day. Floor and I wonder about the different countries in the world, different cultures of people and how they get on. I know more than ever that politics is most important to watch and countries must be generous and learn about each other. We are thinking what we can do.

Henni, I hope it was easy back into school, and not behind in schoolwork. Now you have routine. Everybody would be happy to see you and hear stories.

Too much talking by Jacob.

You are welcome always in Eerste Hugo de Grootstraat.

Your friend

Jacob

                    my desk
                  my own bedroom
                    Home Sweet Home

Dear Jacob,

I got your email. I've written to you many times in
my head, and finally I'm writing it down and I'll send
this letter today. I'm including a poem for you and my
latest squashed work of art. Hope you like them.

Amsterdam seems a long time ago.

Willa said a good memory isn't always a good thing.
Well, an imagination isn't always good either. Jacob,
if I think of Sara and Matius, I can't imagine their
last days and last hours. It's too horrible. I will think
of the moment of that little family photo, and I hope
you do too.

The story of the painting is amazing! First we wonder
about the *Blue Dog* and now we wonder about Bruno
Kreitz. I'm sure there will be a book about him and
his paintings. In the movie you and Floor can play
yourselves!

Amsterdam.

Where do I start?

Well, I know I have two real friends in Amsterdam,
you and Carlijn, and I know Hunter and Hartog
are coming to Australia, but Jacob, I want ALL your

family and Carlijn to come, and I want ALL Stella Street to go to Amsterdam. Everyone is sick of me saying *Amsterdam* this, *Amsterdam* that, *Amsterdam* bikes, *Amsterdam* great! but it wasn't all sunshine as you know, and the ending, well, as the days go by it's sad, but not horrible. When I got home, I missed Willa again in my ordinary life. I told everyone about Willa and the van Veens in the war. Many Jewish families came to Melbourne to start a new life.

The flight back was okay, but if the plane bumped or the engines made a different sound, there went my imagination again.

I was an 'unaccompanied minor'. I felt indignant at first, after being in charge of Willa *and* six pieces of luggage through that turbulent flight I told you about. I thought, *I can look after myself!*

They put me with a kid who babbled on about cartoons till Dubai, then the man in front wouldn't shut up about getting good deals in Amsterdam, changing money, blah blah blah. His neighbour said, 'Did you see any Rembrandt paintings?'

'No,' goes Chatterbox, 'I like window shopping.'

So at the end of those long long flights, I was happy when the crew handed me over to the ground staff who helped me through immigration.

Jacob, it's so nice to be home, with my friends and family and sleeping in my own bed, with the bathroom so close. I know where everything is, and the washing dries outside in the sun, but one thing I notice. So many *cars*!!!!

I see the drivers, tense, stuck in traffic, picking their noses, while I zoom past on my bike. People miss out on so much fun when they don't ride. I have a new bike, made by my friend Rob.

Stellastraat had a Welcome Home pizza night where I gave out the presents and we cooked those bread-pancake things with chocolate sprinkles. We talked a lot about Willa. You know what Willa's job for me was? To write about our time in Amsterdam, which I've pretty much done already!

And now BIG NEWS! Remember I said I wanted to swap schools but Mum and Dad were against it? When I got home I was *determined*! I arranged for us to visit the other school. I argued. I didn't get cranky. And finally they said okay! The new school's further to ride, but it's worth it. The teachers expect us to work and we're more independent.

The school has only two broken bike racks, so three other kids who ride and I have started a petition for new racks. If you weren't so far away I'd make you sign it. You'd be surprised how bold I am now. I'm surprising myself! And we're making it cool to ride to school.

Jacob, I'm talking to you now like I used to talk to God when I was a kid, and God was always there, which was handy, and I believed he listened. So if you hear a voice in your head it's probably me. But you don't have to do anything. Just be there.

Jacob, you can't be sad forever, you can't be angry forever, you can't live forever and you can't stay awake forever, either. I'm tired. I'm going to bed now.

Dag

X

Henni van Stellastraat

Riders flow through Amsterdam
like water round cobblestones.
Like a rushing creek
they sweep round old riders.
Behind Centraal, cross-currents and rapids.
Round Vondelpark we flow like ribbons
transported
by wheels of simple grace.

Meneer Lepelneus (Mr Spoonnose)

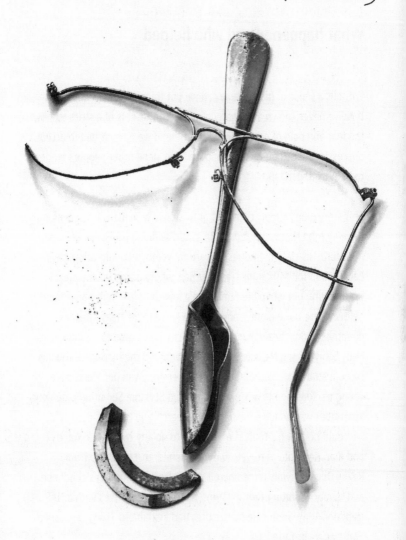

For Bea and Alessandro, who drew us into this lively city

What happened and who helped

Without a sense of history, how can we put things in perspective?
If we've never known a hongerwinter, the dark streets of a strict curfew,
the fear and pain of occupation in wartime; if we haven't had to accept
oppression, or risk our lives to oppose it, we need other people's stories
to help us understand.

This story didn't simply pop up, it grew slowly with many helpers along
the way. John Nieuwenhuizen is an award-winning translator of Dutch
literature. His clear memories of wartime youth, then migration, gave
background for Willa's life. Lies Voerman, whose photo is on page 111,
was a young girl when her family hid a Jewish family in the apartment
below where our daughter now lives in Amsterdam. Haas Kuijper's
directness, honesty and passion for the city was a grounding influence.
Milly Schiferli and Nelleke van de Streek shared their stories. Cartesius
Lyceum students and their English teacher Anne van der Marel gave
young persons' points of view. Mathias and Stefanie Servatius' ingenious
apartment was an ideal base for my research, and Mathias even said
we could borrow his tools if we wanted to do any woodwork. Wendy
and Alan Reid told of travels with grandchildren. Els Scroop from
Roxby Downs vividly remembered stories from her mother's childhood
and family migration. Rob, in Cairns, has a sister who lives with a NAP
trapdoor. Anne-Sophie de Martimprey and I exhibited *Things Squashed
Flat by Cars* in Yarra Park.

Young readers told me honestly what they thought: Violet O'Dowd, and Alphington Primary students, Leo, Luke, Saskia, Sunshine and Darby.

Dear friends Sue Flockhart and Rosalind Price helped guide the story. Andrew McLean introduced me to the joys of illustrating on an iPad. Steady, supportive Andrew Clarke kept the home fires burning and helped with graphics. Our daughter Bea Clarke gave research, editing, encouragement and inspiration.

At Allen & Unwin, Hilary Reynolds nursed the story with intensive care through iso times. Designer Jo Hunt put it on the page.

Here's Henni's Aussie view of modern Amsterdam, where energy, ingenuity, engineering and artistry steer this old city towards an economy within ecological limits – a human place where the streets are fun.

Thank you all, and you too, Queen Wilhelmina.

First published by Allen & Unwin in 2020

Allen & Unwin
83 Alexander Street
Crows Nest NSW 2065
Australia
Phone: (61 2) 8425 0100
Email: info@allenandunwin.com
Web: www.allenandunwin.com

A catalogue record for this
book is available from the
National Library of Australia

ISBN 978 1 86508 454 1

The illustrations in this book were created on an iPad Pro using the
Sketchclub application and an Apple pencil.

For teaching resources, explore www.allenandunwin.com/resources/
for-teachers

Cover and text design by Elizabeth Honey and Joanna Hunt
Set in 11.5 pt Berkeley Oldstyle Medium by Joanna Hunt

Printed in July 2020 in Australia by McPherson's Printing Group

10 9 8 7 6 5 4 3 2 1